# SKE
# FALLING STAR

### A Portrait of Crime Mystery

# SHARON PAPE

### AUTHOR OF *TO SKETCH A THIEF*

BERKLEY
PRIME
CRIME

**$7.99 U.S.**
$8.99 CAN

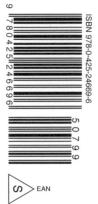

ISBN 978-0-425-24669-6

5 0 7 9 9

S ⊳ EAN

*Berkley Prime Crime titles by Sharon Pape*

SKETCH ME IF YOU CAN
TO SKETCH A THIEF
SKETCH A FALLING STAR

# Sketch a Falling Star

## Sharon Pape

BERKLEY PRIME CRIME, NEW YORK

**THE BERKLEY PUBLISHING GROUP**
Published by the Penguin Group
Penguin Group (USA) Inc.
**375 Hudson Street, New York, New York 10014, USA**

Penguin Group (Canada), 90 Eglinton Avenue East, Suite 700, Toronto, Ontario M4P 2Y3, Canada
(a division of Pearson Penguin Canada Inc.) • Penguin Books Ltd., 80 Strand, London WC2R 0RL,
England • Penguin Group Ireland, 25 St. Stephen's Green, Dublin 2, Ireland (a division of Penguin
Books Ltd.) • Penguin Group (Australia), 250 Camberwell Road, Camberwell, Victoria 3124, Australia
(a division of Pearson Australia Group Pty. Ltd.) • Penguin Books India Pvt. Ltd., 11 Community
Centre, Panchsheel Park, New Delhi—110 017, India • Penguin Group (NZ), 67 Apollo Drive,
Rosedale, Auckland 0632, New Zealand (a division of Pearson New Zealand Ltd.) • Penguin Books
(South Africa) (Pty.) Ltd., 24 Sturdee Avenue, Rosebank, Johannesburg 2196, South Africa

Penguin Books Ltd., Registered Offices: 80 Strand, London WC2R 0RL, England

SKETCH A FALLING STAR

A Berkley Prime Crime Book / published by arrangement with the author

PUBLISHING HISTORY
Berkley Prime Crime mass-market edition / March 2012

Copyright © 2012 by Sharon Pape.
Cover illustration by Cliff Nielson.
Cover design by George Long.
Interior text design by Laura K. Corless.

ISBN: 978-0-425-24669-6

BERKLEY® PRIME CRIME
Berkley Prime Crime Books are published by The Berkley Publishing Group,
a division of Penguin Group (USA) Inc.,
375 Hudson Street, New York, New York 10014.
BERKLEY® PRIME CRIME and the PRIME CRIME logo are trademarks of
Penguin Group (USA) Inc.

PRINTED IN THE UNITED STATES OF AMERICA

10  9  8  7  6  5  4  3  2  1

ALWAYS LEARNING                                           **PEARSON**

*For my husband, Dennis.*
*Who needs a Mount Palomar anyway?*

# Acknowledgments

I want to thank my daughter, Lauren, for brokering many peace accords between me and my computer, thereby saving my sanity.

I want to thank my son, Jason, for "fixing" me whenever I break myself, which is more often than one might think.

# Prologue

Rory was wrestling her suitcase into the trunk of the Volvo when she was startled by a bright little voice wishing her a good morning. She couldn't imagine who else was out and about, much less in her driveway, at six o'clock on a Sunday morning. She popped her head up so quickly that she banged it on the lid of the trunk.

"Oh my," said the owner of the voice, an elderly woman so slight that she might have been blown there by a sudden gust of wind. She had stunning blue eyes that were caught up in a seine of wrinkles and white hair that sprouted in random tufts across her scalp. Although she was wearing a blue terry-cloth robe over yellow pajamas, her feet were bare. The lack of shoes didn't seem to bother her in spite of an outside temperature that was straining to reach forty.

"I didn't mean to scare you," she said, her forehead pleated with concern.

"That's okay," Rory told her, finding it hard to be annoyed with the woman, who had an open, childlike expression, in spite of the years deeply etched into her face. "What can I do for you?"

"I'm Eloise," she said, a smile puffing up her sunken cheeks and twinkling in her eyes.

"Well, I'm Rory." She extended her hand. "Nice to meet you."

Eloise gave it a firm little shake.

"Are you lost?" Rory asked.

Eloise shook her head. "I live over there." She pointed down the block to the brick colonial owned by the Bowman family.

It was close to a year now that Rory had been living in the refurbished Victorian her uncle Mac had left her, and she knew all her neighbors well enough to say "hello," ask after their families and presumably borrow a cup of sugar should she ever need one. But she couldn't recall having seen Eloise before. It was possible that she'd come to stay with the Bowmans recently, as she became incapable of living alone. They probably weren't even aware that their matriarch was out wandering the neighborhood.

Of all mornings too. Rory's alarm clock had chosen that night to stop working, so she'd overslept and was already late leaving for the airport. Thank goodness she'd decided to drop Hobo off with her parents the night before or she wouldn't stand a chance of making her flight. It was going to be a toss-up anyway, and not even her indomitable aunt Helene would be able to convince the airline to wait for her. Still, she couldn't just drive away and let Eloise continue roaming around on her own. She'd have to drop her back home and see her safely inside.

She was about to coax Eloise into the car when she saw Doug Bowman come tearing out his front door with a raincoat over his pajamas and his comb-over standing on end as if he'd just rolled out of bed.

Things were looking up. She just hoped Doug wasn't in a chatty mood.

"Mom!" he yelled, flip-flopping down the street to them in slippers that were in imminent danger of flying off his feet. "Mom, come back here. Mom!" he implored like a man who was mere inches away from the end of his quickly fraying rope. Rory understood that feeling only too well, courtesy of a certain deceased federal marshal who shared her home and her life. Judging by the desperation in Doug's tone, this probably wasn't his mother's first solo flight.

Eloise didn't bother to acknowledge her son. Still focused on Rory, she started giggling with her hand in front of her mouth like a little girl. "You know he's going to miss you," she said in a singsong rhythm.

"My dog?" Rory asked. Eloise had probably seen him out in the backyard or when they'd gone for walks. "Don't worry about Hobo; he'll be fine." She turned away to close the trunk of the car. "He's staying with my mom and dad while I'm away."

When she turned back, Doug Bowman was stumbling up the driveway, holding his raincoat closed and trying to catch his breath. Eloise paid him no mind.

"No, silly," she said, "I mean your Marshal Drummond."

Rory felt the blood drain from her face so fast that it left her a bit light-headed. How could Eloise possibly know about Zeke? Although his ability to travel beyond the house had improved exponentially with her reluctant help, he still couldn't leave the house unless she was with him or at his destination. And unless she'd developed selective amnesia, she was certain she'd never seen Eloise before. It occurred to her that the one variable in this troubling equation was Eloise herself. Unfortunately, Rory didn't have time to investigate the situation further, but it would definitely be number one on her "to do" list when she returned from Arizona.

"Hi, Rory. Sorry about this," Doug wheezed as he reached them. He immediately took hold of his mother's arm as if he were afraid she might slip away again. "Rory can't visit with

you right now, Mom. We'll come by another time, I promise."
He gave her arm a gentle tug. "We have to get home—Jean's
whipping up some of those pancakes you like."

In spite of her fragile appearance, Eloise stood her
ground. "Don't you worry, dear," she said to Rory, giggling
again. "Your secret's safe with me."

Doug looked from his mother to Rory and back again.
"You'll have to excuse my mother," he whispered as if Eloise
wasn't standing beside him and perfectly capable of hearing
every word. "I'm afraid she hasn't been herself since the
stroke."

Rory managed to arrange her face into a lighter, "no
worries here" expression for Doug's consumption. "I'm glad
your mom and I had a chance to meet," she said. She would
have liked to ask Eloise if she'd mentioned the marshal to
anyone else, but that wasn't possible with Doug right there.
At least the Bowman family wasn't likely to buy any strange
tales she might tell.

"Rory, you have yourself a lovely trip," Eloise said, tuck-
ing her arm through her son's. "Come along now, Douglas.
You know I don't like cold pancakes."

Doug wished her a good trip as well, looking relieved
that he didn't have to pick his mother up and carry her home
like a truculent two-year-old. They set off across the lawn
in deference to Eloise's bare feet.

Rory was about to get into her car when Eloise stopped
abruptly and turned back to her. The smile had vanished,
swallowed whole by an expression Rory could best describe
as sympathy.

"Something terrible is going to happen," Eloise intoned
solemnly. Then quick as a wink her childlike aspect
returned, her smile as bright as ever, and without another
word she let her son escort her home.

# Chapter 1

According to the map, Tucson was a straight shot southeast on I-10 from Phoenix. What the map failed to indicate was the amount of traffic that plied the route between those two cities on any given day. Rory had been looking forward to an easy drive, during which she could enjoy the unfamiliar landscape of the Sonoran Desert. Instead, she found herself playing the same unnerving game of "dodge the semi" that she played on the Long Island Expressway. However, at speeds of seventy-five and above, it was the expressway on steroids.

Although she couldn't risk taking her eyes off the road for more than a second or two, she managed to catch glimpses of the desert plain with the hearty scrub that made it unique in the world, according to the tour guide she'd read in preparation for the trip.

Having lived all of her life on a relatively flat island, Rory was enchanted by the way the distant mountains faded into the horizon, like giant roadblocks intended to keep the desert from wandering beyond its allotted space. Everywhere she looked, Zeke was front and center in her thoughts. This was his home, his true place in the world. Or it had been before the twentieth and twenty-first centuries came calling. She wasn't sure he would even recognize it now. For that matter, she was having a hard time imagining the desert as he'd known it, back when buzzards were the largest things that sailed the skies, and a man alone on horseback had only his gun and his wits to keep him alive.

Her thoughts circled back to the reason she was there—her promise to find out who'd killed Zeke by putting a bullet in his back a hundred and thirty-four years ago. The marshal didn't seem to care that the killer was also long dead. He stubbornly refused to move on beyond his present limbo without that bit of knowledge. Rory had done all the research it was possible to do from her home computer, and she'd gone through the newspaper archives in Huntington, but she'd come up empty. Tucson was their last hope.

To set the stage for her trip, she'd told her family that she might be visiting a college friend in Arizona sometime in the spring. She couldn't very well say she was making the trip to find out who'd killed the ghost in her house, or that she was trying to keep a promise she'd made to said ghost, unless she was also interested in an extended vacation in a nicely padded cell. Thanks to Zeke, she could teach a master class in the white lie. Only this time the lie had turned around and bitten her.

"You're not going to believe this," her aunt Helene had said in an enthusiastic phone call three weeks after Rory first mentioned her prospective trip.

Rory had braced herself for whatever was coming. When Helene took on a project, it was total immersion. She'd research it inside out, upside down and sideways. Yet in spite of all her work and best intentions, she often wound up jumping off a cliff without considering the impact of her landing.

"When you said you wanted to go to Arizona, I had this lightbulb moment," her aunt went on.

Uh-oh. The warning sirens were starting to blare. "I haven't actually made any plans yet," Rory said, hoping to defuse whatever bomb was ticking away in Helene's mind.

"That's what I figured. So I've taken care of it for you."

Too late.

"All you have to do is pay your share and show up at the airport."

Her share? Of what? What had Helene signed her up for? With a tangle of questions fighting for air time, a bewildered "What?" was all Rory managed to get out.

Helene was only too happy to fill in the details. It seemed that some of the actors from her Long Island acting troupe, the Way Off Broadway Players, had decided to go on vacation together between productions. But where to go? Enter Helene, stage right, armed with tour books and a soliloquy about the wonders of Arizona.

Once she'd convinced the group that any other destination couldn't possibly measure up, she'd gamely taken on the job of travel agent. She'd spent hours online and then on the phone, but it was all worth it in the end, she'd proclaimed, since everyone was thrilled with the tour package she'd arranged for them.

Rory hadn't bothered to point out that "everyone" couldn't possibly have been thrilled, since "everyone" hadn't been consulted. Of course, she shouldn't have been surprised. She'd learned when she was still quite young that Helene sometimes took hostages when she plunged off a cliff.

In the end, she'd decided not to object. Her aunt's intentions were honorable; plus, she'd freed Rory from the work of planning the trip herself. For all she knew, traveling with the Players might even turn out to be fun. She would simply bow out of their side trip to Gray Wolf Canyon, in the high country near the town of Page, and head down to Tucson on her own.

Zeke had been pleased to hear that she would soon be back on the trail of his killer but somewhat less thrilled about the prospect of rattling around in the house all alone for seven days.

"It's one week—you spent decades alone before Mac moved in," Rory had reminded him. "I'm sure you'll be able to manage."

"Well, I expect I could drop by from time to time to see how you're doin' out there," he'd said, as if the idea had just occurred to him.

So this was where the conversation had been leading all along.

"It'd be mighty nice to see my home again," he'd added with a nostalgic sigh.

Nice touch, Rory thought, not buying any of it. He'd clearly had the whole little act worked out before he'd even opened his mouth. Since he'd improved considerably in the art of traveling beyond the confines of the house, it had become more difficult for her to lobby against his trips. He had the posture and gait of the living down cold. And he hardly ever made the mistake of walking through walls anymore when he was out in public. He'd even updated his wardrobe with some slacks and a few nice shirts so as not to draw attention, although he made no bones about how much he disliked the cut and fit of modern apparel. In the house, he always reverted to the clothing he'd worn when he was alive.

"I understand that you'd like to go back home for a visit," she'd said evenly, "but I'll be able to concentrate better on the investigation if I'm not constantly expecting a three-ring circus to march into town."

"You've got nothin' to worry about, darlin'," he'd assured her. "I'll be stealthy as a coyote with a hankerin' for rabbit."

Somehow the image had brought her no comfort at all.

Rory was so lost in her thoughts that the voice of the GPS startled her with a reminder that the exit for Tucson was coming up. It was a good thing she'd insisted on having a car with a navigation system; Zeke was already messing with her mind.

The Arizona Historical Society Library and Archives was situated just outside the campus of the University of Arizona. Rory parked in a nearby garage and walked the two short blocks to the building, carrying a pad of paper, a pen and a bushel of determined optimism. She wound her way through the exhibits, enjoying the overview of Tucson's past, but it was in the small library that she found her first lead.

When she walked in, the librarian rose from her chair behind the front desk. She was somewhere in her middle years, dressed in a long, gauzy skirt of coral that was topped off with a blouse of similar style and fabric. The name tag she wore introduced her as Wanda Shaw.

She welcomed Rory in a hushed voice, although no one else occupied the library at that moment. Even the smile Wanda produced was low-key, as if more gregarious facial expressions were also discouraged there.

Taking her cue from the librarian, Rory whispered that she was doing research on crime in late-nineteenth-century southern Arizona and that she was hoping they might have newspapers from that era.

"Yes, of course," Wanda replied, "but they're much too fragile to be handled. Luckily, they've all been copied onto microfilm. You're welcome to view them that way if you'd like."

Rory assured her that the microfilm would be fine and that she was primarily interested in newspapers from January through October of 1878.

Wanda excused herself, disappearing through a door in the back where a sign read "Library Personnel Only." When she returned a few minutes later, she was holding several small boxes.

She came out from behind the desk, her skirt swishing softly around her as if it too respected library etiquette. Motioning for Rory to follow, she led the way to a room so tiny that it had probably started life as a supply closet. There was barely enough space to accommodate the desk that held the bulky microfilm reader, a low-tech dinosaur from the days before microprocessors gave birth to sleek computers. Rory couldn't help thinking that if the reader seemed anachronistic to her, then Zeke must be shell-shocked from watching the world's innovations hurtle by him over the years.

Given the room's modest dimensions, Rory watched from the doorway while Wanda threaded the film into the machine.

"I've started you off with the *Arizona Citizen*," the librarian whispered as she and Rory did a little do-si-do to switch places. "It's probably your best bet. It was a weekly newspaper published Saturdays here in Tucson." She pointed out the control for scrolling through the film, then left Rory to her work with a reminder that she was nearby if she was needed.

Rory started scanning through the pages searching for articles about John Trask, the man wanted for abducting and murdering a series of young girls, the man Zeke had been tracking when he was killed. Given the circumstances, Rory figured Trask was responsible for the marshal's death as well. But according to Zeke that wasn't possible, since the bullet had slammed into his back while he'd had the outlaw in his gun sights.

As Rory worked her way through the microfilm, she kept thinking how much simpler it would have been to do a word search on a computer. That thought was quickly followed by another about how beggars can't be choosers, and that she ought to be grateful to have even this kind of access to the old papers.

Two hours later, she pushed her chair back from the desk with little to show for her time and effort. Although she'd gone through every reel of microfilm Wanda had given her, the few articles about Trask were short and grim. Back in the nineteenth century, with no modern forensic tools, the marshal had had little to help him as he'd hunted for the killer. According to the articles, he'd probably only known Trask's name and that he was a loner, a predator who roamed the Arizona and New Mexico Territories, where too few lawmen patrolled far too vast an area. The one valuable clue he'd had was a composite sketch of the killer. Rory stared at Trask's image for several minutes, glad to finally have a face to go with the name. Not much to show for the eyestrain and pounding headache she'd developed from reading the small print, which had already started to fade by the time it was transferred onto microfilm.

Instead of answering her questions, the research had actually added a new question to her list. What had become of John Trask? Although the *Arizona Citizen* had reported the marshal's death, it never mentioned Trask again. Back home when she'd searched the Huntington newspaper archives she'd come across an article that said he'd been wounded in the gunfight that killed Zeke but had escaped. If there was an answer to be found, it might literally be buried somewhere on Long Island.

The only information Rory bothered jotting down was the list of Trask's victims. Three of the girls had come from New Mexico, the other two from Arizona, including Betsy Jensen, who'd lived right there in Tucson, where her family had owned a general store. Although Rory wasn't at all sure how this information was going to help her figure out who had murdered Zeke more than a century ago and some two thousand miles away, on Long Island, an idea was beginning to take shape in her mind.

She rewound the microfilm and brought it back to the librarian at the front desk.

"Is there anything else I can help you with?" Wanda inquired so softly that Rory found herself leaning forward to catch the words.

"Actually I do have a question," she whispered back. "I read that there was a family by the name of Jensen who ran a general store around here in the 1870s. Would you know if anyone from that family still lives in Tucson?"

"It's possible, but Jensen's a popular name around here. There's probably a couple hundred Jensens in the greater Tucson area. Without a first name, it wouldn't pay to look in the telephone directory. In fact, the Jensen you want to find might not even have a listed number. There is something else we can try, though," Wanda said sitting down at her computer. "We keep a file of all the families who've donated items of historical interest. If the Jensen family donated anything, it would be listed here along with the date of the donation and the name of the donor."

Wanda clicked away at her keyboard while Rory waited, trying not to appear as impatient as she felt.

"Yes, here it is!" the librarian said at full volume, momentarily forgetting herself. "Sorry," she whispered, looking chagrined over her lapse.

Rory smiled to let her know she wasn't at all disturbed by the outburst.

"We've apparently had quite a few donations over the years from one particular Jensen family, the first going as far back as 1921 and the most recent in 2007. That last donation was made by Abner Jensen. According to this, he still lives in the original Jensen home over in the historic district near the Presidio." She jotted the address and phone number on a slip of paper and handed it across the counter to Rory, who tucked it into her purse. She might not learn anything of consequence by going to see Abner Jensen, but she was heartened by the simple fact that her investigation hadn't come to a complete dead end once again.

"Would you like to see the articles they've donated?" Wanda inquired, pushing back in her chair.

Rory said she would appreciate the opportunity, after which Wanda once again disappeared into the back storage area. This time fifteen minutes elapsed before she reappeared carrying a large, plastic storage container. She set it down on top of the front desk and opened it. An envelope containing an inventory had been taped inside the lid. Each item in the container was listed there along with the date it had been given to the historical society.

Together, Wanda and Rory spent the better part of an hour looking through the objects, which included antique clothing, books and catalogues, ledgers from the general store, toys and sundries of every sort. But as interesting as these items were, they didn't provide Rory with any useful information.

Wanda was about to place the inventory list back in its envelope when she noticed there was another sheet of paper still tucked inside. It turned out to be a handwritten letter dated 1998, signed by Abner Jensen and witnessed by Harold Winthrop, attorney-at-law. In the brief note, Abner stated simply that as he had no kin, upon his death all of his land and possessions were to become the property of the Arizona Historical Society.

"I'll bet that house has a treasure trove of items," Wanda said, looking like she wanted to dance a jig, albeit a very quiet jig. "There could be letters, diaries, a family bible— things that would paint a real picture of how folks lived in the past, how they felt and what they thought."

Her enthusiasm was so contagious that Rory decided she couldn't possibly leave Tucson until she'd had a chance to speak to Abner Jensen. She thanked Wanda for all of her help and walked back to the parking garage with a hopeful spring to her step. She refused to dwell on how slim the odds were that a great-great-grand-relative of one of Trask's victims would know, much less recall, anything about the murder of a long-dead family member or the marshal who'd been involved in the case. As Zeke liked to say, "You don't know where a lead will take you till you get there." Great. Now she was beginning to think in Zeke-isms.

An angry little grumble from the pit of her stomach made her consult her watch. She was surprised to see that the afternoon had slipped away while she was busy squinting at microfilm. No wonder she was hungry; she hadn't eaten anything since the free continental breakfast that morning in Phoenix. She decided to stop for some fast food on her way over to the hotel she'd booked for the night. Once she was checked in, she'd give Abner Jensen a call. With any luck, he'd agree to see her in the morning.

A half hour later, Rory was sliding back into the rental car, her stomach quietly working away at a quarter pound of beef and greasy fries, when her cell phone rang. She didn't recognize the number that came up. Probably a solicitor or wrong number. She let it go to voice mail. Seconds later it rang again. By the third time, she decided it would be simpler to just answer it and set the caller straight.

Helene was on the other end as close to hysterical as Rory had ever heard her.

"Aunt Helene, calm down. I can't understand a word you're saying."

There was a pause, during which Rory heard her aunt draw a deep, wobbly breath, like a child who's been sobbing.

"We were at Gray Wolf Canyon," Helene said more slowly, her voice high-pitched with emotion. "And suddenly there was water—there was water everywhere, and it was rising so fast, and everyone was screaming and trying to keep their heads above it, and I thought . . . I thought I was . . ." The rest of her words were choked off completely.

"But you're okay?" Rory demanded, anxiety expanding like a balloon in her chest. *"Aunt Helene—are you okay?"*

"Yes, I'm okay . . . I'm okay," Helene replied, "but Preston Wright is dead."

# Chapter 2

"Where are you right now?" Rory asked.

"We're back at our hotel in Page," Helene said, her voice cracking like ice that was too thin to bear weight. "Except for Preston and the three who were taken to the hospital. Stuart had chest pains so they're keeping him overnight for observation. Dorothy has a fractured foot, and Jessica broke her arm, but I think they're due back here soon."

"You mean you weren't all taken to the hospital and checked out?"

"EMTs came, and they were really thorough. Most of us were lucky—just bumps and bruises. Besides, you know how I feel about hospitals."

Rory knew. When Helene was eight, her best friend went into the hospital with bone cancer and never came out again. From that time on, the word "hospital" was synonymous with "death" for Helene. As an adult she understood that the hospital hadn't killed her friend, but somewhere deep inside she still carried the psyche of that eight-year-old, with all its attendant scars. Rory had no intentions of debating the issue with her. She'd just keep a close eye on her in case any disturbing symptoms should arise.

"The police are coming here to interview us," Helene said. "Navajo police, believe it or not. It seems the canyon's on their land. They tried to talk to us back at the site, but everyone was in shock or hysterical. Oh and I lost my shoes and my purse—it had my cell, my wallet, my ID—I can't even remember everything that was in it. But how can I even complain about such trivial stuff with poor Preston dead?"

"You're right—it is just 'stuff,' and we'll take care of it. The important thing is that you're okay," Rory said, feeling as if she'd fallen through a worm hole into an alternate universe where she was her mother—the voice of calm and provider of comfort. "I'll be up there as soon as I can."

They spent the next few minutes going back and forth about Rory's decision to cut short her visit with her "friend" in Tucson so that she could drive up to Page. Helene insisted she'd only called to let Rory know what had happened and to tell her that she was okay. Sure, she was upset—who wouldn't be?—but she was physically fine and didn't need anyone to hold her hand. It wasn't as if she was alone there.

Rory stood her ground. She knew she could have ended the discussion sooner if she'd simply confessed that there wasn't any "friend" in Tucson, but such a statement would have inevitably led to the fact that she was there doing research for her resident ghost. Given all her aunt had been through in the past few hours, this was probably not the best time for her to learn about Zeke.

"How long was the bus ride up there from Phoenix?" she asked, hoping to short-circuit the debate that was already in its fourth go-round.

"Let me see . . . let me see. . . . I'm sorry; my brain is still all muddled. That was just this morning, right? It feels like it was a month ago." She paused again. "Close to six hours, I think, but we stopped for lunch and bathroom breaks."

Rory was a bit surprised that she'd actually managed to derail Helene, who was famous for holding on to her side of an argument like a shark with its first taste of human tartare. She was evidently more frazzled than she was letting on.

"Try to rest and have something to eat," Rory said, briefly reprising the role of her mother. "I'm heading up there now."

She called to cancel the hotel reservation in Tucson, then reprogrammed the GPS to take her to Page. Although adrenaline had drop-kicked the fatigue out of her for the moment, it wouldn't keep her going forever. She had a long haul ahead of her, and it would be turning dark in a few hours. She was going to need lots of strong coffee and loud music.

She was making her way back to I-10, mulling over what Helene had told her about the deadly flood when an image of Eloise Bowman popped into her head. Eloise—slight and pale. "Something terrible is going to happen," she'd said. At the time, the pronouncement had caused an odd little shiver to run the length of Rory's spine, but she'd managed to dismiss the words as the ramblings of a stroke-damaged brain. Now she couldn't help wondering if Eloise had been talking about the flood.

"That's ridiculous," the logical side of her mind declared. "A predication that vague was bound to come true eventually."

"Yes, but Eloise also knew about Zeke," the intuitive side countered. "How are you going to explain that away?"

Although Rory found the voice of logic appealing, she couldn't ignore the fact that it had failed her miserably when it came to the existence of ghosts. With no immediate way to resolve the issue, she left it to simmer on the back burner of her mind as she sped north.

By the time she passed the turnoff to Sedona, night had clamped down so hard that it seemed determined to be more than a temporary resident. Hours earlier, the cacti and desert scrub had given way to mountains and deep stands of conifers. But with the coming of night, all the distinct shapes had melted into a uniform blackness. The traffic had thinned out to the point that Rory felt at times as if she traveled the dark highway alone. If not for the occasional pockets of light from distant houses and towns too small to rightly be called "towns," she might have worried that she'd made a wrong turn and was cruising along a very different road, straight into the depths of *The Twilight Zone*.

In spite of all the caffeine, fatigue was gaining the upper hand, and she was having trouble keeping her eyelids propped open. She wouldn't be much use to her aunt if she missed a curve and slammed into a mountain or went flying off into a ravine. So when she saw signs promising food and lodging at the first exit to Flagstaff, she surrendered to common sense. Had Rory's dear friend and mentor, Detective Leah Russell, been there, she would have applauded that decision and arranged for a ticker-tape parade. Detective Russell had only one quibble with her protégé—that her impulsiveness and general lack of caution would someday get her killed.

"Leah, this one's for you," Rory murmured as she pulled into the first motel she saw. It was part of a well-known, lower-end chain, which was fine for her purposes. She wasn't looking for a glamorous resort, just a place with clean sheets where she could close her eyes for a few hours. She registered and drove around to the room she was assigned, all the while trying to reach her aunt to say she'd be delayed. The switchboard at the hotel in Page seemed to be having trouble keeping up with the volume of incoming and outgoing calls. No surprise. Everyone on the tour had probably lost his or her cell phones to the flood, and by now the media had to be making a bad communications situation much worse.

When Rory finally had her aunt on the line, she was relieved to hear that her voice had lost its hysterical edge. Instead she sounded completely drained and maybe a little numb. Surely that was to be expected in the aftermath of such an ordeal. They talked briefly, promising each other they'd get some sleep; then Rory set the alarm on her cell phone and placed it on the nightstand. She wanted to be in Page by dawn.

Since she'd packed a bag for the trip to Tucson, she had her toiletries and makeup with her as well as a nightgown and a change of clothing. After washing, she left the bathroom light on and the door open a crack so that she wouldn't collide with the furniture should she need to get up during the night to use the facilities. Though she hadn't eaten dinner, between the coffee and water, she'd had enough fluids to keep a cruise ship afloat.

At three a.m. Rory was startled awake by the alarm. As she surfaced from the depths of sleep, it took her a few moments to remember where she was and why she'd set the alarm for such a ridiculous hour. No time to snuggle under the covers. She forced her reluctant eyelids open, then bolted upright in the bed. Marshal Ezekiel Drummond was sitting in the armchair a few feet away, his body outlined by the spill of light from the bathroom.

# Chapter 3

Waking to find Zeke watching her from a chair was like a replay of the night they'd first met. Of course, back then she'd been frightened, angry, bewildered and a whole host of other emotions, all reasonable enough when confronting one's first ghost. But after a year of sharing her home and her life with the marshal, he no longer had the power to scare her. Not even in his blackest moods. Still, it made her uncomfortable to know that she was being watched while she slept, unaware and so completely vulnerable.

"I flickered the lights, but you kept right on sleeping," Zeke said before she could protest that he hadn't used the agreed-upon signal to let her know he'd be appearing.

"What are you doing here?" Rory asked, groping for the switch on the bedside lamp. When she turned it on, the sudden brightness was so painful that she had to close her eyes again to give them a chance to adjust.

"I was hopin' you could tell me, darlin'. The Navajo police called and left a message for you. It didn't sound much like a social call. How did you get yourself in trouble so fast?"

"*I* didn't get into any trouble, for your information," she bristled. Sleeping those few hours hadn't done much to alleviate her fatigue or the irritability that had hitched a ride on it.

She couldn't imagine why the Navajo police would have called her home number unless Helene had meant to give them her cell number and mixed the two up. She'd certainly been upset enough to make that kind of mistake. In any case, it seemed that Zeke had a legitimate excuse for dropping in on her. The phone was still out of the question for him. Whenever they'd tried it, she'd been treated to a scream of static that threatened the integrity of her eardrum. Although he could manage e-mail and texting, he groused about it, saying that when he asked a question he didn't want to sit around and wait for the answer like back in the days of Morse code. He'd become a spoiled brat of technology, go figure. Rory didn't usually argue the matter. She'd learned to pick her fights with the marshal, and this one wasn't worth the hassle.

"So you're sayin' Helene's the culprit?"

"More like one of the victims." Rory told him the bare bones of the story as her aunt had related them to her.

"Page, huh? I didn't get that far north much," Zeke said, after expressing his condolences, "but I sure heard stories about how fast those slot canyons can flood. You say this Preston fellow was the only death?"

"According to Helene."

"Was he gettin' on in years?"

"He was only in his forties and looked like he was in great shape."

Zeke looked at her with a wry, little smile tugging at his mustache. "Great shape, huh? Would that be a professional sketch artist's opinion?"

Rory ignored the remark. "Why were you asking about his age?"

"Well, I imagine there were some older folks on the tour a lot less fit than this Preston fellow, yet he's the only one who died."

"Maybe it was a matter of where he was in the canyon when the flood hit."

"Maybe, but something about this just don't sit entirely right with me."

"I don't see how his death can be attributed to anything more than a random act of nature," Rory said to stanch the speculation. The marshal might be feeling chatty, but she hadn't set the alarm for three a.m. to practice the art of conversation.

"I've known stranger things to happen. There was this one time . . ."

"I appreciate the message service," Rory said as pleasantly as her sleep-deprived mood would allow, "but this really isn't the best time for a visit. I need to get up to Page to make sure my aunt is as fine as she claims to be."

Since her cotton nightgown was neither skimpy nor in any way revealing, she threw back the covers and climbed out of bed. It was obvious that for a moment Zeke thought he'd be treated to a more interesting sight. His disappointment with the gown's utilitarian nature was plainly written across his face. It occurred to Rory that if he'd played poker when he was alive, he must have lost a lot more often than he won.

She grabbed her clothes from the suitcase and excused herself to use the bathroom, with a reminder to Zeke that he wasn't welcome to join her in there. Back home, he wasn't allowed in her bedroom either, but she couldn't very well blame him for joining her in the motel bedroom, since that was all she had at the moment for receiving guests.

After she'd changed, she ran a comb through her hair, which had grown over the winter from a neat auburn cap

that framed her features into an unruly set of layers that
turned and twisted every which way, not unlike Medusa.
Her hairdresser had told her on more than one occasion that
she ought to take advantage of the fact that she looked best
with short hair. According to him, she was one of the lucky
few whose features didn't need camouflaging or balancing.
Rory didn't agree with him. With her one dimple, she
thought she looked about as unbalanced as one could be,
and as far as she knew there was no hairstyle to correct that
particular deficiency. In any case, since she had neither the
time nor the inclination to fuss with her hair on a daily basis,
she was going to have to let him have his way with it. Somehow it had been easier to schedule such things when she'd
worked the regular hours of a police sketch artist. Once she
opened Drummond and McCain Investigations, her work
hours seemed to eat up each day in its entirety.

When she emerged from the bathroom dressed and ready
to leave, Zeke was still sitting in the armchair. Although he
seemed to be staring at the cheap print of Sedona that was
hanging over the bed, his eyes were unfocused, as if he were
actually looking inward instead.

He turned to her. "I'd sure as hell like to take the ride
with you," he said wistfully, "but I'm nearly out of time."
His record for remaining intact when he traveled beyond
the house was presently in the fifteen-minute range. Since
he hadn't yet shown signs of erosion, Rory figured he must
have arrived shortly before the alarm went off. Thank goodness he was at least being reasonable about his limitations.
She had enough on her mind without having to worry about
a passenger who was shedding body parts. She could just
picture the faces in the cars that came alongside them as the
marshal started to disintegrate. No amount of creative lying
could explain away a sight like that.

"Once you're back home, we're goin' to have to work at
increasin' my endurance," Zeke intoned, as if it were a right

guaranteed by the Founding Fathers and protected by the Constitution.

Well, so much for being reasonable. Considering that he needed her cooperation for any traveling practice, she thought he could have phrased it more like a polite request than a demand. Hadn't he learned by now that she didn't respond well to orders?

She tucked her toiletries and nightgown back into the suitcase without comment. Discussions about his traveling always seemed to end in arguments, and this particular one was likely to follow suit. The bottom line was that she didn't want him to increase his traveling time. Fifteen minutes was more than adequate in her opinion. At home she lived with the potential of his appearance pretty much 24/7. Even happily married couples needed time apart.

"Did you come up with anythin' useful in Tucson?" he asked, perhaps believing that her silence meant she'd acquiesced on the matter of traveling.

Rory didn't answer immediately. She was distracted by his right foot, which had become translucent, as if its molecules were flying apart. She watched it shimmer for a few seconds like air caught in a heat wave before evaporating completely. Zeke seemed unconcerned about the loss, but Rory still found the process unsettling. Had he been more wraithlike to begin with, it might have been easier for her to accept this lack of cohesion. But at his optimum the marshal appeared as whole and solid as any mortal, and mortals weren't in the habit of dissolving into thin air no matter how low their energy levels sank.

Knowing that he might wink away at any moment, Rory gave him a quick rundown of her library visit, ending with the fact that Helene's distress call had come before she'd had a chance to track down Abner Jensen.

Zeke frowned. "I don't see what help he would be anyhow."

"The librarian seemed to think there might be old papers or journals in the house that could prove useful. Of course, she had no idea what I was actually researching. But with all that's happened up in Page, I'll have to make another trip out here to follow up with Abner. Preferably minus an acting troupe."

She was surprised to see Zeke's body stiffen. "I'm not interested in anythin' more than the name of the coward who shot me in the back," he said tersely, "and I don't believe this Abner fella would have that sort of information."

Rory had expected him to be excited and upbeat about this new avenue she'd found to explore, but he sounded irritated, almost angry. It made her wonder if he was afraid she might unearth other information—information he preferred to leave buried. Although curiosity was pressing her to pursue the subject, it would have to wait. For now, the tragedy in Page topped her list of priorities.

She did a quick check of the room to make sure she hadn't left anything behind, then zipped up her suitcase. When she looked back at Zeke a moment later, his right arm had vanished, leaving his hand to float in midair like a relative of Thing from *The Addams Family*.

"I'll be out of commission for a time recoverin' from this trip," Zeke said finally, in a nod to his disappearing limbs. "Try not to get into any more trouble, 'cause I won't be around to help you out."

"*I* wasn't in any trouble," Rory reminded him sharply. "And you know damn well by now that I'm perfectly capable of resolving anything that could come up." Before she reached the end of her sentence, the marshal was gone, and she had no way of knowing if disappearing at that precise moment was a matter of metaphysics or personal choice.

# Chapter 4

When Rory stopped into the motel office to check out, the young man behind the desk was staring at a small flat-screen TV, where a weary-looking reporter was reciting Preston's bio with as much enthusiasm as she could muster at that hour.

". . . an only child, he's survived by his mother, Clarissa Carpenter, who still lives on Long Island. Mr. Wright had returned to Long Island two years ago, at which time he joined the Way Off Broadway Players. In past years he'd belonged to a half dozen amateur acting troupes in as many different states. Although he received uniformly good notices from local critics, it seems he never sought a more professional outlet for his talents."

So, Preston didn't like staying in one place for too long, Rory thought as she set her key card on the counter. It occurred to her that she didn't really know much about him, or any of the other Players, for that matter. Helene had made a big fuss over introducing her to each of them after the first performance she attended, but what little information she possessed came from anecdotes her aunt shared with her from time to time.

Since the clerk had run her credit card when she'd arrived, Rory tossed him a hurried "good night" as she turned to leave.

"Sure, no problem," he mumbled, his eyes still glued to the TV. If he was curious about why she was leaving in the middle of the night, he hid it well.

She drove into the small town of Page as the eastern sky was pinking up with first light. She found the hotel where the troupe was staying by the news vans camped along the curb outside its parking lot. Page might be a speck on a map, but the story of Preston's drowning had quickly made headlines all over Arizona and across the country. Although Preston had not sought fame when he was alive, it had come calling upon his death.

Rory was glad to see that none of the reporters were up and about yet. From what Helene had told her, the Navajo police had asked for the hotel's cooperation in keeping the media outside and away from the survivors for forty-eight hours. The hotel management had balked. Since the hotel was not on Navajo land, it was under no obligation to comply with the request. In the end, a compromise had been reached. In an effort to be sensitive to the needs of the survivors at such a difficult time, the hotel agreed to keep the media off its grounds for at least twenty-four hours. And in the spirit of cooperation, the Arizona state police had stationed a man at the entrance to the parking lot to keep out anyone who didn't belong there.

The moment Rory turned into the parking lot, she was stopped by a state trooper, who called to find out if she was expected. Once she was given clearance, she parked her car and headed inside, trailing her suitcase.

Although she'd expected the lobby to be empty at such

an early hour, she spotted Dr. Richard Ames, Adam Caspian and Dorothy Johnson—all members of the Players—clustered together in armchairs on the far side of the room. When they saw Rory enter, they briefly raised their hands in greeting. Rory waved back, managing a little smile meant to convey her sympathies along with how glad she was that they'd survived their ordeal.

On the other side of the lobby, a waiter was setting out complimentary coffee and fixings on a table near the entrance to the coffee shop, which hadn't yet opened for business. The lobby itself was unremarkable. It had been decorated in blues and browns a decade earlier when that palette had first come into style. The carpeting and upholstery were clean, although worn. Vases with silk flower arrangements had been placed around the room in an apparent effort to perk it up. But having faded over time, they now lent the room an air of benign neglect. A lingering odor of ammonia and other cleaning solutions poked through a veil of floral air freshener. It could have been the lobby in any moderate hotel chain anywhere in the nation.

Rory headed for the reception desk. At first glance, there didn't seem to be anyone on duty, but as she drew closer, she could see a man in his seventies dozing in a chair behind the counter, his chin resting against his chest. A dozen snow-white strands of hair had been artfully arranged across his pink scalp in a last stand against baldness. His wire-rimmed glasses had slipped down to the tip of his nose, where one good snore could send them tumbling off.

Rory was about to clear her throat in an effort to wake him gently when a sudden shriek of joy startled her and sent the elderly clerk scrambling to his feet. She spun around right into the outstretched arms of her aunt Helene.

"Rory, you're a sight for sore eyes," she said hugging her niece tightly to her. "Listen to me quoting my grandmother. You never even met her, did you? No, I think she died before you were born. And now I'm babbling as if I'm demented. Tragedy and insomnia will do that to you," she rattled on before releasing her niece.

Rory stood back and took stock of her aunt. The only visible evidence of her brush with death were a few scrapes on one side of her face and a nasty-looking bruise on the fleshy part of her upper arm that would probably turn every shade of the rainbow before eventually fading away. What concerned Rory more was how exhausted she looked. Helene had always been a high-energy person, but this ordeal seemed to have utterly depleted whatever reserves she had. Even her rumpled clothing looked too tired to keep up appearances. What remained of the eyeliner and mascara she'd applied the previous morning was flaking off, specks of it sticking to her face like a 3-D game of "connect the dots."

"Have you been able to get any sleep?" Rory asked.

"Not much. Every time I close my eyes I see a replay of what happened, and that gets my adrenaline going again. I imagine at some point exhaustion will trump memory, or maybe I'll just run out of adrenaline." She issued a thin laugh that could have passed for a sob.

"Why don't you go sit down while I register," Rory said. "Then we can grab some coffee and talk."

"Register? Don't be silly, you're going to share my room. It's not like I can sleep in two beds at once."

"Okay, then it's straight to the coffee." She threaded her arm through her aunt's and headed for the table, where the waiter was setting out a platter of miniature Danish. Once they'd fixed the coffee to their liking and each chosen one of the breakfast pastries, Helene led the way to a couple of unoccupied chairs.

"Have the police finished interviewing everyone from the troupe?" Rory asked as they sat down and set their food on the little table between them.

"I think so, but they made it clear they want us to stay put here until they tell us otherwise. In fact," she said lowering her voice and leaning closer to her niece, "one of them is still here at the hotel. I guess they're afraid we might make a run for it."

Rory smiled. "I'm not surprised—you're certainly a shifty-looking bunch."

Helene smiled back, and some of the tension in her face relaxed. She took a hearty bite out of her cherry Danish.

"I don't suppose the police mentioned where they were going or what they were looking into?" Rory tasted the coffee, which was anemic in spite of the grounds floating on the surface. She would have tossed it, but it was the only available source of caffeine at the moment.

Helene wiped a bit of frosting from the side of her mouth. "Funny you should ask," she whispered. "I overheard them say they wanted to talk to the people at the weather bureau again—something about a breakdown in communications."

It certainly sounded as if Preston's death was heading toward a verdict of "accidental," with the catchall of "human error" shouldering the blame. If the investigation was able to get past all the inevitable finger-pointing and half-truths, the person or persons who'd committed that error would most likely be fired. The Navajo had to protect the important tourist trade. People making plans to visit the state and the slot canyons needed to know that not only had justice been served, but that they and their families would be safe to vacation and sightsee there in the future. In spite of Zeke's sense that Preston's death was not as open and shut as it seemed, Rory was confident the autopsy and evidence would prove her right. After all, planning a successful murder by flash flood had to be harder than winning the lottery.

She was enjoying a surprisingly good cinnamon-raisin Danish when a man in a dove-gray police uniform entered the lobby through the front door. His uniform was fresh and stiff, the crease in his pants so sharply pressed that he had to be a rookie. Rory figured him for twenty-three, tops. He was lean but solidly built, his black hair pulled back in a leather thong. Her eyes were immediately drawn to the high cheekbones that anchored the broad planes of his face. As an artist, she'd always been fascinated by the topography of the skull and the way it shaped a person's appearance.

Helene bobbed her head in the officer's direction as if to say there's one of them right now. If she was trying to be discreet, she missed the mark entirely. The officer gave her a brief nod in return as if he thought she was greeting him.

"Oh great," Helene groaned softly. "Now he probably thinks I'm flirting with him."

"I wouldn't worry," Rory said. "You didn't break any laws, even if you are old enough to be his mother."

Helene laughed for real this time, her hands flying to her mouth to muffle the sound in consideration of the recent tragedy. Rory felt all the tight muscles in her body relax a little. Her aunt was already on her way back to being the upbeat, quirky woman Rory knew and loved.

She washed down the last of the Danish with a swallow of coffee that was now tepid as well as weak. Telling Helene she'd be right back, she headed over to the table, where the officer was filling a cup for himself. She waited until he'd finished stirring in sugar and milk before addressing him.

"Hi. I'm Rory McCain," she said, extending her hand. "Helene Brody's niece."

"Walter Begay. Pleased to meet you." He gave her hand a good firm shake, which caused the coffee in his other hand to slop up to the rim of the cup. His English sounded a little off to Rory, but it took her a minute to figure out why. Although he spoke with a typical southwestern accent, the rhythm beneath the words was different, no doubt a holdover from his native Navajo tongue.

"I was in Tucson when my aunt called to tell me what happened," Rory said. "I drove up immediately."

"A terrible, uh, a really terrible thing," Walter said, glancing down at his shoes as if they suddenly required his undivided attention. "My, uh, condolences."

Rory tried to put him at ease. "Thanks. I know how difficult it can be to deal with a deceased's family and friends when you're trying to investigate a case."

Walter looked up, bobbing his head in agreement and apparently relieved to move past the awkward etiquette of death.

"I worked as a detective back on Long Island," she went on, slurring over "worked" so that it might as easily have been "work." She was hoping he'd consider her a fellow officer and let down his guard. "How's the investigation going?" she asked before he could think too much about what he'd heard.

"Pretty much routine," he said, hitching up his trousers with his free hand. "Except it's been a long time since anything like this happened. Those canyons are so narrow and winding—if you get a good rain going up north of there, the water will flood them out in next to no time."

"I heard there was some kind of mix-up in communications at the weather bureau," Rory pushed. She felt a bit guilty for taking advantage of a newbie but not guilty enough to stop.

Walter tried his coffee and seemed fine with it. There was truly no accounting for taste.

"You see," he said in an easy tone of camaraderie, "how it works is that the weather bureau sends advisories to the companies that run the tours through the canyons. Slightest chance of rain shuts them right down, no two ways about it. But yesterday that warning either didn't go out in time or it didn't reach the right people. Somewhere the chain broke down."

So simple, so nice and clinical. But Rory had learned firsthand—when her uncle Mac died suddenly—that one person's detached statement of fact was another person's devastating loss. For the first time since Helene's hysterical phone call, she wondered about Preston's family. What had their phone call been like?

# Chapter 5

Exhausted and with little else to do at that early hour, Rory and Helene went to their room, hoping to grab some much-needed sleep. Two hours later, the telephone on the nightstand jolted Rory awake as effectively as the alarm on her cell phone had less than eight hours earlier. She located the receiver by Braille and issued a grudging "hello," trying to remember where she was. Too many hotel rooms in too few days. The sound of her aunt Helene snoring loudly from the bed next to hers quickly reeled in her memory. Either Helene hadn't heard the phone, or she figured Rory could handle it. In any case, the call was for Rory—the Navajo police were requesting an interview. She tried to tell the caller that she wouldn't be able to add anything new to their investigation, but he remained insistent, and since it was never a good idea to argue with the police, she decided to let them discover that truth for themselves.

She pulled on the clothes she'd been wearing when she arrived and splashed her face with cold water to clear out the last cobwebs of sleep. She shoved her room key and cell phone into her pocket and left Helene still snoring away, a fact she would surely deny if it ever came up. Since there was no point in them both being awake, Rory put out the "Please do not disturb" sign before going down to the lobby for her command performance.

What a difference a few hours made. The lobby was buzzing with life, although not the kind with microphones and TV cameras. That was still several hours away. The elderly night clerk had been replaced by two vivacious young women, who were helping guests register or check out. As people learned that the slot canyons wouldn't reopen until the police completed their investigation, there was some grumbling and scrambling to make alternate plans. During her tenure with the police department, Rory had found that most people reacted to a fatal accident with compassion and sympathy until it inconvenienced them. Preston's death was no different.

Looking around she saw that four actors from the troupe were now seated where the three had been when she'd first arrived. Adam Caspian's daughter Sophia had joined them, and someone had arranged for another chair to be set up to accommodate her. They all had the dull, dazed look of survivors, grateful to have escaped Preston's fate but unsure why they'd been spared. Rory scanned the lobby again but still didn't see anyone who looked official. She was wondering how to go about locating the detective who wanted to speak to her when she heard her name. She turned and found herself looking into eyes as hard and black as river rock.

"I'm Detective Daniel Joe," the owner of those eyes said. He was dressed in a uniform similar to the one his rookie was wearing. He gave her a quick dip of the head in lieu of a handshake; she reciprocated in kind. "We've been using the manager's office to conduct our interviews," he went on, heading off in that direction before Rory could summon up a comment or question. She followed behind him, thinking his young rookie could teach him a thing or two about the social graces, when the phone in her pocket started to vibrate. She took it out and saw that it was her friend, Leah. She'd get back to her after her chat with the detective.

The manager's office was directly off the main hall, just steps from the lobby. Joe stopped at the door and ushered her in. The room was on the small side, a desk and three chairs making it seem more cramped. A keyboard and monitor dominated the desk, which held several neat stacks of paper along with some framed family photos.

The detective went around the desk and sat in the high-backed, padded chair behind it. "Take a seat," he said, nodding to the two lesser chairs in front of the desk. Rory thanked him and sat down. He might be socially inept, but she had her standards.

Joe leaned back in the chair and studied her for a minute. Rory had to restrain herself from telling him point-blank that although this little act of his might succeed in intimidating others, it didn't stand a chance of working on her. In fact, if he wanted an affidavit to that effect, she knew a certain federal marshal who would be happy to supply one. She actually found herself wishing she could summon Zeke to materialize right then and there.

"I assume you have some questions you want to ask me?" she said instead.

Joe's eyes narrowed with irritation, as if this were a scripted scene and she'd had the audacity to step on his lines.

"Detective?" she prompted.

He leaned forward, settling his arms on the desk and causing a pile of papers to cascade onto the floor. "Lying to a police officer doesn't get you started on the right foot around here," he said finally. "But then you should already know that, Ms. McCain, having *been* one yourself."

Rory hadn't seen that coming, and she definitely didn't

like being sucker punched. "Excuse me?" she said stalling for time to consider the best response.

"You told Officer Begay you're a detective back in New York."

So her little word dance had twirled around to stomp on her toes. She was surprised Joe had actually checked her out. Didn't he have better things to do with his time—like investigating Preston's death?

"I told him I *worked* as a detective, which is absolutely true," Rory said, realizing that Leah's call had probably been to give her a heads-up. "I can't be responsible for what Officer Begay thought he heard."

"He was mighty sure about it," Joe insisted, clearly unwilling to let go of the subject.

"Again, I can only tell you what I said, not what someone else might have heard." If she'd thought Begay would repeat their conversation to his superiors, she would never have spoken to him. Okay, who was she kidding? She'd wanted information, and Begay had been the quickest path to it at the time.

"I don't know how things work in the Big Apple, what with all the corruption you've got there, but out here things are a lot simpler. We take our officers at their word, and we don't take lightly to folks looking to play us for fools."

"That was never my intention," Rory said. She didn't bother to explain that Long Island wasn't technically part of New York City. She was pretty sure he wasn't in a learning frame of mind. "I apologize if I gave you or officer Begay that impression." Sometimes it was just smarter to act contrite. To be fair, Detective Joe had probably dealt with one too many smart-aleck tourists over the years.

"Where were you at the time of Preston Wright's death?" he asked, abruptly switching topics.

"In Tucson, doing research," she replied evenly. The way things were going, she couldn't very well lie and say she was visiting a nonexistent friend unless she was interested in some new accommodations at the local Navajo jail. "I'm sure the librarian at the Arizona Historical Society will vouch for me."

Joe wasn't taking notes, which told Rory that he wasn't actually interested in her answers. He was just trying to make her sweat as payback for her transgression. She toyed briefly with the idea of breaking down in tears and confessing that she'd arranged for the rain and the flood specifically to kill Preston. But since Joe didn't seem to have a sense of humor, she decided it wouldn't be in her best interests to bait him further.

He asked her how well she'd known the deceased and how she'd describe his relationships with the rest of the troupe. She said that she'd barely exchanged two sentences with the man and that she had no idea about how he interacted with the other actors, since she wasn't even part of the troupe. He seemed about to follow up with another question from his bottomless bag of tricks when his cell phone rang. He took the call and listened for less than ten seconds before hanging up. Rising from his chair, he dismissed Rory as if he were suddenly eager to be rid of her; he exited the office while she was still seated. Curious, she followed him out of the room and into the lobby, wondering what bigger fish had just beached itself on his shore.

# Chapter 6

As Rory watched, Detective Joe strode across the lobby in the direction of his rookie. Begay was standing near the entryway beside a trim blonde who appeared to be in her sixties. She was wearing the same shell-shocked expression as the members of the troupe and kept dabbing at her red-rimmed eyes with a tissue. Begay was once again examining his shoes, the floor, any place other than the woman's face. He looked even more uncomfortable than when he'd expressed his sympathies to Rory earlier, which led her to assume that the blonde was a close relative of Preston's, probably his mother. That would also explain Detective Joe's eagerness to meet her. He'd probably been waiting for her to formally identify the body and perhaps fill in some blanks in his report.

After a moment's debate, Rory started walking nonchalantly toward them, hoping to get close enough to overhear what they were saying. She told herself she wasn't looking for trouble. As far as she knew, there was no law against walking around a public space like a hotel lobby. Besides, Joe's back was to her.

She saw Begay introduce the blonde to his boss, who not only dipped his head, but also shook her hand——VIP treatment, coming from Joe. Before Rory had navigated half the distance to the three, the officers whisked the woman out the front door.

Robbed of her destination, Rory stopped where she was, a human jetty to the ebb and flow of people moving through the lobby. She was trying to decide what to do next when she noticed that Sophia Caspian was waving her over to join them. Sophia, who was two years Rory's junior, had been seated next to her on the flight west, and the two young women had spent most of the time in conversation. She was bright and funny, and to Rory's artistic eye, quite beautiful. Although her individual features would never earn a ten by any plastic surgeon's standards, the combination was striking, the whole much more than the simple sum of its parts.

It didn't take Rory long to decide that some idle chitchat with Sophia and the others was vastly more appealing than listening to her aunt snore, so she headed in their direction. Once they'd all exchanged greetings, Dorothy Johnson excused herself and rose from her seat with the aid of a cane. Her left foot was encased in a bootlike contraption that was making it difficult for her to maneuver. Whenever Rory had seen her at the theatre, she'd been as vivacious and spry as the younger members of the troupe. Even in her present condition, it was hard to believe she was courting seventy.

"I'm off to see if I can catch me a sandman," she said, shaking her head. "The older I get, the more sleep eludes me. And after our little skirmish with mortality, well . . . enough said . . . I'll see you all later." She limped off to the elevator.

As Rory settled into the empty seat, Richard Ames, pathologist and amateur actor, inquired how she'd enjoyed being interviewed by Detective Joe. The trademark British accent he'd held on to in spite of some thirty years in the United States added a delightful kick to his sarcasm. Tall, with graying hair and a strong jawline that had only started to soften now that he'd hit middle age, his accent suited him so thoroughly that it seemed to have been etched into his DNA.

"The detective is nothing if not thorough," Rory replied. Until she had a better sense of these people, she didn't want to be the first to cast any weightier stones. It was a concern that became academic the moment Adam Caspian opened his mouth.

"If you ask me, Joe's like the dictator of a two-bit banana republic," Adam said, with a snap to his words that Rory hadn't expected. Whenever she'd seen him in a play, he was cast in the part of the slightly nerdy, kindhearted friend of the lead. He had a round, open face exaggerated by round wire-rimmed glasses and a rounded paunch where his waist should have been. Sophia had clearly inherited her looks from her mother. Rory wondered how often she thanked her lucky stars.

"He's in his glory now that he's got himself an audience," Adam went on, "and even though I've never met the man before, it's obvious that he's enjoying the hell out of the power trip."

"Come on, Dad," Sophia rebuked him. "That's not fair. The guy's trying to do his job. And it can't be easy with all the media scrutiny."

Adam looked at Rory and sighed a father's sigh of love and bemusement. "My daughter adores the underdog even if he's biting off her hand."

"You don't need to be patronizing," Sophia said, her dark eyes flashing with indignation. "I know you're probably glad that Preston's dead, but that doesn't mean the police can just shirk their responsibility. If I'd been the one who drowned, you'd be all over Joe to search through every needle in every haystack before they labeled my death accidental."

Rory's ears had perked up at Sophia's accusation. Why would her father be glad Preston was dead? And how could she find out what Sophia meant by that remark without coming across as impossibly nosy and rude?

"I'd be a bit more careful with comments of that nature," Richard said, lowering his powerful tenor to a whisper. "No need to give Detective Joe more grist for his mill, if you take my meaning."

Sophia's olive complexion paled a shade or two. "I didn't actually mean my father would ever, could ever . . . I just . . ."

"Hey, it's okay, sweetheart," Adam said patting her hand. "I know you weren't implying anything. But Richard does have a point there. I don't think any of us wants to stay cooped up in this hotel longer than necessary."

The questions were still alive in Rory's mouth; words like tiny battering rams seemed determined to push their way through her lips. She'd nearly convinced herself she could live with being a little rude when Richard's warning stripped away that option. She doubted Detective Joe had had the hotel bugged since it wasn't on Navajo land and he was only there at the pleasure of the management, but that didn't give her the right to take a chance with someone else's reputation. Her curiosity would have to wait for a more discreet time to demand satisfaction. In any case, there was another matter campaigning for her attention.

"Does anyone know the name of the blonde who left with the police?" she asked.

"Clarissa Carpenter," Adam said. "Preston's mother." The others murmured their agreement.

"Carpenter," Rory repeated. "I guess she remarried somewhere along the way. What's she like?"

He shrugged. "I only met her once, after a performance

of *Guys and Dolls*. She seemed standoffish, but to be fair she didn't know me."

"I had much the same impression that day," Richard said. "And I think it's noteworthy that she didn't give her son so much as a peck on the check. Not one 'bravo' or 'well done,' either."

"Not all families are huggy-kissy," Sophia pointed out, "especially in public." She seemed calmer to Rory now that Clarissa was the center of the discussion.

"I'm proud to say that *my* family most certainly is," Helene chimed in as she came up behind Rory. She bent to kiss the top of her niece's head.

"Ah, if it isn't Rip van Winkle," Richard said. "The rest seems to have done you good."

Rory was thinking the same thing, minus the literary reference. Her aunt was quickly returning to herself.

"Am I the only one who's famished?" Helene asked. "Or is it inappropriate to talk about eating at a time like this?"

"I could eat," Adam said, and the rest of them quickly seconded the idea.

"I must say I've had quite enough of the hotel's cuisine," Richard added. "Dare we venture out and risk capture by the media hordes?"

"I say we gird our loins and have at them," Adam said, getting into the spirit of things.

"'One for all and all for one.'" Rory checked her watch. "Detective Joe's twenty-four hours is nearly up anyway."


The intrepid little group returned from lunch in an upbeat frame of mind, quite proud of how well they'd run the media gauntlet. They'd answered every question that was thrown at them with a smile and nothing more, except for Helene, who'd ground her high heel into one reporter's foot when he tried to grab her arm. They'd escaped into a small luncheonette around the corner, where the owner not only barred the press, but gave the survivors free desserts with their meals.

"I think I could get used to this celebrity treatment," Helene announced as she slid the last piece of cinnamon-rich apple pie into her mouth. Rory led the others in a round of good-natured booing that quickly turned to laughter, her aunt laughing so heartily that she almost choked on the pie. Rory knew that the emotional issues Helene and company were struggling with in the aftermath of the flood weren't likely to resolve themselves in a week or even a month, but the laughter was a fine indication they were headed in the right direction.

As they made their way back into the hotel, they were again assaulted by a barrage of questions. This time, the reporters played it safe and kept their distance from Helene's lethal footwear.

Inside, a hand-lettered sign had been posted atop the reception desk announcing that the Navajo Police Department would hold a press conference at two fifteen in the conference room. Well-timed, Rory thought. The police injunction would run out at two anyway, marking the start of open season on the survivors. The media was sure to be in attendance, cameras and microphones at the ready.

Rory and her lunch group headed to the conference room, which turned out to be a relatively small space with a grandiose title. The rest of the troupe was already in attendance, along with the hotel manager, who was supervising the removal of the twenty or so chairs that were usually in there. In order to accommodate more people, the briefing would be standing room only. He left one chair off to the side for Dorothy Johnson, who wasn't supposed to stand for too long on her injured foot.

At exactly two o'clock the media laid siege to the hotel. One minute the lobby was peaceful; the next it was swarming with reporters and cameramen, cursing and shoving each other out of the way in a mad dash to reach the survivors and get on air with their story before their colleagues did. When they reached the conference room, they were pleasantly surprised to find all the survivors waiting there as if they'd been corralled expressly for their purposes. In less than two minutes, every member of the troupe had a microphone thrust in his or her face. Rory lost count of how many eager reporters she disappointed with the fact that she hadn't been in or even near the canyon at the time of the flood. She finally slipped away from the chaos and went back to the lobby to wait for Detective Joe's arrival.

He and Begay arrived a few minutes late without Preston's mother in tow. Presumably she'd already identified her son's remains and been given the official police report, including the cause of death. Rory would have liked to believe that Detective Joe talked Clarissa into skipping the press conference because he had a kind, well-intentioned heart and wanted to protect her from the feeding frenzy going on at that moment in the shark tank otherwise known as the conference room. But with one look at the hard set of his face as he hurried past her, Rory let that particular fantasy expire.

She followed the two policemen back to the room, which came to order as soon as the detective appeared on the raised platform. The reporters stepped back from their subjects; all eyes turned to Daniel Joe.

"I'm going to read a brief statement," he said, "after which I'll take some questions." He withdrew a piece of paper from his shirt pocket, unfolded it and started reading slowly and without inflection. "The investigation into the death of Preston Wright at Gray Wolf Canyon on April 14th has been completed. It is the opinion of the medical examiner that Mr. Wright died of drowning. The various contusions and abrasions he sustained are consistent with a body being thrown against the walls of the canyon by the force of the water. Particles of canyon rock were found inside the largest gash, at the base of his head. It is most likely that that injury knocked him unconscious and led directly to his drowning."

Joe looked up from his paper. "As many of you are aware, there is a system in place meant to prevent this type of tragedy from happening. The tour company that takes people into the canyons shuts down whenever the weather bureau predicts rain north of here. From what we have uncovered, it appears that the warning did go out to the other slot canyons in the area yesterday but not to Gray Wolf Canyon. The person who was ultimately responsible for making that call claims to have become distracted by another matter, and by the time he remembered to issue the warning for Gray Wolf, it was too late. That person's employment with the weather bureau has been terminated. If you have any questions, I'll take them now."

Rory raised her hand. She didn't actually have any questions, but she knew that Zeke did. As he wasn't in a position to ask for himself, she decided to ask for him. Joe nodded in her direction.

"What can I do for you, Ms. McCain?" Rory was sure she heard a note of disdain in his voice. Well, she knew exactly what he could do with it, but she kept that graphic thought to herself. "Doesn't it strike you as a little strange that a man like Mr. Wright, who was fit and in the prime of his life, was the one casualty?" she asked.

The detective shrugged. "It might be as simple as his location in the canyon when the flood hit. Beyond that, no one can account for the whims of fate, not even you, I imagine."

Rory counted to ten . . . then to twenty. At twenty-five her anger finally boiled down to a low simmer. "Thanks for that pithy observation," she muttered to herself. Richard Ames, who was standing next to her, chuckled.

"Remind me not to ever get on your bad side," he whispered.

"What bad side?" she whispered back with a smile.

For the next five minutes, Joe answered questions from the press related to the procedures for flood warnings and the issue of whether another layer of precaution needed to be put in place.

"There is one other piece of information I want to leave you with before I wrap up this briefing," Joe said when the Q&A was over. "During our investigation we discovered that Preston Wright was not actually the deceased's name, but one of several aliases he's been known to use. His actual name is Brian Carpenter. That's all I'm prepared to say about it at this time."

Leaving an armada of questions in his wake, Daniel Joe left the podium and exited the room with Walter Begay at his side.

# Chapter 7

Rory was in complete agreement when the Way Off Broadway Players voted to cancel the rest of their ill-fated trip. Their hearts weren't in it anymore, and they felt they should be home to attend Preston's funeral. Of course, he'd never technically been Preston. But since they'd known him for nearly two years by that name, they were all having a hard time thinking of him as "Brian," and a harder time still trying to make sense of his need for an alias. They'd spent much of the flight home conjuring up all kinds of elaborate scenarios that would explain it, from the Witness Security Program to more colorful possibilities, like a serial killer. What none of them could fathom was why a person who needed an alias would jeopardize his anonymity by performing on a stage for all the world to see. Well, parts of Long Island anyway.

Upon arriving home from the airport, each member of the troupe found a voice mail from Clarissa Carpenter with the pertinent details about Brian's wake and funeral. She apparently subscribed to the actor's motto that the show must go on. And the sooner the better. Rory suspected that most of the troupe would be attending the wake not only to pay their respects to their colleague, but also in the hope that they could learn more about his secretive past. After all, you never knew what a distraught relative might slip and say at such a time.

When Helene called to see if Rory wanted to go with her to the wake the next day, Rory took a few moments to decide. She'd already mapped out a full day of buying groceries, doing laundry, playing with Hobo and catching up on her current cases. In the end, curiosity trumped nearly all of that. She reasoned that if Brian hadn't died, they would all still be in Arizona anyway. Her "to do" list could wait another day to be done, with the exception of Hobo. He wouldn't be cheated out of a single belly rub, throw of the tennis ball or general hugging and cuddling.

Although it was late when their flight landed at JFK, she'd gone directly to her parents' house to pick him up, unwilling to spend her first night home without him. He'd been deliriously happy to see her, dancing around in circles and barking with joy, his whole shaggy body wagging in counterpoint to his tail. Her father had feigned heartbreak, claiming Hobo had led him on.

"There was a lot of bonding going on between the two of them," her mother had explained with a wink. "They played ball together. They sat together on the couch every night watching TV. They shared snacks. Aside from a few unsavory habits, Hobo is the son your father never had."

Rory had promised to bring him back soon for a play date.

That first night back home Hobo had sniffed his way into every corner of the house and every inch of the backyard before he was satisfied that nothing was amiss. Rory had done her own walk through each room checking for Zeke, not that she'd expected to find him there. He was probably still recovering from his trip to Flagstaff.

When she brought her suitcase upstairs, the bed looked so inviting that she wanted nothing more than to snuggle under the covers and drift off to sleep. Unpacking could wait for the morning. Hobo had already jumped onto the bed and was busy arranging the quilt to his liking. Then he turned around three times in a primitive doggie ritual before collapsing into a heap. Rory changed into her nightgown and climbed into bed too. When she tugged part of the quilt out from under him, he didn't even stir.

She closed her eyes, savoring the special contentment of being in her own bed again. The stress of the past few days was slowly draining away. She was on the threshold of sleep, the place where thoughts unravel into dreams, when she thought she heard someone whisper, "Welcome home."

Trading the lively sounds and brightness of a sunny spring day for the dim quiet of the funeral home had an immediate effect upon the psyche. The step automatically softened, the voice lowered, as if not to disturb the eternal rest of the departed. Rory had long suspected it was a subconscious effort to keep the angel of death from knowing you were in the neighborhood.

When she and Helene walked into the room designated for Brian Carpenter, they were surprised to see how few people were there. Clarissa had made it clear the wake would only last one day. Maybe some people had stopped in earlier, and others were planning to come by after work, but that wasn't enough of an explanation to suit Rory. When a person in his forties died under such tragic circumstances, there was usually a great outpouring of sympathy from even the most casual of acquaintances. Of course, that depended largely upon whom Clarissa had informed about the passing of her son. If he'd been in the Witness Security Program or was a serial killer on the lam, it was understandable that she might have chosen to keep it as low-key as possible.

Given how empty the room was, Clarissa was easy to locate. She was standing to one side of the casket talking with an elderly man who was nodding solemnly at what she was saying. Since Rory and Helene didn't want to interrupt their conversation, they slid into the last of several pews behind the three members of the troupe who were the only others presently in attendance. Amy and Greg Renato, the newest members of the Players, were sitting beside Andrew Dobson, the troupe's director. According to Helene, Rory's only authority on the subject, Andrew was a moody, frustrated playwright who taught high school English to pay the rent and hated to be called "Andy." The few times Rory had seen him before the trip, he'd always been wearing the same, sour expression, as if he'd taken a bite out of life and found it bitter with disappointment.

"It's not exactly standing room only in here," Helene whispered, leaning closer to her colleagues.

Amy twisted around in her seat. "I know. We've been here forty minutes, and that guy with Clarissa is the only one who's come in."

"Actually I'm glad you showed up," Greg said, "because we need to get going; we just didn't want to leave Clarissa alone in case that guy doesn't stay long."

Rory nodded. What could be sadder than holding a lonely vigil at a loved one's wake?

Andrew was already standing. Tall and thin with hunched shoulders and a beak of a nose, he reminded Rory of a vulture looking down at them. "Well, I'm afraid it's hello and good-bye for me," he said, edging out of the pew past his companions. "I'm late for a dentist appointment. I'll see you three at rehearsal Monday. Rory, I hope to see you at our next production." He was gone before Rory could assure him she'd be there.

Amy and Greg stayed to chat for a few more minutes, leaving just before the old man did. Now that Clarissa was alone, Helene and Rory made their way down the aisle to pay their respects, hoping someone would show up eventually to relieve them.

Clarissa appeared far more composed than when Rory had last seen her, across the lobby of the hotel. Her makeup was flawless, her short blond hair liberally streaked with highlights. She looked a good ten years younger than she had to be, considering her son's age.

"Thank you so much for coming," she said after they'd introduced themselves and murmured their condolences. "Are you both in the troupe?"

"I am," Helene told her. "My niece plays a supporting role by being in the audience."

Clarissa sighed. "I wish I'd made it my business to come out here to see more of Brian's plays. One of those pointless regrets, I guess."

"So you live on the Island?" Helene asked.

"New Hyde Park. My husband and I bought our first house there. We meant to move on to something bigger and grander, but we never got around to it," she said with a little shrug.

"I've been a widow for five years now, and at this age, I don't have the energy to start uprooting myself. So my first house will most likely be my last house too. Besides, where would I go? Brian was my only child." Tears rose in her eyes, but she clenched her jaw against them and held on to her composure.

Rory tried to think of the right thing to say to bridge what was fast becoming an awkward silence. But aside from a few platitudes, she came up empty.

"The troupe and the audiences will miss Brian," Helene jumped in. "He was really talented—like a chameleon the way he became the characters he played."

Clarissa smiled ruefully. "I can't say that I'm surprised." She turned to Rory. "So how do you spend your time when you're not an audience member?"

"I have a small PI firm," Rory said, thinking that all the mourners she'd known wanted to talk about their lost loved one. Yet Clarissa had changed the subject as if to avoid such a discussion.

"And she used to be a sketch artist for the police department," Helene added proudly.

Clarissa's face brightened. "You're not going to believe this, but after Brian is . . . well . . . settled, I was going to look for a private investigator. And you know what they say—there's no such thing as a coincidence."

"I've always subscribed to that theory myself," Helene said. "And you won't find a better investigator anywhere. In fact, you may have read last summer about how Rory solved two murder cases the police hadn't—"

"Aunt Helene," Rory interrupted sweetly, "let's not bore Clarissa with my résumé."

"That's okay," Clarissa said. "I really think you're meant to be the one. Do you mind if we talk business for a few minutes?"

Although Rory didn't think it was the right time or place for a business meeting, she supposed it was up to Clarissa to decide on the proper etiquette for her son's wake.

Helene promptly excused herself to give them some privacy, and a moment later, Rory found herself seated beside Clarissa in the first pew, feet from where Brian lay in repose.

"As a rule I refrain from talking about my son," Clarissa began stiffly, "so this is going to be a bit difficult for me."

"Take your time," Rory said, "and please be assured

that anything you tell me will be kept in the strictest confidence."

She nodded and produced a lopsided, little smile as if she had half a mind to continue and another to cut and run. Rory watched the inner struggle play out on the woman's face.

"Okay," Clarissa said finally, "here goes. My son could be both utterly charming and absolutely despicable. As a result, he had a fair number of enemies, which is why he moved around a lot and used aliases."

Apparently, Clarissa didn't believe in not speaking ill of the dead. Rory thought she might have at least waited until her son wasn't in the same room.

"I've been expecting this day for the last twenty years," Clarissa went on. "I knew Brian would die in a violent way, though I didn't anticipate it happening quite like this."

"Are you saying you believe Brian was murdered?" Rory asked, hoping her voice didn't betray how ridiculous she found the question.

"Yes, I think it's a distinct possibility."

"But you do know that he was killed in a flash flood, right?"

"I do."

"And that the police investigation and coroner's report all confirmed that it was an accident caused by a horrific mistake on the part of someone at the weather bureau?"

"Yes." A bored expression had settled over Clarissa's features as if she were waiting for the inevitable questions to run their course.

"The odds of someone succeeding at murder by flash flood must be astronomical," Rory pointed out.

"Which is why the killer didn't plan any of it."

"An opportunistic murder?" she asked. "Someone wanted Brian dead and was willing to wait until the perfect scenario might present itself?"

Clarissa nodded.

"People bent on revenge aren't generally known for that kind of patience," Rory pointed out. "And even if you're right, how did someone manage to drown Brian while not also succumbing to the flood? Brian was probably the strongest, most able-bodied person in the canyon that day."

"Believe me, I've considered every one of your questions and others you haven't thought of yet. And no, I haven't completely lost my mind."

"I didn't mean to imply—"

"I know, dear, but let's just assume for the time being that he was murdered."

The old saying that the customer was always right popped into Rory's head. "Okay," she said, although she thought it was a waste of time.

"Even though Brian may have deserved what he got," Clarissa said, "I can't live out the rest of my days without knowing what actually happened."

"That's certainly your right," Rory said thinking she wouldn't have much of a business if people didn't feel the need for closure.

"This may sound strange to you, but I'm not looking to put his killer in prison. The truth of the matter is that Brian would have gone on hurting and ruining innocent people if he'd lived."

"If I agree to take on the case, I need you to understand there's a good chance I won't succeed in finding what you're looking for."

"In other words," Clarissa summed up, "you doubt you'll be able to find his killer, since you don't believe he was murdered."

Rory nodded. "That being said, I'll set my bias aside and make every effort to track down his killer if in fact there was one."

"Fair enough. How much do you require as a retainer to get started?"

Rory spent a minute explaining her fees, and Clarissa insisted on writing her a check on the spot.

"I'll need you to tell me everything you can about your son's relationships with the people who were in the canyon with him. Sometimes what seems trivial winds up being pivotal in solving a case."

Clarissa shook her head. "I'm afraid I won't be much help. My son didn't stay in regular contact with me." She spoke dispassionately, as if she'd sealed the painful emotions in a deep vault a long time ago. "And when I did hear from him, I had to take whatever he told me with the proverbial grain of salt. I don't think he actually understood the difference between lying and telling the truth." She paused for a moment as if to gather the strength to continue.

"Something was missing in Brian," she went on stoically. "I realized it when he was only five. Chances are it was there before then, but I simply refused to see it. No mother wants to accept—" she interrupted herself as two other members of the troupe entered the room. "I guess we'll have to leave it there for now," she whispered, popping a demure smile in place as Brett Campbell and Jessica Krueger walked up to them.

If Brett had sustained any injuries in the flood, they were hidden beneath his clothing, but Jessica had a cast on her left forearm, along with a sling to hold it in a neutral position against her body.

Since other reinforcements might not arrive for hours, if at all, Rory took that opportunity to excuse herself and say she'd be in touch. She found Helene sitting on a stone bench just outside the funeral home enjoying a chocolate-covered ice-cream bar from one of the trucks that trolled the streets that time of year. During the half-hour ride home, she let her aunt hold up both ends of the conversation while she thought about Brian Carpenter. Some stones were just better left unturned, and she suspected that what lay beneath his was dark and ugly. Maybe she should have refused to take the case. But it was too late now; her curiosity had already set up shop.

# Chapter 8

"It's good to have you and the mutt home." Zeke grinned, the slash of dimples around his mouth like fissures carved into the planes of his face by time and adversity. He was standing in the backyard with Rory watching Hobo retrieve the tennis ball she'd thrown for him.

Minutes earlier, the marshal had appeared fresh from rehab, causing Rory to literally jump with the surprise of finding him right in front of her. They had to think of a better way for him to announce his arrival when there were no electric lights for him to flicker. On one occasion, he'd tried saying her name, but she'd been just as startled by the unexpected sound of his voice.

Hobo, on the other hand, wasn't at all taken aback to see his former nemesis pop out of the ether. After Zeke helped save his life, Hobo had wholeheartedly accepted him into the pack without bias against his lack of flesh and bone. In his worldview, there were no gray areas. You were either good or bad, part of the pack or not.

As soon as Zeke had materialized, he'd requested an update on the events in Page, which Rory provided in great detail, including the fact that Clarissa had hired her and finishing with the strange news that Preston's name was an alias.

"This case just gets more and more interestin'," he'd said, almost licking his chops like Hobo at dinner time hoping for a windfall of steak.

Rory had to bite her lip to keep from laughing at the image that came to mind. The marshal didn't have much tolerance for being the butt of jokes.

Hobo dropped the ball at Zeke's feet with a bark, clearly requesting that he throw it. Chuckling, the marshal focused his energy, scooped up the ball and sent it burning across the yard, causing Rory to wonder if there was any rule against ghosts pitching in the major leagues. She watched Hobo joyfully bound after the ball. Six months earlier, she would have taken all bets against the two "men" in her life ever getting along. Now the three of them were like a family, albeit an unorthodox one. A family complete with arguments and slamming doors. Of course, she was pretty much the only one who slammed them. Zeke generally just disappeared in a huff, and Hobo had to rely on barking his displeasure, since he lacked an opposable thumb.

"Clarissa claims her son had a lot of enemies," Rory said. "She's absolutely convinced one of them used the flood to conceal his murder."

"So I'm not the only one who thinks fate might have had a helpin' hand that day."

"Which doesn't automatically make you right," Rory pointed out. "Clarissa could be crazy as a loon."

"You've seen evidence to that effect?"

"You mean during my one and only conversation with her? Not really, but we didn't talk for more than a few minutes and not under the best of circumstances. Her son's casket was only a few feet away."

When Hobo returned with the ball, he dropped it in front of Rory as if he were making an effort to be fair and alternate between them. As she bent to pick it up, she heard the house phone ring. She'd forgotten to take the handset out with her and had to run inside to answer it. She knew Zeke would be all right without her as long as it wasn't for more than five or six minutes. After that he'd be snapped back into the house as though he were tethered to a temperamental bungee cord. If that happened she could depend on his grousing about it for days. In spite of how hard he'd tried to push that particular envelope, he hadn't met with any real success. His ability to travel or stay outside the house without Rory seemed to be an immutable boundary, and Rory prayed it would stay that way.

She made it back outside just under the wire to find Zeke talking to Eloise Bowman. For a quiet neighborhood, things could sure change in the blink of an eye. Warning Zeke about the latest addition to their neighborhood had been the next topic on Rory's agenda, but Eloise had beaten her to it. From what Rory could tell as she flew out the kitchen door, so far things were under control. They might have been any two neighbors in any American town who'd stopped to chat on a lovely spring day. But, of course, they weren't. One of them was a ghost, and the other a stroke victim with extra-sensory abilities.

Eloise looked somewhat more presentable than she had the day Rory first met her. The tufts of white hair had been combed flat against her head as if someone had tried to tame them into a style but eventually gave up and settled for making them neat. She was wearing shapeless, green polyester pants with a purple tee shirt tucked into the elastic waistband, like a toddler who'd insisted on dressing herself and didn't know how to coordinate colors. This time her feet weren't bare but clad in sneakers. Given her proclivity for escaping from the Bowman house, it seemed to Rory that another type of footwear might make better sense.

As she came up beside Eloise she heard her saying, "You need to learn how to forgive yourself, Ezekiel." Her words were solemn, nothing little-girl-like in her tone. This was the Eloise who'd warned Rory about the impending trouble on her trip. Bad timing squared.

Zeke's jaw was clenched so hard that Rory imagined she could hear the sound of teeth grinding on teeth. Aware of it or not, Eloise had shot an arrow straight into the darkest corner of his soul—a place Rory had been tiptoeing around for months. She sent him a silent plea not to vanish into thin air out of anger. The last thing Eloise needed was more fodder for her addled brain.

"Eloise, what a nice surprise," Rory said brightly, hoping to diffuse the situation. "Does your family know you've gone out for a walk?"

"I like to walk," Eloise replied, back to her happy-go-lucky self. She picked up the ball Hobo had dropped at her feet when he'd come to sniff out her intentions. "Can I throw it for him?"

"I'm sure he'd like that. Did you tell anyone you were leaving?" she tried again.

Eloise clapped her hands when Hobo caught the ball and brought it triumphantly back to her.

"I had a dog when I was eight," she said. "His name was Arnold. No, wait; that was the cat's name." Her forehead rippled with the effort of rummaging around for the right memory.

Rory took her by the hand. "Why don't I walk you home? Hobo has to go in and take a nap now anyway."

"Are you going inside too, Marshal?" Eloise asked as Rory started to lead her away.

"Everyone's going inside, *right*?" Rory glared at him when he didn't immediately respond.

"Yes, ma'am, I'll be goin' inside," he grumbled, "seein' as how I don't have any choice in the matter."

* * *

"What were you thinking?" Rory demanded when she returned from escorting Eloise home. "You should have vanished the second you saw her heading this way. She's not exactly quick on her feet, and I'm sure that at her age her eyesight isn't great either."

Zeke was sitting on the third riser of the staircase. She could hear Hobo in the kitchen noisily lapping water from his bowl. Zeke must have "pushed" the door open to let him in.

"I was thinkin' I'd be neighborly and practice my conversation skills," Zeke said hotly, as if to let Rory know that he wasn't the defendant here. "But that woman knew my name before I had a chance to introduce myself. You should've cleared it with me before you started advertisin' my presence."

Rory swallowed her not-so-righteous indignation. "I didn't tell anyone about you," she said. "I met her the day I left for Arizona, and she already knew who you were. If neither of us told her, then she must have some kind of psychic ability."

"Ain't that just dandy," he muttered.

Rory repeated what Doug Bowman had said about his mother's stroke, along with the fact that no one actually believed the strange stories she'd been coming up with ever since then.

"So for now at least I don't think we have anything to worry about."

"Be that as it may, I refuse to have any more to do with her," Zeke announced with finality. He rose and came down the steps to Rory. "I don't want you around her either."

Rory was about to back away as she usually did when they were in tight quarters. She'd never come in contact with Zeke, and she had no desire to find out what such an ectoplasmic experience might be like. Some things were better left to the imagination. But this time she stopped herself and stood her ground. She didn't want Zeke to interpret her withdrawing as a sign of backing down and obeying. He didn't get to decide who she could or couldn't see. It was a good thing she'd never been conscripted into the military. She would have made one lousy soldier.

Even if she'd wanted to comply with his order, it would have been difficult to do. They lived on the same block, and in spite of the Bowmans' efforts to keep their matriarch under lock and key, she seemed to be channeling Houdini.

"You were with her for less than five minutes, Marshal. Why do you find her so threatening?" Rory asked, knocking the fight back into his court.

"Threatening? I'll have you know, Aurora, that there ain't a soul on this earth who's ever scared me. I just don't cotton to folks who can read my mind. It's unnatural."

"You know I don't like being called 'Aurora,'" she reminded him. It had been awhile since he'd used her full given name, and it was clear he was doing it now just to irritate her.

"I know," he said, a smile cracking his stony expression. "I'm fairly sure that's why I find it so charmin'."

"Really?" She shrugged. "Well, that's fine, because I've decided I don't care anymore." She made the statement out of pure pique, but as she said the words, she realized they were actually true. "You have my blessing to call me 'Aurora' whenever you like." She watched the smile desert him, leaving bewilderment in its wake. She could even feel a subtle shift in the balance of power that was always seesawing between them. When she'd told him she hated the name, she'd basically handed him a weapon with which to needle her. Disarming him was so simple—why on earth hadn't she thought of it months ago?

"Now," she went on, since he still seemed at a loss for words, "regardless of whether or not I have your permission to see my aunt Helene, I have an appointment with her in a few minutes, and I fully intend to keep it."

# 1878

## The New Mexico Territory

Marshal Ezekiel Drummond made his way to the Albu-querque blacksmith's shop on legs that threatened to give out at any moment. When he'd been brought in to Dr. Walter Abbott more dead than alive, his horse had been taken to the smithy, where it was stabled to await the marshal's eventual recovery or demise. Although still weak from the gunshot that had nearly killed him, Drummond had insisted on leaving his sickbed within hours of regaining consciousness. To his way of thinking, he had no choice. Too many days had already passed, and once again, the unthinkable had happened. While he'd lain senseless in bed, another young girl had been abducted. He knew without a doubt that John Trask was responsible. Only one question remained—was she still alive, or had Trask already killed her?

Dr. Abbott was a pragmatist as well as a quick study. He'd realized that no matter what he said, he would not be able to change the marshal's mind. So he'd seen to it that his patient ate a decent meal before he left, and he sent his son, Henry, along to carry the marshal's saddlebags down to the stable. At first, Drummond had declined even that help, announcing that he was perfectly capable of managing the bags himself. But Mrs. Abbott had stocked them so full of provisions that when he'd tried to lift them, he'd fallen back against a conveniently situated wall. Acknowledging that pride alone wouldn't get the job done, he'd finally accepted Henry's help.

The two-block walk to the smithy was difficult for Drummond, who was winded before he even left the house. It took every bit of his concentration to plant one foot in front of the other and remain upright. Every rock in the road, every rut could easily prove to be his undoing. Henry walked close beside him, brows pinched with concern, ready to jump into action if the marshal should stumble or otherwise require his assistance. Under most circumstances, the marshal would have chafed at being the focus of such attention, but it was somehow more palatable in that young Henry was himself training to be a doctor.

Although the day was not overly warm, by the time they reached the smithy, a fine sweat coated Drummond's body and glistened on his face. Nausea had set his stomach to roiling like a boat riding heavy seas, and it was questionable whether his lunch would stay with him. He stopped to lean against a wall of the smithy until his body reached a decision.

"Mr. Drummond, is there something I can do for you?" Henry asked, clearly troubled by his patient's current state. "Perhaps you should reconsider and stay on with us awhile longer. We'll have you fit as a fiddle in no time, I promise you."

"I'm sure that's true, Henry, since you and your father seem to have brought me back from death once already. But I have responsibilities and obligations I can't ignore. And if I don't take care of them, I'd just as soon be dead."

Henry shook his head but kept his counsel to himself, for which the marshal was deeply grateful.

Once his stomach had quieted sufficiently, he bolstered himself with as deep a breath as he could manage given the pain in his shoulder and drew away from the wall. For the first time he noted the dense smell of horses. Dense but not offensive, an important distinction that meant the stable was clean, the horses well cared for. It lifted his spirits to know that the chestnut had been treated properly during his incapacity. With Henry by his side, he made his way through the courtyard, where the blacksmith sometimes shod horses in good weather, and entered the building. The inside space, which was loosely divided between the forge and the stable, was larger than Drummond had expected. And there was a back door near the stable that provided good ventilation for its occupants.

He'd barely stepped foot into the relative darkness of the smithy when the chestnut started to whinny. He recognized the sound instantly, in the way that a mother can pick out the sound of her child's voice from a thousand others in a crowd. A smile pulled at his mouth. He hadn't smiled in so long that his skin felt too tight, as if it could no longer accommodate that expression. With a spryer step Drummond followed the whinnying to where the chestnut was doing an excited little dance in the narrow confines of his stall, his head bobbing up and down with joy.

The horses in the other stalls watched with ears pricked forward as Drummond ran his hand along the side of the chestnut's head, then laid his cheek against his muzzle. The animal immediately calmed, nickering softly in contentment. At that moment, the blacksmith entered the stable through the rear door. He was a burly man with the look of health in his plump, rosy cheeks. Henry introduced him to Drummond as Barrel Williams.

"Pleased to see that you've recovered," Barrel said over

a firm handshake that sent a shock of pain through the marshal's shoulder.

"Thank you," Drummond replied, rescuing his hand at the first opportunity. "Much obliged for taking such good care of my horse."

"I do the best I can for these fine creatures," Barrel said. "Never once has a horse disappointed me. That's a heap more than I can say about my own kind," he added with a chuckle.

Under other circumstances, Drummond might have enjoyed a whiskey and lengthier conversation with the smith, who apparently shared some of his own philosophy. But things being what they were, he paid Barrel for the chestnut's board and with Henry's assistance saddled the horse. Henry laid the saddlebags across the horse's withers and led him outside. Drummond managed to swing up into the saddle but nearly fell off the other side when a wave of dizziness gripped him. He gritted his teeth, holding on with sheer determination until the world stopped spinning around him. Then he thanked Henry and bid him and Albuquerque good-bye.

Late in the afternoon of his second day on the road he met up with the search party that had been out looking for the missing girl. They were as grim a group of men as he'd ever come across. Their words confirmed what their faces had already told him. They'd found the girl but too late to do her any good. Drummond hammered them with questions, but in the end, all they could tell him was the place where they'd found her and the fact that her killer had left no tracks. Despair in their eyes, they wished him Godspeed.

Whatever reserves of strength had seen Drummond through the last two days sluiced out of him, along with hope. Trask had another notch in his gun belt and time enough to disappear forever into the consuming vastness of

the country. Weary of body and spirit, Drummond made
camp for the night. Had he been a different sort of man, he
might have prayed for death to come while he slept. Instead,
he prayed for the strength to go on.

# Chapter 9

H elene had insisted that the meeting take place in Rory's office. She wanted the experience of being interviewed by a PI to be as authentic as possible. Either she'd found her interview with the Navajo police wanting or she was just trying to broaden her repertoire. Rory didn't know exactly what her aunt was expecting. If it was a grilling under a naked lightbulb, she was going to be sorely disappointed.

Zeke had abruptly retired after their little argument, and Hobo was busy snoozing from his romp outside, so Rory went out the kitchen door alone to meet her aunt. She found Helene waiting near the old carriage house that now held the office of Drummond and McCain Investigations.

"How long have you been waiting?" Rory asked as she hurried across the yard to her.

"Only ten minutes or so." Helene was decked out in a gray suit, complete with stockings and high heels. Her hair was pulled back in a tidy bun that didn't do her face any favors.

Rory was surprised when her aunt didn't immediately envelop her in an embrace. She was generally an enthusiastic hugger. Instead she greeted Rory with a rather formal "hello" and a handshake. Something was definitely up, but since Helene always had a specific method to her madness, Rory was willing to wait and see where she was headed.

"Why didn't you just ring the bell?" she asked as she unlocked the office door. "You could have waited for me in the house."

"I want to play by the rules, or it's no fun playing at all," Helene whispered as she stepped inside. "Not that Preston's—excuse me—Brian's death has been fun," she quickly recanted. "But you know what I mean."

Rory wasn't entirely sure that she did. Her best guess was that her aunt was using their meeting as an impromptu little drama in which she played a character witness in a murder case. The acting bug had taken its pound of flesh.

Doing her best to play along, she offered her aunt a seat.

Helene thanked her and sat down in the armchair, smoothing her skirt demurely over her knees.

Rory took her seat behind the desk. "I asked you to come because I'm hoping you can give me a sense of Brian Carpenter's relationships with the others who were in the slot canyon the day he died. I'm also interested in hearing your thoughts about the man himself."

Helene adjusted her position in the chair and cleared her throat. "Well, if I had to describe him in one word, I think that word would be 'slick.'"

"Slick? In what way?"

"He reminded me of a politician. He was always smiling and knew just what to say to ingratiate himself. I had the feeling he was acting even when he wasn't on stage. And I don't mean like what I'm doing today," she whispered in another aside.

"That's okay," Rory whispered back, "I understand."

"Having said that, I want to point out that initially at least he was extremely easy to like. Apparently, even to love." Helene smiled slyly as if she knew her niece would pounce on the tasty little morsel she'd just set out.

Rory's eyebrows arched with interest. One thing she'd learned during her short career was that love often played a role in murder. "Can you give me a name?"

"You mean names."

Zeke was right—this case was getting better and better. "I'm listening."

"There were plenty of rumors flying around, and lots of drama as you can imagine with a group of thespians, but I'm going to stick to the facts as I know them."

Rory waited, pen poised over notepad.

"As far as I could tell, Brian was never without female companionship. He was like a chain-smoker that way. His first conquest in our troupe was Jessica Krueger. When that liaison cooled off, he hooked up with Sophia Caspian. They were together quite awhile. Her father wasn't thrilled, to say the least, but I'm not sure if it was because of the big age difference between them or for some other reason. In any case, by the time of his death, Brian had moved on again to Amber Luft, who wasn't on the trip with us."

"I assume he ended one affair before starting another?"

"There could easily have been some overlap, judging by how out of joint certain noses were at times."

"It must have been hard for all of them to work together under those circumstances."

"Not as hard as you might think. As actors we're used to putting ourselves aside and adopting other personas," Helene said, as if she'd been on the stage for thirty years instead of two. "It's part of our job description."

"Would you happen to have phone numbers for the two women and Adam?"

Helene opened her handbag and pulled out a sheet of

paper. "This is a list of the whole troupe with their numbers and addresses. I put a check mark next to the ones who were on the trip in case you've forgotten who's who."

Rory thanked her and set the paper on the desk. She shouldn't have expected any less from her aunt. "You said that Brian was well liked by everyone in the beginning, but that Adam Caspian had no use for him even before he dumped Sophia. Who else defected from his fan club?"

"Jessica, of course, after he dumped her. She's carried that chip on her shoulder for so long now it might need to be surgically removed."

"And Sophia?"

"Sophia may be young, but she's a smart cookie. I mean it was obvious she was upset when it was over, but she seemed determined to remain friendly with Brian. In my opinion, she was trying not to make too much of it, because her father was so irate. And he did mellow to some degree when he saw that she was okay."

Irate Adam moved straight to the top rung of Rory's ladder of suspects. "Anyone else?"

"Those are the only ones I know about in the romance department," Helene said.

"There were other departments?"

"There must have been, because Richard Ames and Brett Campbell also jumped off the bandwagon, although months apart."

"It sounds like it was easier to despise Brian than to like him, in spite of his initial charm," Rory said. Clarissa was apparently right about her son's talent for cultivating enemies.

"Even Dorothy Johnson turned on him," Helene added as an afterthought. "One day she's baking him ginger-spice cookies, and the next she won't even say 'hello' to him. I've never figured out what happened between them. I asked her one day when my curiosity got the better of me, but she shrugged it off and changed the subject."

Rory was about to ask if Brian ever talked about his past when the recessed lighting in the office started to flicker. Uh-oh. "Not now," she said emphatically. She knew her aunt was going to wonder why she was scolding the light fixtures, but in the end, it would be easier to plead temporary insanity than to explain an appearance by Zeke.

"Excuse me?" Helene said on cue.

Rory dropped her pen and pad and pushed back from the desk. "Sorry. The lights in here have been driving me crazy lately. I really have to call an electrician. But, no harm—we were pretty much done anyway." She walked over to the door and opened it. "Thank you so much for coming in." For her aunt's sake, she was trying to remain in character as she rushed to end the scene before Zeke could give it a paranormal twist.

Helene stood up, her mouth open as if she were trying to figure out what to say now that her costar had skipped past several pages of script. By the time she reached the door, she'd rounded up her composure. "I'm glad I've been able to help. Feel free to call me if you have any other questions."

"That's very kind. Why don't I walk you to your car?" Rory said following her out. "I'll take care of the problem in here later," she added, ratcheting up the volume so that anyone in a five-mile radius would have heard her.

Helene came to an abrupt stop and turned back to her. "Are you okay, dear?"

Why? Can you see the steam coming out of my ears? Rory managed a smile and hoped it was convincing. "Yes, I'm fine."

"Well, if you're sure. . . ." Helene pulled her into a tight hug. "Thanks for playing along with me. It was really terrific, even though I thought it was going to be more intense."

"You definitely would have gotten more bang for your buck if this was the police station and you were an actual suspect. But please don't take that as a suggestion," Rory said with a lighthearted laugh meant to reassure her aunt nothing was wrong. After Helene drove off, Rory marched back to her office minus the smile, with a very different sort of conversation in mind.

She found Zeke perched on the arm of the couch waiting for her. "What was that all about?" she asked, not bothering to sit.

"Some good old-fashioned eavesdroppin'," he said, sounding quite pleased with himself. "It would be a lot simpler if I could just hear things firsthand, at the same time you do."

Rory was about to object, but she stopped herself. What was she doing? Either he was her partner or he wasn't. She couldn't have it both ways. She'd grown so accustomed to arguing with the marshal that it had become a reflex. Surely he'd earned the right to have his thoughts given consideration and not rejected out of hand. "And the flickering lights?" she asked.

"It seemed only right that I should let you know I was around," he said, "although I can see as how we need a different signal when I'm plannin' to stay out of sight."

"Thank you. It might keep me from acting like a complete idiot again."

Zeke grinned, eyes twinkling with mischief. "Well now, that's a pretty tall order, and there's only so much I can do."

Rory shook her head and laughed. Maybe a little more patience and restraint on her part would actually work. Hey, it was worth a shot.

"There you go," Zeke said, "you didn't leave your sense of humor out west after all."

"Shouldn't we be having this conversation in the house?"

she asked, since he seemed to expend far too much energy even commuting the short distance to the office. From what she could tell, there was little if any correlation between measurements of time and distance in her world and the dimension he inhabited.

"Thoughtfulness *and* a sense of humor. Are you tryin' to stun me into submission?"

"If only."

O nce they were seated at the kitchen table, Rory summarized her conversation with her aunt, since Zeke had only heard the tail end of it. He was right. It definitely made more sense for him to hear and see things firsthand, complete with facial expressions and body language. As long as he didn't take the inch she was offering and stretch it into a mile. She shook off the little voice in her head that was second-guessing her decision. If she wasn't willing to trust him, their relationship was never going to work in the long run.

"We're sure as hell not lackin' for motives," Zeke said, already wading knee-deep in the possibilities of the case.

"Assuming it was murder," she reminded him.

"I'll bet there are other motives in the troupe Helene's not even aware of," he went on, as if she hadn't spoken. "You're goin' to have to interview everyone who was in the canyon. And bein' actors, they're likely to be real talented at hidin' the truth."

Rory got up for a glass of water. When the marshal was fired up, it was just easier to let him run out of steam than to try to stop him.

"I'll tag along as often as I can, energywise. It'll be like havin' an extra pair of eyes and ears with you."

As long as that wasn't in the literal sense. Rory had a brief but horrible vision of Zeke's eyes and ears blossoming out of thin air while she was interviewing someone. She told herself that would never happen, that he only appeared by choice. At least he'd always made it seem that way. Who was she kidding? She had to know for sure.

"You can't materialize by accident, right?" she asked.

"I don't believe so."

She suppressed a groan. Why couldn't he have simply said "'right'"—a firm, unequivocal "'right.'" "What if you were so focused on listening to a conversation that you let down your guard a bit—could it happen then?"

"I imagine almost anythin' can happen given the proper circumstances, darlin', but the odds are you've got nothin' to worry about."

And right then and there she started worrying.

# Chapter 10

When Rory started calling the members of the troupe to set up interviews, the number one name on her list was Adam Caspian. According to the offhand comment his daughter had made, he was glad Brian was dead. That sounded like a man with a motive to Rory's way of thinking. Now, if she could just tease a confession out of him, she wouldn't have to bother interviewing anyone else; the case would be closed in record time. But when she reached Adam by phone, her hopes were quickly dashed.

"I heard Clarissa hired you," he said after Rory identified herself. "She really believes her son was murdered, huh?" Apparently the troupe's grapevine was as efficient as a posting on Facebook.

"Yes, that's true."

"Then I have some good news for you," he said cheerfully.

"What's that?" If it was a confession, Rory swore she'd go back to believing in Santa Claus and the tooth fairy.

"You can cross Sophia and me off your list of possible suspects."

So much for childhood fantasies. "Why would you assume you were on such a list?" she asked, thinking she might reap some useful information by playing dumb.

Adam chuckled as if he'd just heard a good joke. "Come on, Rory. How naïve do you think I am? Clarissa hires you to catch a killer, and out of the blue you call me. We've never said more than a few words to one another. Am I wrong? Did you call to ask me out to dinner or a movie?" The chuckle was still there behind his words.

"Okay," she said, "so why is it I can cross you off this supposed list of mine?"

"You know what they say—location, location, location." Adam was positively jolly. "And throw in an eyewitness for good measure."

"You've definitely got my attention," she said, wishing they were having this discussion in person so that she could read his face as well as his voice.

"Sophia and I were the last ones into the canyon," he said, sobering quickly as he began to recount the details of that day. "And we were the first ones out when the flood hit."

"Just a happy coincidence?"

"Not entirely. We'd been chatting with Jerry, our guide, on the walk to the canyon entrance. Sophia had asked him about the history of the area, and Jerry was obliging but a bit long-winded. Anyway, he was still answering her question as the rest of the group started filing inside, so we wound up being the last ones." Adam paused, either for effect or because the horror of the day had seized him again. "We couldn't have been there for more than a few minutes when the flood swept in. I credit Jerry with saving our lives. And now it seems we also have him to thank for providing us with an alibi."

"You were lucky on several counts that day," Rory said,

thinking it all sounded too pat. "Would you mind if I called and spoke to this Jerry? You know, due diligence and all for my investigation."

"No problem." Adam's buoyant tone was back as if he'd shaken off the memory the way Hobo shook the rain from his coat. "I actually took down his number in case something like this came up." Talk about being prepared. Adam must have made a fine Boy Scout.

"So you're just crossin' the Caspians off the list?" Zeke asked incredulously after Rory told him about her conversation with Adam.

"Not 'just,'" Rory came back. "I called the guide and had a long talk with him. He verified everything Adam told me and then some. If ever a job suited a person, his does. That man sure loves talking. I was even treated to a lesson about how the slot canyons were discovered before I was able to get off the phone."

"Well, that's all fine and dandy, but did it occur to you that maybe Adam paid him for his cooperation? I doubt tour guides up there on Indian land earn a heap of a lot. A chance to make some extra cash could be awfully tempting."

"Of course I thought of that," she said, annoyed by the defensiveness that immediately infiltrated her tone. "Jerry sounded very relaxed, not at all nervous or rehearsed."

"Money can have that kind of calmin' effect."

"Short of kidnapping and torturing the man, how would you like me to make sure he was telling the truth?"

"By keeping Adam and his daughter on that list for now."

Rory had to admit that what the marshal was suggesting made a certain amount of sense. But putting them back on the list made her feel like the investigation was moving in reverse, which it pretty much was.

*  *  *

After the Caspians, Rory had no particular order in which she wanted to conduct the rest of the interviews. As a result, the first actual interview was with Richard Ames, MD, simply because he was the first one to answer the phone when she called. She'd tried four of the other actors before him but wound up leaving four voice-mail messages. Either they were a busy bunch, or some of them were screening their calls. Technology wasn't always the boon it was cracked up to be.

Although Richard wasn't on her aunt's list of those with known grudges against Brian, Rory couldn't afford to ignore any Player who'd been in the canyon that day. She still didn't believe Brian had been murdered, but Clarissa did, and she was the one paying the bills.

She arranged to meet Richard at his home in Lido Beach at seven o'clock that evening. He'd sounded surprised to hear from her and more surprised to learn that she'd been hired to investigate Brian's death. It appeared the grapevine hadn't reached him yet. Rory told him she just wanted to get his insights into Brian and his relationships with the other members of the troupe. She'd decided to use the same excuse with all the Players she interviewed. People opened up more easily when they weren't on the defensive.

As soon as she hung up, she did a Google search on him. Apparently Richard Ames was a popular name on planet Earth. It was a good thing he was also a doctor. That narrowed the parameters substantially, leading her to Richard Ames, pathologist and member of the Way Off Broadway Players. From what she could see, there were no red flags. Nothing specific to jot down and inquire about when she talked to him.

Zeke had been keeping a low profile since she'd agreed to let him be her invisible fly on the wall, with "invisible" being the operative word. She still had some trepidation about opening that door to him, but in the interest of harmony she'd adopted a wait-and-see attitude. For his part, Zeke had been conserving energy in order to be at maximum readiness to play his new role. He'd worked out a signal to let Rory know when he was in the room—a gentle tap on the shoulder. They'd tested and refined it a dozen times, since tapping by remote-control energy was hardly an exact science. By the time Rory was satisfied that the pressure was enough to catch her attention without startling her, Zeke was grumbling under his breath about a princess and a pea. She let his words hang in the air without rebuke, proud of her self-restraint.

She arrived at the Ames' home with a few minutes to spare, the trip south to Lido Beach having taken more than an hour in the last of the evening rush. The houses on the block were large and clearly expensive but built so closely together that it was hard to discern any beauty in the jumble of different architectural styles. Since land there was a commodity in short supply, if you wanted to be on the water you had to make sacrifices.

Richard's two-story contemporary overlooked the calm waters of Reynold's Channel, while a quarter-mile directly south of it, the waves of the Atlantic Ocean pounded the shore. Since it was only late April, the summer crowds were still months away, which meant parking was not a problem. When Rory emerged from her car, it was fully dark, even though they were already on daylight saving time. A sharp wind was whipping off the ocean, heavy with salt and the pungent smell of low tide. She tugged the sides of her leather jacket together. She'd forgotten how much cooler the temperature on the south shore could be, a benefit only in the heat of summer. She climbed the bullnose-marble steps to the Ames' front door and rang the bell.

To her relief, Richard answered the door in a matter of

seconds. "Come in, come in," he said. "I have hot water up
for tea. It's that sort of night, isn't it?" He chattered on about
the weather as he led her past a formal living room and
dining room and down a wide center hallway to a gourmet
kitchen that flowed into a spacious family room. Rory
couldn't help thinking that it was a lot of house for a wid-
ower whose only daughter was away at college—information
Helene had eagerly imparted when Rory called her on the
way to the interview.

"You have a beautiful home," she said, accepting a seat
in an armchair that faced a broad bank of windows. She was
sure the view in front of her had to be spectacular during
the day, but at night, with only a few, dull lights in the distance, it was like having a ringside seat at the edge of the
abyss. When Zeke gently tapped her on the shoulder a
moment later, she literally jumped several inches off her
seat. For once, she couldn't put the blame on him.

Luckily, Richard was in the kitchen with his back to her,
busy making their tea and providing a lively little tutorial
about the proper preparation of tea and the great American
sin of using bags rather than leaves.

"Milk or lemon?" he inquired, turning to her.

"Just sugar, thank you." She was surprised her voice
wasn't quivering like her insides.

Richard placed a cup on the table beside her. With his own
cup in hand, he sat on the couch, with his back to the daunting
view. Rory thought about asking if they could switch seats,
but she didn't know if he would be offended. In all likelihood
he'd offered her what he considered the best seat in the house.
So she picked up her cup instead and dutifully sipped the tea,
proclaiming it superior to any she'd tasted before, although
in reality she couldn't detect much of a difference.

Richard beamed, the thin skin around his eyes crinkling
like finely shattered glass. "Precisely my point. You'd be
amazed by how many people can't tell the difference."

Rory shook her head, thinking she wouldn't be amazed at all.

After several minutes of sipping tea and polite but inane conversation, she felt another tap on her shoulder. It took all of her willpower not to snap at Zeke out loud. She wanted to get on with the interview as much as he did. But if he didn't work on his patience, he wouldn't be accompanying her in the future. Courtesy might not count for much in his world, but in the world of the living, it was still held in fairly high esteem.

Rory waited for a natural break in the conversation, at which point she said politely, "We can get started—if that's okay with you?"

"By all means." Richard leaned back against the cushions as if he was settling in for an evening's light entertainment.

She set down her cup and withdrew a small pad of paper and a pen from her handbag. When she looked up again, she focused on Richard's face so that she wasn't distracted by the barren darkness beyond him.

"How well did you know Brian?" she asked.

"Not as well as I should have, as it turned out. You've heard the saying 'Keep your friends close and your enemies closer'?"

Talk about an attention grabber. That was quite an opener for someone being interviewed in a murder investigation. In her experience, even innocent people withheld that sort of comment for fear that it might be taken the wrong way. Either Richard had no reason to worry or he wanted to give her that impression.

"How do you mean?" She kept her tone neutral with a dash of ho-hum, as if she heard that sort of remark in every case she investigated. She called it her "you have nothing to fear from me" gambit.

"Over time, it became apparent to me that he wasn't the person I thought he was," Richard said. "I believe you'll find that sentiment echoed by a number of the other Players."

Rather than press him for details, she finished jotting a few notes then looked up at him expectantly. It was a subtle ploy that had served her well in the past. The interviewee almost always felt the need to fill the silence and answer the questioning look on her face.

Richard was no exception. "This is somewhat embarrassing for me," he said, his cheeks and neck pinking up nicely in support of his disclaimer. "Brian told me that he'd invested in a green company, a start-up specializing in renewable power sources like solar and wind. He was very enthusiastic about it, dazzled me with statistics and projections. Gave me a copy of the company's prospectus. It appears that even at my age, I'm still a naïve fool." He looked down and wagged his head as if he were giving himself a silent scolding. "Although I daresay most people would be intrigued by the prospect of easy money. But that's neither here nor there. I was so busy at work that instead of researching things for myself, I begged him to get me in on the ground floor too. I'm sure you can guess the rest—the company was stillborn. And I have mostly myself to blame."

"That's horrible," Rory sympathized as she scribbled more notes. "After it all went south, did you try to verify what he'd told you about it?"

"Yes, well, I'm quite good at closing barn doors after the horses are long gone. In any case, I did find out that the proper papers had been filed by a company with that name. Bottom line—I could hire an attorney to try to recoup some of my losses, but the odds were against there being any money to recoup, which meant that I'd just wind up with big legal bills. So I licked my wounds in private and vowed not to be so damn trusting in the future."

"Did he apologize to you, try to make it right?"

Richard laughed, a tight knot of a laugh with no humor. "Actually, he did a rather splendid 'woe is me' act and claimed he lost a lot more than I did. To listen to him you'd think we were just two fools caught up in the same despi-cable scam. Brian was a slick operator."

There was that word "slick" again. "Do you know if anyone else in the troupe had business dealings with him?"

"I don't think so, but I can't be sure. People tend to be pretty closemouthed when it comes to finances. And I was feeling so ashamed of being taken that I certainly wasn't going to bring it up."

"It must have been difficult seeing him and working with him since that happened," she said. "I give you a lot of credit. I probably would have left the troupe or lashed out at him in a fit of rage." She'd added the last to see his reaction. Sometimes that kind of commiseration was just enough to pop the cork on a magnum of bottled-up confession.

But Richard just shrugged. "Look, it's not as if it left me destitute, and as I said—I blame myself most of all. Truth be told," he added with a sheepish grin, "I couldn't bear to leave the troupe. I do so love acting—all the strutting and fretting, you know." He drained the last of his tea and set the cup down on the inlaid mahogany coffee table in front of him.

"You mentioned earlier that some of the other Players didn't care for Brian either. Why was that?"

"Mostly soap-opera stuff—liaisons, heartbreak, the usual."

"Nothing specific? Nothing that made you think one of them was heartbroken enough to be interested in revenge?"

"No, that didn't even occur to me at the time of the flood. Let's face it—what normal person hears that someone died in a flash flood and immediately thinks, 'Aha, sounds like murder to me'?"

Rory would have loved to see Zeke's expression at that moment. She was pretty sure he'd take exception to being classified as abnormal. Her next thought was that he'd damn well better not show his displeasure by tossing objects around the room. She breathed an internal sigh of relief when everything in the room went right on obeying the laws of physics.

Richard seemed to be momentarily lost in thought. "I suppose I could pick the Player I think the likeliest to resort to such an extreme measure," he said finally, "but it would be a rather arbitrary guess. And I'd probably be doing that person a grave injustice." He chuckled. "Pun not intended but quite delightful nonethe—my apologies," he cut himself off, his smile vanishing. "That was dreadful of me. I certainly didn't mean to treat Brian's death or your investigation as fodder for grade-school humor."

In spite of Rory's assurances that he was being too hard on himself, Richard looked chagrined and miserable. Given his mood and the fact that she'd run out of questions anyway, she wrapped up the interview and thanked him for his time. Just because he wasn't devastated by Brian's death, it didn't automatically mean he was guilty. If that was how justice worked, a majority of the world's population would be doing hard time.

When Rory climbed back in her car, it was well past rush hour, and the traffic had thinned out dramatically. With her radio tuned to her favorite FM station, Rory merged onto the Meadowbrook Parkway and was settling in for the trip home when the dashboard lights flickered, and she was no longer alone in her car.

# Chapter 11

"Are you sure you want to be wasting your energy this way?" Rory asked the marshal, who was now occupying the passenger seat. Any time away from the house was problematic for Zeke, and he'd already spent more than an hour at the interview with Richard Ames. Although he didn't expend as much energy when he was invisible and therefore didn't need as much time to recoup, they still had a long list of suspects ahead of them.

"I'm not stayin' long. Just wanted to get your thoughts on the doc while they were fresh."

Rory shrugged. "He seems like a nice enough guy, pretty laid-back, and like he said himself—a bit naïve for his age."

"Maybe a bit *too* naïve for his age? He's no Easter Bunny, you know."

"I think you mean 'spring chicken'," Rory said, trying to keep a straight face. "I suppose that's possible. On one hand, you wouldn't expect doctors to be naïve, what with all the miseries they see. But on the other hand, some of them are so wrapped up in the medical world that their social skills aren't what they should be."

"Just don't you forget these people are actors, darlin'. The doc might not actually be a nice guy. He might have just learned how to act like one."

She considered that possibility for a minute but found it hard to accept. "Are you saying you think he's guilty?"

"Nope, I'm sayin' you can't be gettin' bamboozled by a snappy accent. I imagine the redcoats we fought gettin' our independence sounded every bit as charmin' as this fella."

Rory was about to protest that she would never be taken in by such a superficial trait when it struck her that he might be right. Had she been judging Richard more favorably because he sounded so polished and civilized?

"I can tell you about the time we arrested two cattle rustlers," Zeke went on, falling into his 'good old days' voice. "Same evidence on both of them. One had a fancy French accent, and the other never had a day's schoolin'. The jury let Frenchie go and hanged the other man. Turned out Frenchie was the brains behind the whole thing. The man they hanged had hooked up with him that very day just to earn a dollar so he could eat."

"Point taken," Rory said, not interested in being regaled with more stories. "Getting back to Brian, though—it's obvious that he dabbled in a variety of unethical, and possibly illegal, enterprises."

"Love and money—it'll be interestin' to see what we turn up next."

"Then you should go tuck yourself into whatever passes for bed and get some rest."

"My thought exactly," Zeke said, apparently pleased that they were of the same mind. "I surely did enjoy this outin' with you."

Rory was about to warn him not to vanish while there was a car in the lane to their right, but he left before she could open her mouth. When she stole a peek at the other driver, the light from his dashboard was just enough to illuminate the look of horror on his face.

Four days after the funeral, Clarissa called Rory. She wanted to finish the conversation that had been interrupted when Jessica and Brett arrived at the wake to pay their respects. Rory had been prepared to give her a week to tie up whatever loose ends Brian had left behind before calling her. Clarissa was definitely a "taking care of business" kind of gal. She suggested they continue their talk right then and there over the phone, but Rory had found that being face-to-face with an individual almost always provided helpful and often unexpected insights. In deference to what should have been Clarissa's period of mourning, Rory offered to drive out to her home in New Hyde Park.

Zeke was still away restoring and refreshing himself, and since Clarissa wasn't a suspect, there didn't seem to be any point in trying to contact him even if she'd known how to go about it.

She'd never brought up the subject, because he generally seemed to be there when she needed him, as well as plenty of times when she didn't. But since it seemed like something she should know in case of an emergency, she made a mental note to find out.

She arrived at Clarissa's home at nine o'clock the next morning, having braved the morning rush hour, when a thirty-minute trip could take a leisurely hour or two. The house was in a cookie-cutter development, a trend that started on Long Island with the building of Levittown, after World War II. Clarissa's house sat in the middle of the block, a cute Cape Cod with gable dormers like all of its neighbors. What made it stand out from the rest was the meticulous, updated landscaping. The overgrown bushes from the fifties

had been ripped out and replaced by newer, dwarf varieties
that were in proper proportion to the dimensions of the
house. It reminded Rory of a man with a well-trimmed beard
standing in a row of ZZ Top wannabes.

Inside, the house had the polished look of a model home
or designer showcase, everything in its proper place, right
down to the perfectly spaced fringe on the Persian rug in
the living room. Rory found it all strangely sad. It was as if
no one lived there, no one to leave a stack of newspapers on
the table or an unwashed glass in the sink. No pet to leave
hair on the couch or drip water across the floor from its bowl.
It was beautiful in a sterile sort of way, but it didn't feel
much like a home.

Clarissa seemed inordinately pleased that Rory was on
time. She invited her into the kitchen, where a carafe of
coffee waited on the sparkling granite countertop alongside
a plate of crumb cake. Rory politely declined both; she'd
already had breakfast, and given the impeccable state of the
house, she suspected her client might be distracted by the
possibility of a crumb or spill.

Clarissa set the cake on the table in case Rory changed
her mind. Once they were both seated, Rory opened her
notepad to a fresh page.

"Okay," Clarissa said. "Here's the Bad and the Ugly.
Unfortunately, there isn't any Good."

There was nothing Rory could say after such a remark,
so she simply waited with what she hoped was a neutral
and understanding expression until the older woman con-
tinued.

"Ten years ago Brian hit what I consider a personal low
when he was convicted of mail fraud and had to do time in
prison."

"Was that his only conviction?" Rory asked.

"The only one I know about. Brian was always a quick
learner, and he seemed to become more careful in his

dealings after that. He moved around a lot and kept changing his name. The only communication we had was by cell phone, but he changed that number frequently too. Months would go by when I wouldn't hear from him, and then out of the blue, he'd start calling again. I have to admit," she added, "that I gave up trying to stay in touch with him in the last few years. It became too painful. It's hard enough to lose someone you love once; I lost Brian over and over again." Those words coming from someone else's mouth would likely have been fraught with emotion. But Clarissa's voice was as stoic and steady as if she were discussing a set of keys she'd misplaced and given up on ever finding.

Rory wondered how far down one would have to dig to reach the wellspring of the real Clarissa, the young mother buried for decades now beneath the crushing mound of disappointment and hopelessness. Although Brian's sudden death had caused a crack in the bulwark, the bleeding had been brief and quickly stanched. Everything back in its proper place.

"How did he make a living?" Rory asked.

"I have no idea. He never brought it up, and on the few occasions when I asked him outright, his stock answer was always 'finances—it's too complicated; you wouldn't understand.' After his conviction, I decided I'd be better off not knowing."

"Did he ever go for counseling?"

Clarissa had cut a small wedge from the crumb cake and was nibbling on it, one hand cupped under the other to catch any wayward crumbs. "I took him to at least a half dozen therapists over the years," she said, abandoning the cake to a napkin as if she'd already lost interest in it. "Thousands of dollars and about as useful as putting the money through a paper shredder. By the time he reached his teens, he refused to go at all. How do you help someone who doesn't believe he needs help?"

Since the question was purely rhetorical, Rory wagged her head in empathy and waited a suitable few moments before pressing on with her own questions. "I'm having trouble reconciling Brian's efforts to avoid more jail time with the risk he took every time he appeared on stage. What if someone in the audience had recognized him from an earlier scam?"

"I know it seems counterintuitive, but from what the therapists told me, it actually fit right in with my son's diagnosis."

"May I ask what that diagnosis was?"

"He was a classic psychopath," Clarissa said grimly. "Bright and charming, but without a conscience. He didn't know guilt or remorse. You'd be horrified if I told you some of the things he did as a child." She closed her eyes and took a deep breath as if trying to exorcise those memories. "Anyway," she went on, "he needed to be the center of attention, and appearing onstage seemed to feed that need. So he convinced himself it didn't put him in jeopardy. After he got out of prison, he told me the police would never catch him again, because he was onto their game, whatever that was supposed to mean."

Listening to her, Rory felt as if she'd unearthed something slimy and foul in her garden and was deeply relieved to find that it was dead. Distressed by the intensity of her reaction, she tried to shake it off. Whatever else Brian Carpenter may have been, he was Clarissa's son, and she shouldn't have to deal with Rory's emotions on top of everything else.

"When was the last time you spoke to Brian?" she asked, once she trusted her voice to sound normal.

"Two days before he left on the trip to Arizona," Clarissa said, a little frown pinching the skin between her eyes. "It actually struck me as strange. After all the years of moving from place to place and living under different aliases, he suddenly wanted to let me know he was going to be away for a week."

"Did he say he was concerned something might happen to him? Did he seem nervous or agitated?"

Clarissa shook her head. "He didn't say anything like that, and to be honest, I don't think Brian knew what it meant to feel nervous. It was part of what was missing in him."

"So nothing else about that conversation set off flares?"

"Well, I don't know if this is in any way connected or relevant, but he did say he was thinking of moving off the Island."

Taken together, the two remarks made Brian sound like a man who'd sensed a shift in the wind and wasn't planning to wait around until the hurricane blew ashore. For the first time since hearing about his death, Rory began to believe in the crazy possibility that Clarissa and Zeke might actually be right—that the flash flood provided a would-be murderer with a once-in-a-lifetime opportunity.

"He didn't say anything about a business deal or romance gone sour?" she asked, hoping to jog something loose in Clarissa's memory.

She laughed as if to say "you've got to be kidding." "Those were two subjects he never discussed with me."

"Did you ask him why he was thinking of moving away again?"

"Why bother?" She shrugged. "I'd played his games long enough to know he wasn't going to tell me the truth." She glanced at her watch, then back at Rory. "I think I've told you everything I know that might help the investigation. If you have no other questions . . ." she said, rising from her chair. "As you can imagine, my schedule's all backlogged, what with everything that's happened."

Rory had a mental image of Clarissa checking items off a list: buy cake—check; conversation with PI—check;

mourning—check. She immediately chided herself for being judgmental. The woman had clearly done her mourning long before her son's physical death.

Clarissa was walking her to the door when she came to an abrupt stop in the middle of the living room. "I almost forgot—tomorrow morning I'm going over to Brian's apartment to clear out his belongings. I thought you might want to meet me there. Maybe you'll find something useful to the case."

"Absolutely," Rory said, buoyed by the prospect of an actual clue.

Clarissa gave her the address, and they agreed to meet at the apartment at nine thirty the next day. Rory had just reached her car when her cell phone signaled that she had a new e-mail. It had come from her home computer and was only two words long: "COME HOME."

# Chapter 12

The sender of that message had to be Zeke, unless Hobo had recently acquired a new skill. She considered writing him back, but that was always more frustrating than it was worth. If he wasn't at the computer, he wouldn't receive the message. And even if he was still there, it was never a quick process. He'd proven to be obtuse when it came to learning the abbreviations that were common in that form of communication, although she suspected it was the principle of the thing more than any real inability on his part. He often complained that the present generation was murdering the English language and that he refused to help dig its grave. Rory had come close to pointing out that he was often guilty of the same crime. In any case, she wasn't in the mood to listen to another of his lectures about the deficiencies of the modern age.

The trip home took a quarter of the time it had taken during rush hour, which was still more than enough time for Rory to imagine several terrible reasons for the marshal's

abrupt message. When she arrived home, she found out she'd
been wrong on every count.

Hobo met her at the door with all of his normal, fur-flying
enthusiasm. He jumped up in his version of an embrace,
with his front paws on her shoulders, and started lapping
her face. At least nothing was wrong on the canine front.
With Hobo still up on his hind legs, she did a little sidestep
dance with him to the keypad to turn off the alarm.

Zeke popped in while she was trying to convince the dog
that four legs on the floor were preferable to two. She threw
in a promise of ear scratches to seal the deal. With Hobo
back on the ground, she turned to face the marshal.

"Okay, I'm here—what's the big emergency?"

Zeke's expression was grim. "We've got trouble."

"Could you narrow that down a bit?" she asked, walking
over to the bench beneath the stairs to kick off her shoes.
Being home meant being barefoot.

"Someone broke in while you were gone."

"But the door was locked. I had to use my key to open
it," she said, trying to make sense of this information. "And
the alarm was set."

"I wasn't here at the time so I can't tell you how he got
in. I heard the mutt carryin' on somethin' awful, but I didn't
pay it no mind 'cause he does that with the mailman, the
paperboy and every squirrel he sees trespassin'. But then
he got quiet too suddenly. None of the easin' down like he
usually does. You know, what you call his grumblin'. That's
when I dropped in to see if he was okay."

Rory tried to push away the memory that sprang to mind
of Hobo nearly dying from the poisoned meat someone had
thrown into her yard back in the fall. "And?"

"He was merrily chewing away on one of those stuffed
toys he loves."

"He does that all the time." Exasperation was seeping
into her voice.

"Not with a frog. You never bought him a frog, did you?"

"No," she said, her brows bunching together with a mixture of concern and confusion. "So someone broke in here to give Hobo a present?"

"I never said it made a lick of sense."

"I guess I should be grateful that the intruder likes dogs."

"It's sure a heap of a lot better than the last time."

"But why break in at all?" she murmured thinking out loud.

"I've been rollin' that around in my head. I think the intruder's tryin' to tell you that you're bein' watched. That he can get to you if he wants to."

"That's pretty damn creepy. Sort of sounds like a stalker."

"No, I don't think so. I can't say for sure, but the timin' leads me to think this has to do with Brian's death. Could be he wants you to stop your investigatin'."

"Then why be so vague about it? Why not just throw a brick through my window threatening to kill me if I don't drop the case?"

"Who knows how any of these guys think. Maybe he's just playin' a game in your brain."

"I think you mean 'playing mind games'."

Zeke scowled at her. "This is serious, darlin'. He's probably been stakin' out the house to get a handle on your schedule so he could break in when you weren't home. That tells me that he's not lookin' for a confrontation just yet."

"And you're sure he didn't leave a threatening note or maybe a bomb somewhere?" she asked, only half kidding.

"No, ma'am, I went through this house from stem to stern, and far as I can tell, he didn't take anythin' or leave anythin' except the frog."

"Did you—"

"Course I did. I checked that toy every which way as soon as I saw the mutt chewin' on it."

Rory had run out of questions, with no answers in sight.

It was bad enough that someone had broken into the house and managed to turn off the alarm in less than a minute, but how on earth had he or she reset the alarm without knowing the code and then relocked the front door without the key? She felt as frustrated as when she watched a highly skilled magician. There had to be a trick to it, but she couldn't figure out what it was, and that drove her a little crazy.

She padded into the kitchen with Hobo at her heels, the frog still stuffed in his mouth. Zeke was already sitting at the table waiting for her. "What's goin' on in that pretty head of yours?" he asked warily.

Rory opened the freezer and rummaged around until she found a pint of strawberry ice cream hidden behind a frozen pizza. "There's got to be a way to find out who broke in here, but I'm coming up empty." She popped the lid off, and grabbing a spoon, she joined him at the table. Hobo dropped the frog and settled down next to her waiting for a handout.

"I guess I could dust the house for fingerprints," she said, digging into the container, which was only a quarter full, "but whoever did this was way too professional to make such a rookie mistake."

"You're overlookin' a bigger concern," Zeke said. "How are we goin' to keep you and the mutt safe from someone who ain't stopped by locks and alarms? I don't mind standin' guard for you, but I can't keep that up without rest."

"Maybe I should buy a junkyard dog to protect us," she said without humor.

"Now hold on there; one dog's my absolute limit."

"Just kidding."

"I think maybe you should stay with your folks until we get this sorted out."

"I'm not running and hiding," she said, scooping a bit of the ice cream into her hand for Hobo to lick, which he did with gusto.

"What about askin' Leah to arrange for some protection?"

Rory finished the last spoonful and got up to toss the container in the garbage and the spoon in the sink. "I'd like to see where this is headed before I start crying wolf."

"You think maybe this is goin' to escalate into flowers and candy?" Zeke asked, not bothering to hide the sarcasm.

Rory didn't respond. A strange-looking tag on the stuffed frog had caught her eye. She picked up the toy, soggy with Hobo's saliva, to get a better look. There was the usual tag, like the ones that came on clothing and generally listed fabric content, washing instructions and the name of the country where it was manufactured. But beside it was a second, larger tag, which on close inspection had clearly been sewn on by hand, a very unskilled hand. Someone had used an indelible marker to write a message on it. Unfortunately, the tag had been so badly mangled by Hobo's teeth that it was indecipherable.

"What've you got there?" Zeke asked, appearing beside her.

Rory held the tag out so that he could see it without coming any closer.

"Damn, how'd I miss that?" He sounded chagrined at his failure.

"Hey, I almost missed it, and I'm familiar with the tags they use these days. But on the positive side, this tells us something else about the intruder." With any luck she might be able to detour the marshal from the safety debate.

"Is that so?" Zeke said, smiling at her as if she were a prize student.

"Whoever did this never owned a large dog, or he would have known his message wasn't likely to survive."

"Which isn't such good news for us in the end," Zeke pointed out, his expression dead serious again. "We don't know what this guy's after or what he's expectin' of us, but now he thinks we've gotten his message. That could lead to some problems."

"I think there's actually a computer program that may be able to reconstruct what was on the tag," Rory said. "It's at least worth a try."

"Would Leah have access to somethin' like that?"

Rory could tell he was already trying to maneuver back to the topic of her safety. "Possibly. But my money's on BB's friend Reggie."

"You're goin' to ask some guy you never met, rather than your best friend?" Zeke sounded testy.

"It's just less complicated that way," she said, trying not to be drawn into an argument. "I'll tell you what; I'll give BB a call right now." She stepped around Zeke to pluck the phone from its wall mount and started to punch in numbers before he had a chance to raise any more objections.

When Rory reached the office of the Suffolk County Medical Examiner, she was told that Dr. Browning, otherwise known as BB, was away for the week. If she liked, she could leave a message on his voice mail. After she did that, Rory checked her address book for BB's home number, since a week off didn't necessarily mean a week away. Although she also had his cell number, she had no intentions of using it. If he was out of town on vacation it didn't seem right to bother him with anything short of an emergency. Zeke might consider this to be one, but she didn't. As it happened, BB answered his home phone on the first ring.

"Rory, dear girl, *mon amie*, what a lovely surprise."

"I'm really sorry to disturb you at home," she said, even though he didn't sound at all disturbed. In fact, he sounded like someone who'd fallen overboard and was grateful to be thrown a life preserver.

"No, no, not at all, *no hay problema*. How may I be of help?"

Rory explained the strange circumstances about Hobo's gift and asked if Reggie might have the necessary tools to decipher the note attached to it.

"I believe he just might. I'll pop over to your house tomorrow and pick up the item."

"You've already gone out of your way for me so many times," she protested. "Why don't I drop it off for you?"

"Truth be told, I'm bored beyond endurance," he admitted. "It turns out I don't do 'idle' very well."

"In that case, I'd love to show you my new office," she said, hoping he wouldn't ask to tour the house as well.

"Just say when, and I'll be there bearing cupcakes. I've become quite the connoisseur of those dainty treats."

# Chapter 13

Brian had been renting a furnished one-bedroom condo in Melville. The unit was on the second floor of a two-story building in a large, gated complex. All of the buildings were identical. Winding roads wove through the development as if the builders had belatedly realized that the complex was crying out for a touch of grace. Unfortunately, they wound up creating a confounding maze with roads that circled back on themselves or led to unexpected dead ends. To make matters worse, the address numbers on the buildings were too small to be seen from a passing car, and some of the street signs were missing. Even the navigation system in Rory's car seemed confused. Once she was inside the complex, it took her an additional ten minutes to find Brian's building and that was after two phone calls to Clarissa and a couple of U-turns. When she rang the bell, Clarissa took so long to open the door that Rory was starting to wonder if she had the correct apartment after all.

"Don't worry," Clarissa said in lieu of "hello" as she let

Rory in. A roll of large trash bags and empty boxes of various sizes were scattered across the living room floor. "I haven't touched anything important. I've just been cleaning out the fridge."

Rory realized her face must have given away what she'd been thinking. She produced a smile and assured Clarissa that she hadn't been worried at all. Clarissa nodded absently and without another word headed back to the kitchen as if her thoughts had already turned down a different corridor. She seemed a lot less poised than usual, although far from the Clarissa who'd flown into Arizona to identify her son's remains. When she saw that Rory had followed her into the kitchen, she became flustered.

"Oh Rory, oh my goodness," she said. "I just left you standing there, didn't I? You'll have to excuse me today . . . I'm not myself . . . I guess being here with all of Brian's belongings has had more of an impact on me than I expected."

"No need to apologize." Rory remembered only too well how difficult it had been to put her uncle Mac's affairs in order after his sudden death. It had to be much harder for a mother after the unexpected death of a child. Even a child who'd turned out like Brian. "Is it okay if I start looking around?"

"Of course, of course. You have carte blanche to do whatever needs doing. Nothing is off-limits."

Rory thanked her and started with the small dining area just beyond the kitchen. There was a table that might have been Formica posing as wood and four upholstered chairs. A hanging lamp of 1980s vintage completed the ensemble. She checked beneath the furniture in case Brian had secured important papers to the undersides and came up empty-handed. Not that she'd expected to find anything.

The dining room flowed into the living room, which was dominated by a sectional sofa in a dark, tweed fabric that

was no doubt good for hiding the dirt and stains of numerous
tenants. Mounted on the wall across from the couch was a
forty-inch flat-screen television. If Brian was like most
single people, when he ate at home, he did so sitting on the
couch and watching TV. Rory looked behind and under all
the cushions. Once again she came up empty. Unless she
was planning on prying up the hardwood floor, there was
nothing else in the room to inspect. She headed down the
hallway in search of the bedroom.

Brian had apparently been using the room as his office
as well as his sleeping quarters. A laptop computer and
printer occupied the top of an otherwise uncluttered desk.
When Rory opened the desk drawers, she found them to be
neatly organized. Brian had used the larger bottom drawer
as a filing cabinet for a small stack of manila folders. With
Clarissa's permission, she'd take the laptop and folders
home, where she would have more time to go through them.
The upper drawer held the usual miscellany of office sup-
plies: rubber bands, paper clips, pens and pencils, each in
its own little receptacle. Everything in its place. Rory wondered if Clarissa had noticed that at least in this one respect,
her son had taken after her.

Across the room was a queen-size bed, the linens balled
up in the center as if Brian had been running late to catch
the plane that would carry him to the end of his days. The
only other furniture in the room was an armoire, its legs
scarred from years of combat with a vacuum cleaner. On
inspection, the chest and closet revealed the basics of a
man's wardrobe minus whatever casual clothing he'd had
with him on the trip. The clothes that were there had high-
end labels and were clearly well made. Rory checked all the
pockets in case Brian had left anything important in them.
All she came up with was some loose change and candy
wrappers. He seemed to have been partial to Butterfingers.
Rory would have figured him for a Godiva sort of guy.

Before returning to the kitchen, she stopped to check out the small bathroom. In the cabinet beneath the sink, there was a comb, shaving cream, a pack of disposable razors, a toothbrush and toothpaste, mouthwash and soap. The only medication was a nearly empty bottle of Advil. Brian may have been immune to emotional pain or pangs of guilt, but he hadn't been immune to physical pain. Rory found that thought strangely comforting.

Clarissa was still in the kitchen tying up the trash bag that now held the contents of the refrigerator and pantry. "I want to show you something," she said when Rory walked in. She picked up a plastic zip-top bag that was lying on the counter. "This was inside an open box of Cheerios. I was emptying the cereal so I could recycle the box when it fell out."

Even before Rory took the bag from her, it was clear that it held the phony drivers' licenses and other forms of identification Brian had used to support his various aliases.

"Whoever did these for him was very good," Rory said as she shuffled through them. She counted seven different names in all. "If you don't mind, I'd like to take these to the police. It might help them close some cold cases." She'd also ask Zeke to do a Google search on the names and see if he came up with a lead that might point to someone who wanted Brian dead.

"Yes, of course. I want to do whatever I can to make things right," Clarissa said with a determined lift to her chin, once more the self-possessed woman Rory had come to know. Perhaps finding evidence of her son's subterfuge had snapped her out of her nostalgia and reminded her why she'd written him off years ago.

"I'd also like to take Brian's laptop and files with me," Rory said. "Once I'm finished, I'll return all of it to you unless the police need it."

Clarissa told her that would be fine. Rory thanked her

and slipped the bag of IDs into her handbag. Then she went back to the bedroom for the laptop and folders before letting herself out.

Zeke was still resting up from the interview with Richard Ames. The intruder had interrupted the process, setting him back several hours. With that in mind, Rory figured she could count on a pleasant, uneventful meeting with BB. If they stayed in her office, there was a good chance Zeke would never even know the medical examiner had been visiting. Since BB was bringing cupcakes, Rory felt obliged to supply the coffee or tea. She wasn't sure which he preferred, but she did remember seeing him drink coffee, so she settled on that.

She decided to brew the coffee in the house and take just the carafe out to the office. As soon as she opened the back door, Hobo was at her side, ready for whatever adventure presented itself. Since he'd been alone all morning while she was at Brian's apartment, she decided to let him tag along. She remembered that BB had once spoken fondly of the dog he'd had as a boy, so there was a good chance he'd enjoy Hobo's company.

She set the carafe on a small hot plate atop the filing cabinet and laid all the fixings out beside it. At two o'clock on the dot, Hobo jumped up from his place on the couch and started barking. Rory hadn't heard the SUV pull into the driveway, but she'd learned to trust the dog's ears over her own. When she went to open the door, Hobo squeezed in front of her, nearly knocking her off her feet. She wasn't sure whether he wanted to protect her or be the first to welcome their visitor.

Once she managed to open the door, BB was standing there, smiling broadly and holding a cake box large enough to easily accommodate a dozen cupcakes. Hobo, who was always excited to meet someone new, was especially thrilled when that someone came bearing treats. Rory grabbed for his collar a moment too late as he launched himself into one of his two-legged embraces. Before she could change his trajectory, his right front leg grazed the box. BB stumbled back a step, juggling the cupcakes for what seemed like five minutes but in reality was only seconds. Just when it looked like gravity had the upper hand, the medical examiner snatched the box back from its downward tumble. Given Hobo's love of all things edible, Rory couldn't help wondering if he'd planned his strategy from the moment he'd smelled cake.

In spite of the whirlwind welcome, BB appeared truly happy to meet Hobo. He passed the box to Rory and hunkered down to the dog's level, where he administered ear scratches and received a good face washing in return. Once man and dog were both satisfied with their greetings, BB stood up with a few heavy grunts.

"My knees don't work so well anymore," he explained stepping into the office. "But then neither does my memory, or I'd remember not to squat like that."

Rory laughed. It was well known throughout the police department that the medical examiner had a brilliant intellect and a memory like a steel trap in spite of his self-deprecating remarks. "Dogs can make you think you're a kid again," she said, "especially dogs like Hobo."

"Yes, remarkable creatures, *formidable, increíble*. I'm quite sure the human race doesn't come close to deserving their unconditional love and esteem."

Rory closed the door behind him, taking care not to snag Hobo's tail. The small office seemed uncomfortably crowded with the three of them standing there. She'd never felt that way before, but BB was a large man, in both height and girth. And most of Hobo's DNA had clearly come from the larger, shaggy breeds. She invited BB to have a seat, at which point Hobo laid claim to the couch.

"I see he's fluent in English." BB laughed. She started to shoo the dog off, but BB stopped her. "Let him be, let him be; it happens that I'm more of a chair person anyway." As if to prove the point, he settled himself in the generous armchair with a deep sigh of pleasure.

Rory offered him coffee, which he accepted with a splash of half-and-half but no sweetener. She took hers black, a habit from her college days. When she opened the cake box, she found the cupcakes a little worse for the juggling routine. Rainbows of icing smudged the sides and top of the box. She had to restrain herself from swiping a taste with her finger.

"I'm afraid they didn't fare too well from Hobo's greeting," she said, holding the box out to BB.

"Not to worry—they'll taste just as fine," he assured her as he reached in and selected one that was now only modestly covered in chocolate.

Rory went for the pink one, hoping it was strawberry.

Since Hobo appeared to be drooling his way to dehydration, she broke off a piece to give him. He thanked her with a wave of his plumed tail and eyes that begged for more.

Although the cupcakes lived up to BB's hype, one was Rory's limit. By the time they'd set their cups aside, BB had polished off four of them as well as a second cup of coffee. While they ate, Rory filled him in on the Brian Carpenter case, ending with the intruder and the toy frog.

She'd stowed the toy, along with a replacement for it, in the empty bottom drawer of her desk. She pulled the two stuffed frogs out now, handing the original one to BB and tossing the new one for Hobo to catch. The dog gave it a couple of tentative chews before dropping it and staring longingly at the mutilated frog that BB was examining.

"Sorry—I'm afraid Hobo made it a little soggy," she said. "I thought of cutting the tag off the toy, but I was afraid I might compromise the writing on it even more."

"What's a little drool between friends?" BB said, squinting at the tag in question. "I can't make out a single word either. But don't despair—if it's decipherable, there's no one better than Reggie to do it. I must say, whoever thought of this has a good imagination. I've never seen a threat conveyed in quite this manner. Not in twenty years of investigating death in every conceivable form. Of course," he added, "we're not sure this actually contains a threat."

"Why else would someone risk a breaking-and-entering conviction just to give my dog a toy?" Rory asked.

"Why indeed?" BB murmured, absently licking a smudge of icing off his hand.

# Chapter 14

Rory was at her kitchen table searching through Brian's laptop for any clue that might lead them to a potential killer. Zeke was sitting across from her trying to calibrate his energy to the task of going through the file folders. Since there were no handbooks to teach a ghost how to get along in a world meant only for the living, he did all his learning by trial and error. The lighter or more delicate an object, the more difficult it was for him to hone his energy to the point where he could manipulate it without accidentally vaporizing it. Rory had seen more than a few of her belongings sacrificed to the process.

"Hot damn!" Zeke said, clearly pleased with himself for opening the top folder on the third try without so much as a rip or a wrinkle. But when he tried to flip through the sheets of paper inside, he scattered the pages to every corner of the room.

"The papers are lighter than the folder they're in," Rory said without looking up from the computer.

"Thanks for that timely reminder." Zeke vanished from his chair to reappear near the center island. Using his energy like a leaf blower he swept the papers into a disorderly pile near Rory's feet. "I'd be obliged if you'd pick them up, seein' as how I'm likely to scatter them again if I try to do it."

"In a minute. Take a look at this," she said pointing to the monitor.

Zeke, who was positioned beside her, leaned in to see the screen, causing her to rock back in her chair rather than take the chance of letting their heads touch. "What is that," he asked after scanning the page, "a love letter?" He shook his head and frowned. "There's somethin' just plain wrong about sendin' a love letter on a machine," he grumbled finally.

With so much of life lived online these days, that thought had never occurred to Rory. But now that he'd mentioned it, she could see his point. A handwritten letter was more intimate in many ways. Not only was the penmanship unique to the sender, but mailing it the old-fashioned way required more time and effort. With e-mail, all one had to do was click on the word "send." Although a case could surely be made for the speed and convenience of e-mail, she had to agree that at its core, it was colder, more sterile and probably not the best form of communication where love was concerned.

"You old romantic, you," she said with a grin. "I'll bet you did a fine job of courting the ladies back in the day."

"You pokin' fun at me?" Zeke studied her face as if trying to read her real intent.

"Believe it or not, I actually agree with you, love-letter-wise, but that's not why I wanted you to see this particular e-mail. It's from Jessica, and it sounds as if she was completely besotted with Brian, to use a phrase from your era. Here's a fortysomething actress whose career flatlined when she hit her thirties. She had to be devastated when Brian left her for someone so much younger—it was like another door slamming in her face."

"Sounds like motive to me," Zeke agreed, stepping back. "All she needed was opportunity. That flood might have been the answer to her prayers."

Rory leaned forward again, setting the front legs of her chair back on the floor with a thud. "Unfortunately, this letter alone won't convict her."

"True, but I expect it's at least earned her a visit from us."

A fter multiple attempts to reach the lovelorn Jessica by phone, Rory decided it was time to drop in on her unannounced. Zeke was all for the idea until she pointed out that it made no sense for him to tag along until she'd made sure the suspect was home. Why waste his time and energy for nothing?

"I'll ring the phone here once if I get inside to talk to her. Then you can pop right over and join me. How's that?" Rory asked, thinking he couldn't possibly have any objections to such a sensible plan. After all, it wasn't her fault he no longer had mortal flesh in which to travel about the world.

"I imagine it'll have to do," he said stoically. "Meanwhile, I'll keep lookin' through the files." Rory was both relieved and surprised that he was taking such a reasonable approach to the situation. Although it was in his own best interests not to squander his energy, that realization alone was rarely enough to prevent his frustration from reaching critical mass.

She grabbed her purse and left the house before he could change his mind. Of course, if he did, there was nothing to stop him from popping into the passenger seat and once again treating people in nearby cars to the shock of their lives.

She shoved this worry into the storeroom of her mind, which was already jam-packed with other concerns over which she had no control, and slammed the door shut. If there'd been a sign on that door, it would have read "Marshal Ezekiel Drummond."

She programmed Jessica's address into her navigation system and headed east to Commack. Twenty minutes later, and still without a passenger, she pulled up in front of a sprawling ranch-style home with landscaping worthy of a *Better Homes and Gardens* photo shoot. Either Jessica came from money or she'd invested wisely during her brief romp with success in Hollywood.

There was a late model, white Cadillac Escalade in the driveway with its rear hatch open and several grocery bags inside. The front door to the house was open as well. The actress had apparently just returned from a shopping trip. This day, at least, she hadn't been home screening calls.

Rory parked and locked her car. She was walking up the driveway when Jessica came out the front door wearing a cleavage-baring silver shirt, skintight black jeans and her signature stiletto heels. Unfortunately the white cast and sling on her broken arm did nothing to enhance the look she was clearly aiming for. The actress, who'd tiptoed over the forty-year mark with no public fanfare, was still a striking woman, with dark eyes canted up at the corners and long red hair of a shade not normally found in the human genome. Tall and slender, she carried herself with the confident grace of a model or an aristocrat. And from the little Rory had seen, there was a good chance she was her own most ardent fan.

When Jessica noticed her visitor standing there, the neutral expression on her face instantly morphed to surprise and then in quick succession to curiosity, bewilderment and wariness.

"Hi," Rory said, giving her best impression of an innocent smile. She stopped when she was at the back of the SUV and waited for Jessica to approach her. If she had any

hope of being invited inside, she had to let the actress feel
that she was in control of the situation, the alpha female.

"Hi." Jessica tried to produce one of her dazzling smiles
in return, but her mouth wasn't cooperating.

"I was in the area, so I thought I'd stop by to say hello."
Rory threw in a little girl shrug. No cause for concern here.

"Well, that's . . . that's nice," Jessica said still juggling
expressions.

Rory had seen her perform in enough of the troupe's
productions to know that she was a far better actress when
she had lines to memorize and knew what was coming in
the script. Ad-libbing was clearly not her forte.

"Let me help you with these," Rory said, reaching into
the SUV before Jessica could protest. "It must be difficult
managing with one arm." She picked up two of the grocery
bags and stepped back so the actress could grab the last one.
Without another word, Rory followed her into the house.
That was a whole lot easier than she'd anticipated.

Once the perishables had been stowed in the refrigerator,
Jessica thanked her for helping, then made the tactical error
of offering her a cold drink. Rory knew it was just a reflex,
civility having no doubt been drummed into her head from
the day she'd learned to speak. She saw dismay supplant the
other expressions still vying for air time on Jessica's face.
It was clear her reluctant hostess was hoping she'd decline
the offer.

Rory almost felt bad for her. Almost. Which is why she
said that water would be great even though she wasn't actually thirsty. She needed to stay there long enough to engage
Jessica in conversation and any excuse would do.

While Jessica was filling a glass from the spigot on the
refrigerator door, Rory excused herself to use the bathroom.
She was told she'd find it down the hall. As soon as she
closed the door behind her, she hit the speed dial for home.
After it rang once, she hung up. The ball was now in Zeke's

court. She counted to twenty, then flushed the toilet to make her trip to the bathroom seem legit.

When she returned to the kitchen, Jessica was putting the rest of her groceries into the walk-in pantry. She'd left the glass of water on the counter for her guest.

"Thanks," Rory said, taking a long drink. She was setting down the glass when she felt the marshal's tap on her shoulder. Her tension level instantly ratcheted up several notches, and she wondered if she'd ever be at ease with Zeke as her wingman. She was certainly getting to know him better with each passing day, yet in many ways he was still an unknown quantity, a land mine you didn't realize was there until you stepped on it.

"I'm always dehydrated for days after flying. Isn't that weird?" she said with a laugh that sounded hollow and phony even to her own ears. Lesson learned—she shouldn't try laughing when she wasn't actually amused.

If Jessica took note of her lame attempt at humor, she didn't show it. She carried a box of Cheerios and a jar of almonds into the pantry without comment. But there was a tight set to her mouth that told Rory her visit there would soon be coming to an end. Any moment now Jessica was going to plead a headache or a dental appointment or some other polite excuse to get rid of her. If Rory was going to make her play, it was now or never.

"It's now or never," the marshal whispered too loudly in her ear.

Great, an echo—just what she needed. Hopefully Jessica hadn't heard him.

"Is someone else here?" Jessica asked as she emerged from the pantry. "I thought I heard a man's voice."

"No, just me clearing my throat," Rory said, wishing she could slam an elbow into Zeke.

The actress was looking around the room clearly puzzled. "That's not what it sounded—"

"Listen, Jessica," Rory cut her off before she could dwell any longer on what she'd heard. "Part of the reason I stopped by today was to express my condolences to you on Brian's death. I wasn't aware how close you and he had been." There, that should get the denial train rolling nicely along.

As if on cue, Jessica's eyes narrowed. "A word of advice, *honey*," she said, her tone thick with sarcasm and a dash of anger. "I don't know who told you that, but if you want to make it in the PI business, you really ought to find yourself a more reliable source."

Rory had to bite her tongue to hold back the words that were rioting in her mouth. She wanted to say that her source was her aunt and therefore unimpeachable. But calling Jessica a liar to her face could only end one way—badly. Plus, the fallout would compromise Helene's position in the troupe. Rory would eat humble pie for a month before causing that.

"Fact one," the actress went on, "Brian and I split up over a year ago. Fact two, it was never more than a fling for either of us. We both knew the parameters going in. And just to be clear, I don't ever wish anyone ill—karma stamps that sort of thing 'return to sender.'"

"Then you weren't upset when he hooked up with Sophia?" Rory knew she'd crossed the line from polite interest to nosy jerk. A close friend or a cop could get away with an intrusive question like that, but she was barely an acquaintance. And after today, that status wasn't likely to improve.

"Sophia?" Jessica coughed up a laugh that wouldn't have won her any Oscars. "Why would I have been upset about her? I'd already moved on."

Hardly the same version she'd heard from Helene. The actress was either trying to save face after being dumped or she was hoping to distance herself from consideration as a suspect in Brian's death.

"So I assume you know that Clarissa hired me." In for a penny, in for a pound, as her father liked to say.

"I don't see what that has to do with anything," Jessica snapped, pointedly checking her watch against the clock above the sink. "Look—I don't mean to be rude, but I'm already late for the dentist." She grabbed her keys and handbag from the counter and headed for the door.

Although Rory was pretty sure this was just an impromptu little skit designed expressly for her consumption, she had no choice but to follow the actress out of her house.

With a curt good-bye, Jessica climbed into her SUV and backed out of the driveway. She was already out of sight when Rory reached her car and slid into the driver's seat.

"You there?" she asked, addressing the empty seat beside her. When there was no response she assumed the marshal had chosen to go straight home, since that was his only other option. Just as well. They could discuss Jessica later. For now Rory wanted to play out a hunch. She drove to the far end of the block and parked again. She waited there, eyes glued to the rearview mirror, expecting Jessica to return once she thought it was safe. Half an hour later, Rory gave up and left. Maybe the actress had gone to the dentist after all.

# Chapter 15

Rory had just arrived home when she got Jean Bowman's call. After skimming over the usual pleasantries, Jean begged her to come right over. The poor woman sounded desperate, and since Zeke appeared to be otherwise occupied, Rory relocked the front door and headed down the street.

"Thanks so much for coming," Jean said, her voice weary as she held the front door open. Her usually neat-as-a-pin, brown pageboy was in disarray as if she'd been trying to pull it out in frustration.

"It's no problem," Rory assured her, stepping inside. She'd only been in the center-hall colonial on a couple of occasions, but as always she was impressed by the eclectic blend of antiques with contemporary and period pieces. Either Jean had a natural flair for interior design or she had a great decorator.

"I think you know that my mother-in-law has been a handful since her stroke. She's more work than a toddler sometimes. I'm afraid there's no diverting or calming her once she fixates on an idea, and today, I'm sorry to say, that idea is you."

"No need to apologize," Rory said, wondering what Eloise had in store for her this time.

"She's in the family room watching an old movie," Jean said as she led the way there. "It's the first time all day she isn't trying to sneak over to your house or badger me into calling you, and that's only because I told her you were coming over."

"And she didn't say why she needed me?"

"No, I don't have a clue. To be honest, a lot of what she says these days makes no sense at all to me."

Rory decided not to share the fact that whatever Eloise had told *her* so far had made perfect, if troubling, sense.

The moment they crossed from the open kitchen into the family room, Eloise popped up from the couch where she'd been sitting. She wobbled and swayed on her feet for several seconds until she got her balance. Jean was at her side instantly to help steady her.

"Mom, you've got to get up more slowly. Remember what the doctor said?"

Eloise pulled away from her daughter-in-law like a rebellious child and turned her attention to Rory. "Where have you been?" she admonished. "I've been waiting all day for you."

"I rushed right over here as soon as I heard you wanted to see me," Rory said. "Is there a problem?"

"Not exactly, but I can't be expected to remember things for too long at my age. You know I'm not sixteen anymore."

Jean rolled her eyes for Rory's benefit and said she'd be in the laundry room if she was needed.

"Why don't we sit down together, and you can tell me all about it," Rory suggested, trying to gently maneuver Eloise back to the couch. But as frail as she looked, she resisted as if she were rooted to the spot.

"You're going to need paper and a pencil," Eloise said as if that should have been self-evident.

"Excuse me?"

"How are you going to draw her without paper and a pencil?" she asked impatiently.

"I don't know what I was thinking," Rory said, having no clue at all what they were talking about. She'd never even told Eloise that she was an artist, although she might have heard it from Jean or Doug. But more to the point, who could she possibly want Rory to draw? "One minute, I'll see if Jean has some paper and—"

"No, no, she doesn't have that kind of paper," Eloise interrupted, her voice heavy with exasperation. "You need your sketch pad!"

"Of course. How silly of me. I'll be back in a flash," Rory promised. "But I think you should wait for me on the couch, okay?"

"I suppose." Eloise sighed, shuffling off in that direction. "But hurry up; I'm not getting any younger."

Rory stopped into the laundry room, where Jean was folding towels, and explained where she was going. Jean wagged her head as if to say, "Welcome to my world."

At home Rory grabbed her pad and pencil and made it out the door again in under twenty seconds. Thankfully, Zeke hadn't chosen one of those seconds to drop in for a chat. The last thing she needed right then was another confrontation about her seeing Eloise. As for Hobo the watchdog, he'd opened one sleepy eye to confirm that Rory wasn't an intruder before promptly falling back to sleep.

She called out, "I'm back," as she let herself into the Bowmans' house again.

Eloise was on the couch, but the television was off, and she was staring at the kitchen, clearly waiting for Rory's return. Her blue eyes brightened when Rory appeared, sketch pad in hand.

Rory sat down beside her, opening her pad to a clean sheet of paper. "So who is this person you'll be describing to me?"

"I don't know her name," Eloise said, brushing off the question as if it were of no importance. "Things just sort of come to me—people mostly, sometimes places. They pop right into my head with no rhyme or reason." She shrugged her shoulders. "A lot of them are hard to see, like when the TV used to get all snowy. But some of them, like this lady, look as real as you do sitting there next to me. And if they ask for my help, I try to accommodate." Eloise smiled and nodded, clearly pleased with the service she provided.

"Okay, I guess we should get started then," Rory said, feeling far from enlightened. She still had a basketful of questions, but she suspected Eloise had used up her entire stock of answers. "How old would you say this woman is?"

"She's young, like you, but not as pretty," Eloise said touching Rory's cheek.

Rory felt the color rise in her face. She'd been taught to accept compliments graciously, but somehow the lesson never stuck. Compliments made her so uncomfortable that if she sensed one coming, she'd jump in and spin the conversation in another direction. But Eloise had caught her by surprise.

"Can you tell me the shape of this lady's face?" Rory asked, eager to move on.

"Round . . . no." Eloise closed her eyes for a moment as if to reboot the picture in her mind. "More . . . oval. Yes, that's it, oval." Her eyelids fluttered open again. "And her hair is long and dark, but she mostly wears it away from her face."

"That's good. Very good. Can you describe the shape of her eyes?" Rory prompted as she began sketching.

"Almond-shaped. I remember reading that in a book once, and when she appeared in my head, I said to myself, 'Look at that, Eloise. She has almond-shaped eyes.'"

"Deep set or shallow?" Rory could tell from Eloise's frown that she didn't know what that meant. Rory explained the difference, after which Eloise settled on "shallow."

Proceeding in that fashion, Rory led her through each of the woman's features until Eloise declared the drawing to be a perfect likeness.

Unfortunately, the woman looking up at Rory from the page didn't resemble anyone who'd been on the trip. And if she had nothing to do with the investigation, why on earth was it so urgent for Rory to know about her? Maybe she was only a figment of a stroke-addled brain after all, a composite of people Eloise had known in her life, seen on television or read about in books. Maybe Eloise had simply made a lucky guess about the fatal flood. Life being what it was, a prediction of bad news was bound to come true—and probably sooner than later. She was starting to buy into the stroke theory when she remembered that Eloise had known about Zeke. Logic couldn't explain that any more than it could explain the lingering spirit of the marshal himself. And after that merry ride aboard the logic carousel, Rory found herself right back at square one.

"Am I supposed to know this person?" she asked, trying to keep the lid on her growing frustration.

"Yes," Eloise said with a relieved sigh now that her obligation had been satisfied. She reached for the TV remote that was lying on the end table next to her and turned on her movie again.

Rory made a few more attempts to coax information out of her, but Eloise was focused on the TV now, no longer interested in anything else.

"Jessica was awfully hostile for someone who's innocent; that's all I'm saying." Rory poured two big scoops of kibble into Hobo's dish. The dog was watching intently, but when she put the dish on the floor for him, he sniffed it, then padded away, his big head hanging down. He looked as disappointed as a kid who discovers that the lollipop he's been coveting is broccoli flavored.

"She didn't do it," Zeke said. "I can feel it in my gut." He'd hunkered down to scratch Hobo's ears with fingers of energy, an activity that had taken hours of practice on inanimate objects. Hobo gave a low groan of contentment.

"You don't have a gut anymore," Rory reminded the marshal with a little "gotcha" smile.

"I don't have ears anymore either, and yet here I am listenin' to you jabber. I'm tellin' you, Jessica's just worried because she thinks she's the only one with a motive for murderin' Brian. I'd bet my boots she doesn't know anythin' about the scam he pulled on Ames, or that Sophia Caspian was hidin' a broken heart to keep her father in check. Of course, I'm takin' your word on the last one, since I wasn't privy to that conversation."

Rory let the implicit dig go unchallenged. After all, it was true that she hadn't told him she was going to interview her aunt Helene. And although he didn't know it yet, that wasn't her only transgression. Less than an hour ago she'd hidden the sketch of Eloise's mystery lady behind her headboard so he wouldn't find it. She'd told herself that she was just trying to avoid another argument over Eloise and that she'd show it to him eventually. But she knew concealing information from her partner in a case they were working together wasn't right no matter how many ways she tried to spin it.

"For all we know, everyone in that canyon had a reason to kill Brian," she said, picking up where the marshal had left off.

"It's surely startin' to seem that way. How many of the troupe were there that day?"

"Eight, not counting my aunt and Brian."

"So we're assumin' Helene's not guilty?"

"Don't even think about going there," Rory warned him. "I'd suspect myself before I ever suspected her."

"Well, it wouldn't be the first time you misjudged a person's character."

Rory knew by the sly grin on Zeke's face that he was referring to her nearly fatal relationship with Vince Conti the previous fall. But she had no intentions of digging up those old bones and going another round in the "who saved Rory" debate. She gave herself an imaginary pat on the back for not latching on to the marshal's bait.

"The bank statement!" Zeke said, switching tracks so abruptly that he left Rory behind. "I almost forgot about it."

"What? What bank statement? What are you talking about?"

He vanished from the room only to reappear at the kitchen table so quickly that Rory could swear she briefly saw two of him.

"I found it when I was going through Brian's files," he said, setting one of the folders on the table in front of her and flipping through the papers in it without scattering a single one. "I don't know much about banks and finances these days," he said, "but take a look at this page here."

Rory picked up the paper he'd uncovered. It was a statement from Brian's savings account listing all the deposits and withdrawals for the month of October the previous year. The statement was unremarkable until she reached the middle of the page.

She issued a low whistle. "I see what you mean." On October nineteenth, fifty thousand dollars had been deposited into the account. Based on what Brian had told his mother, he'd worked in the financial field. Based on his conviction, not in a legitimate fashion. "Did you find any regular monthly deposits that might have come from a salary?" she asked to cover all bases.

"Not a one."

"What about any other large deposits?"

"Nothin' near that amount. Back in my day, if a body suddenly came into a large sum of money, it was from an inheritance, a winnin' night at the poker table, or the proceeds from a bank robbery."

"I'd add the lottery and blackmail to that list. But since I haven't heard of any bank robberies or lottery winners around here, and Clarissa didn't mention the passing of a rich relative, I'm leaning toward blackmail."

"Blackmail . . . huh."

While the marshal was still busy kicking the tires of this intriguing possibility, Rory was already taking it out for a spin. "The question," she said, "is which member of the troupe has a secret worth fifty thousand dollars? *And* enough money to keep it a secret?"

# Chapter 16

B B called the next morning to say that Hobo could have his frog back. He asked Rory to meet him in front of the Forensic Sciences Building at one o'clock. When Rory arrived, the medical examiner was waiting outside with a brown paper bag in his hand, looking like an overgrown schoolboy waiting for the bus. She waved to him and motioned that she was going to park the car. It wasn't always easy to find a spot in the busy complex of government buildings, but since it was still lunch hour, many of the people who worked there were out eating or using the time to run errands.

As soon as she emerged from the car, she was glad she'd thrown the denim jacket over her sweater before leaving the house. Having lived on Long Island all her life, she knew better than to trust the month of April. The day had seemed warm by early spring standards, but when the wind blew, it carried a sharp reminder of winter. She took the shortest route from her car to BB, trotting across the grass that was just beginning to green up.

"I hope I didn't keep you waiting," she said when she reached him.

"You're exactly on time, *a l'heure, a tiempo,* as always," he said handing her the small bag, which at close range appeared to be adorned with grease stains. "I apologize for the packaging, but I didn't want to walk through the building holding a mangled, stuffed frog. I already have a reputation as something of an eccentric. So I rummaged around in my desk drawers for an appropriate receptacle and discovered that bag. I have no idea how long it was in there or what it originally carried, but I'm pretty sure it was some type of food. I should probably clean out my desk more often."

"It's perfectly fine," Rory assured him, sidestepping the issue of his cleaning ethic. She was hardly qualified to judge anyone, since last night's dinner dishes were still in her sink waiting to be washed. "Was Reggie able to make any sense of the writing on the tag?" she asked to nudge him back to the purpose of their meeting.

"As a matter of fact he was. Do you mind walking while we talk?"

"Not at all," she said stoically. Except that she would have taken her winter coat if she'd known their meeting was going to be al fresco and longer than two minutes. BB and Reggie had done so many favors for her, it seemed petty to complain about the windchill factor. She'd defrost with coffee or hot cocoa on her way home. Bolstered by that thought, she buttoned her jacket and plastered a smile on her face.

"Doctor's orders, I'm afraid," BB explained glumly as they set out to make a circuit of the building.

It occurred to Rory that she'd never seen him sad before. It was like seeing a clown without his happy makeup. "Is it something you want to talk about?"

"Ah, if only talking were the solution. I'd filibuster better than any ten senators. It seems that I have to exercise and shed some weight to get my blood pressure and cholesterol under control."

"Ouch." She didn't know anyone who enjoyed food quite as much as BB did.

"To put it mildly," he said summoning up a bleak smile. "If you don't mind, I'd actually prefer to talk about your frog. With any luck it will distract me from my stomach's grumbling over what I can only loosely call lunch."

As they turned the corner of the building, a cold blast of wind almost knocked Rory off her feet. Deep in his misery, BB didn't seem to notice it.

Rory leaned into the wind to regain her balance. "Did Reggie tell you what was written on the tag?" she asked in the spirit of distracting him and satisfying her gnawing curiosity. The wind swallowed her words, forcing her to raise her voice and repeat the question.

"He was able to make out enough of what was there to be 95 percent certain about his accuracy," BB said, pumping up the volume of his voice too. But as the sentence left his mouth the wind fell silent, and he found himself shouting as if he were trying to reach the upper decks of a football stadium without benefit of a microphone. He glanced around, clearly relieved to see there was no one else in the area.

"That's great news," Rory said, forgetting about the goose bumps that were marching up and down her arms. "It was such a mess that I didn't know if he'd be able to figure it out at all."

"The man never fails to amaze. Not only does he have an amazing mind, but he also has an innate ability to see things that others of equal experience and training discount or miss entirely."

"So did he tell you what was written on the tag?" she pressed him, unable to restrain herself for another moment.

"*Mais oui, por cierto*, yes, of course. You must be dying to know and here I am just rattling on. He actually gave me a note spelling it out." BB came to an abrupt stop while he checked the pockets of his pants. He came up with an old, scuffed wallet, a handful of coins and a crumpled tissue with a questionable past. "I know I had it here somewhere."

Rory had a mental image of herself grabbing and shaking him until he produced the information without further delay.

"Ah, here it is," he declared triumphantly, withdrawing a single, folded sheet of paper from his shirt pocket and handing it to her. "It appears that whoever tampered with your frog has literary leanings."

"Literary?" she said, thoroughly bewildered. "You mean it wasn't a threat?"

"Not unless playwrights scare you."

'Hell hath no fury like a woman scorned.' What's that supposed to mean?" Zeke asked, frowning at Reggie's note as if he could coerce it into disclosing more by the sheer force of his will.

"It's a paraphrase of a famous quote," Rory said. "It means you'd better watch your back if you do your woman wrong."

"Thanks, professor," Zeke said dryly, "but I want to know what it means turnin' up on the mutt's gift frog."

"BB doesn't think it's a real threat," she replied between sips of coffee that were helping to thaw her out. They were upstairs in the study, she behind the desk and the marshal in the old armchair where she used to sit and read while her uncle Mac worked. Hobo, who'd followed them upstairs, was lying on the area rug using his teeth to comb out a mat of fur on his left haunch.

"BB doesn't, huh? When was the last time this fella found himself lookin' down the business end of a .45?"

"I don't see why that matters," Rory said, rushing to the medical examiner's defense.

"It matters because BB ain't the one at risk here; you are. Everythin' about the break-in was top-notch professional. And no one with that level of trainin' breaks into a house without havin' a damn good reason for doin' it."

"Then why use such a vague threat? If what you're saying is true, why be so timid with the note?"

Zeke ran his fingers through his hair as he wrestled with her question. "Because it's more than a threat," he said finally. "I think it's also meant as a clue."

"Someone broke in here to leave me a clue? They could have sent me a letter or given me a call." As theories went, this one had holes big enough to drive a double-decker bus through without nicking the paint job.

"Like I said before, the breakin' in was to show you how vulnerable you are. The note's to point you in a specific direction. For some reason, the intruder doesn't want to threaten you outright, but he's lookin' to get the most bang for his buck."

Rory clamped her lips shut to hold back a grin. She didn't think she'd ever get used to hearing modern expressions roll off the marshal's tongue. But this wasn't the time to indulge her amusement. He'd be doubly annoyed that she was taking her safety so lightly. So she ironed the would-be smile into a suitably sober expression before speaking.

"Okay, let's say you're right. How do we know if the note is a clue or misdirection? Is it pointing to the killer or protecting the killer by trying to frame someone else?"

"There's no tellin' yet."

She sighed. "What if you're wrong about this intruder? Maybe he's eccentric. Maybe he's trying to help us in his own crazy way."

"Let's get one thing straight," Zeke shot back, "anyone

who tampers with your alarm system and just sashays on in here is already a dangerous criminal."

Although Rory didn't like what he was saying, she knew he was right. She could change the alarm code and the locks on the doors, but she suspected that wouldn't even slow down an intruder as sophisticated as this one seemed to be. She picked up the coffee, which had cooled to room temperature, and swallowed it down in a few frustrated gulps.

When the doorbell rang an hour later, Rory was alone in the study writing progress reports on two of her more mundane cases. Zeke had retired to his niche between worlds, and Hobo was enjoying the comforts of the living room couch. By the time Rory came down the stairs, the dog was stationed at the front door barking his displeasure. Although he'd never met a person he didn't like, with the understandable exception of the man who'd killed his first owner, his bark was sincere and ferocious enough to make strangers reevaluate their need to be there. On more than one occasion Rory had opened the door to find salespeople or poll takers scuttling off to the next house without looking back. She just wished she could teach Hobo to cut the Girl Scouts some slack. She really loved their Samoas.

"Good boy," she whispered to the dog as she put her eye to the peephole. She drew back with a puzzled frown. What was Stuart Dobson doing there?

She opened the door just as the director was about to press the bell again.

"Hey," he said. "There you are. I didn't know if you'd be home."

"Here I am," she said pleasantly, wondering why he hadn't tried calling first. "What can I do for you?"

"I was in the area so I thought I'd drop by. Do you have time for a quick chat?"

She'd used that same ploy herself enough times to be wary of the reason behind it. "I do have a few minutes before my next client," she said. There wasn't actually a next client that day, but she wanted an excuse to keep their impromptu meeting from dragging on for too long.

She stepped aside to let Stuart enter. Hobo was wagging and doing his happy little tap dance now that Stuart had apparently passed muster. The director ignored the dog, even though it would have required the bare minimum of effort to provide a scratch or two as a gesture of goodwill.

The entry area was small, certainly not the most comfortable place to hold a discussion. But Rory had no intentions of moving the meeting farther into the house or outside to her office. Whatever Stuart wanted to discuss, they could discuss right there. She knew she was being less than hospitable, but there was something about Stuart that irritated her even though she'd never spent more than a couple of minutes in his company at any one time. The fact that he'd snubbed Hobo wasn't going to win him any points from her either.

"I understand Clarissa Carpenter hired you to look into her son's death," Stuart began once he realized he wasn't going to be invited inside to sit down.

"That's right," she said.

"Well, the investigation seems to be having a deleterious effect on my troupe."

"Really?" Rory was immediately more interested. "In what respect?"

"They're moody, on edge, snapping at each other, even arguing with me." He said the last with haughty indignation.

"That's just awful," she commiserated without much sincerity. "But I don't know what I can do about it." She'd only interviewed three of the players, not counting Helene, and tensions were already on the rise? Finger-pointing and fear of being falsely accused were no doubt promoting the general malaise. With any luck, that kind of behavior might even prove helpful in ferreting out the killer.

"I was under the impression that the medical examiner labeled Brian's death accidental," Stuart said.

"He did, but Clarissa doesn't agree with him. I'm pretty sure she has the right to her own opinion under the law," Rory added sweetly. She could tell by the way Stuart's eyes narrowed that he'd caught the sarcasm beneath the candy coating. "And as long as she's willing to pay for my services, I intend to help her find whatever closure she needs."

Stuart opened his mouth then closed it again without uttering a sound, obviously at a loss for words. "I get it," he said finally. "She has the right to hire you, and you have the right to investigate for her. But I also have some rights here. Like the right to protect my interests. Our little theater doesn't exactly come rent free. And I can't be expected to mount a quality production with a bunch of surly actors who can't remember their lines."

"Then it's in everyone's best interests for me to proceed at full steam and finish up the investigation as quickly as possible," Rory said brightly.

Stuart wasn't doing any cartwheels over her solution. Had he actually expected her to be so abashed by his plight that she would close the case, return Clarissa's money and never darken the theater's doorstep again?

"At the very least," he said, glaring at her, "I expect you to stick to the facts that are germane to the case and avoid pitting the actors against one another unnecessarily."

"Do I hear an 'or else' in there?" Although she knew it wouldn't serve anyone's purposes to ratchet up the animosity between them, the words spilled out before she could stop them.

•

"Of course not. I would never stoop to threats." The director's lips almost slipped into a smile before he shut them down.

"I'm glad to hear that," Rory said, "because I don't respond well to threats. Probably left over from my days as a detective." She could tell from Stuart's face that he'd received her message loud and clear. "And I'll do my best to keep your guidelines in mind," she added. She would have preferred to tell him where he could stuff them, but it wasn't lost on her that he could easily retaliate against her via her aunt. Helene would be devastated if she were relegated to minor roles or sidelined completely.

Since Stuart seemed to have run out of momentum, Rory took the opportunity to wrap up the meeting. She said she was glad they'd had a chance to discuss their positions, and the director mumbled a few words that sounded roughly like 'Thanks for nothing.' "

He'd turned and was starting toward the door when he suddenly stumbled. Flapping his long arms in a desperate effort to stay on his feet, he looked like a gooney bird on takeoff. After several, comical seconds, gravity won out, and he slammed onto the hardwood floor, his knees and hands taking the brunt of the impact. His head missed the door frame by inches. Rory and Hobo had jumped back before he could take them down with him.

"Are you all right?" she asked, kneeling down at his side.

Stuart gathered his gangly legs into a sitting position with a grunt. "What the hell did I fall over?" he asked, looking at the floor around him. Rory saw Hobo's tennis ball at the same moment the director did. It was lying against the nearby wall where it had come to rest after he'd tripped on it.

"Where'd the damn ball come from?" he demanded. "It wasn't there when I came in or I would have seen it."

"I have no idea," Rory said, trying to look as perplexed as he did. "But it couldn't have just appeared out of thin air."

Of course, it might have been transported there by rather unconventional means, but she had no intentions of sharing that bit of information. She extended her hand to help him up, but he ignored the offer and dragged himself to his feet on his own.

"Can I get you anything?"

"No, nothing," he grumbled. "I'd just like to get out of here in one piece." Keeping his eyes on the floor in case any other objects decided to make their debut, he limped out of the house without another word. Rory was about to close the door behind him when she noticed a police cruiser driving slowly past her house. She watched it continue down the street until it disappeared from sight beyond the curve. The police were not a common sight in this neighborhood. A security alarm or a resident must have alerted them to a potential problem. Rory wasn't sure whether it was instinct or simple curiosity that caused her to remain at the door, but less than a minute later, she saw the cruiser come down the block again. This time it pulled to the curb directly across the street from her house and parked.

# Chapter 17

As Rory approached the police car, the patrolman opened his window. He was young, around her age, thirty tops, with blond hair that made him look like a California surfer with a bad sense of direction. She'd never seen him before, but that didn't surprise her. When she'd worked for the department, she'd been assigned to headquarters out east in Yaphank. This guy was from the local precinct and junior enough to pull protective surveillance.

"Ms. McCain," he said smiling and clearly giving her the once-over.

"Officer . . . ?" Because of her angle, she couldn't make out the name on his steel ID tag.

"Cooper, Todd Cooper. Pleased to meet you." He reached awkwardly across his chest to offer her his right hand. "I hear you were a detective before going the PI route."

Rory gave his hand a quick shake. "Yes, a sketch artist."

"Ah, an artist, huh?"

She could tell from his tone that she'd dropped several

notches in his esteem with that admission. She tightened the lid on her already parboiled anger. Todd might be deficient in the social graces, but he wasn't the source of her irritation.

"Who assigned you to watch over me?" she asked, doing her best to remain cordial.

He shrugged. "Some detective at headquarters."

"Does the name Russell ring a bell?"

"Yeah, now that you mention it, Russell sounds right. Anyway, you've got nothing to worry about. I'm here to keep you safe."

"How nice," she said. "I'll finally be able to sleep tonight."

If Officer Todd heard the sarcasm in her tone, he chose not to respond to it.

W hen Rory left her house the next morning, she saw that another cop had taken Todd Cooper's place across the street. She didn't bother to introduce herself. If she had anything to say about it, he'd be gone before she returned.

The parking lot was mostly empty when she arrived at the Suffolk County Police Headquarters in Yaphank before eight o'clock. She parked in a spot designated for visitors and went inside. Being in the building again felt both familiar and strange, like the time she'd gone back to visit her elementary school after moving on to junior high. She knew the location of every loose floor tile, every scuff mark on the wall, yet she didn't belong there anymore.

She'd planned on grabbing a few minutes with Leah before her friend was inundated with work and swept out of reach for the rest of the day. But she hadn't factored people into the equation. Since she'd only been gone six months, nearly everyone she knew was still there. And nearly everyone wanted her to stop and chat. By the time she made it over to Homicide, Leah was already working at her computer and engaged in a testy phone conversation. Her face lit up with surprise when Rory walked in. With one eyebrow arched as a question mark, she held up her index finger to indicate she'd be with her in a minute. Rory signaled back that she'd wait for her in the break room.

The break room was unoccupied, everything exactly as it had been. The walls still needed a fresh coat of paint and the furniture a trip to the landfill. The coffeemaker hadn't budged from its spot on the smaller of two tables with chipped Formica tops. The carafe was half full. Beside it were the coffee fixings and a box of chocolate-covered doughnuts with its top pushed back. Four mismatched chairs, two metal filing cabinets and a small refrigerator completed the decor. Seeing the room again, Rory remembered she'd left her coffee mug behind when she'd cleared out her personal effects. She opened the single cabinet above the refrigerator and there it was, waiting patiently to be rescued. She took it down and was pouring herself a cup of coffee when Leah walked in.

Leah came straight to her and gave her a hug, gentle enough to keep the coffee from sloshing out of her cup. When she stepped back, her brow had lowered into a frown. And Rory knew why. She'd automatically tensed at Leah's touch. Although she'd meant to leave her irritation at home and have a quiet, rational discussion with her friend, it had hopped aboard anyway, riding shotgun to her best intentions.

"Okay, what's going on?" Leah asked, studying Rory's face for clues.

"Look, I know your motives are beyond reproach," she said trying to keep her voice from tightening too, "but this time you've overstepped your boundaries."

"I don't know what you're talking about." Leah sounded so genuinely bewildered that Rory had a moment's hesitation. But there was no getting around the fact that a police cruiser had been stationed across the street from her house since the previous evening.

"Do the words 'police protection' jog your memory?" She set her coffee on the table, no longer in the mood for it.

Leah's expression morphed from confusion to concern. "Rory, I arranged for the protection after you requested it. Please tell me you remember doing that."

"I didn't request any such thing."

"Here, I'll show you." Leah pulled her phone out of her pocket, scrolled down and handed it to her:

Urgent—received note threatening dire consequences if I pursue current case. Need protection.

As soon as Rory read the e-mail she realized what was going on. Zeke was once again trying to protect her. She didn't know whether to laugh or scream. But first she had to come up with an explanation that Leah would buy.

"Did you honestly think I sent this?" she asked, handing back the phone. "It sounds like a telegraph in an old B movie."

"Well, I did think it was peculiar, but all I really focused on was the 'threatening note' part. Yesterday was like a three-ring circus around here, and then I had to leave in the middle of everything because Jake fell out of a tree and broke his arm again. I literally arranged for the patrol car on my way to the hospital. I figured I'd call you today and find out what was going on."

"Whoa, I had no idea," Rory said feeling both foolish and insensitive. "How is he?" At eight, Jake was Leah's youngest, a fearless daredevil who was always stumbling into, or out of, one kind of trouble or another.

"He's fine." Leah sighed. "I, on the other hand, am the proud owner of a fresh new crop of gray hair. So tell me, what gives with the weird e-mail?"

"I think my dad must have sent it. He was at my house when I got the note. But it wasn't a threat; it was a quote that didn't even make sense to me. Someone must have dropped it in my mailbox by mistake. Listen, I apologize for my dad and for me. I should have known you wouldn't order protection for me without asking me first. Or at least trying to bully me into it," she added to lighten the mood.

Leah was still frowning, not yet ready to let the matter go. "Was there an address on the envelope? Writing of any kind?"

"There was no envelope."

"We should at least check the note for prints."

Rory shrugged. "I was so sure it was nothing that I threw it away." She couldn't very well say she'd turned to Reggie for help instead of her best friend.

Leah closed her eyes briefly and took a deep breath as if she were counting to ten. "Okay," she said evenly. "Humor me—what was the quote?"

"The old 'hell hath no fury like a woman scorned' thing."

Leah laughed. "Have you been dating a married man in your spare time?"

"I would never do something like that and not tell you," Rory said, laughing along with her. "I think the note was meant for someone else and wound up at my house by mistake. Trust me, Leah, if I thought—"

At that moment she was saved by Leah's partner, Jeff, who appeared in the doorway. "Good to see you Rory," he said. "Sorry to break up the homecoming, but we've got a body that's decomposing as we speak." He was gone before the last word left his lips.

"I'm there," Leah called after him. She turned back to Rory and locked eyes with her. "You're 100 percent the note wasn't a threat?"

"It was just a quote, and not even an accurate one. You can call off the troops."

* * *

There was no patrol car to be seen when Rory drove down her street an hour later.

"Why did you call off the police?" Zeke demanded, materializing only inches away as she stepped inside. He hadn't even bothered to flicker the lights first, an omission no doubt meant to further unnerve her. No way was that going to work. In fact, she had some complaints of her own to lodge.

"Why did you contact Leah behind my back?" she asked. Although he hadn't left her much wiggle room, she maneuvered around him to deposit her handbag on the bench and her loafers beneath it.

"Someone had to. And you weren't showing any inclination to do it."

"I don't need the police to babysit me," she said, turning her back on him and padding off to the kitchen in her socks.

Zeke was leaning against the center island when she got there, arms crossed in front of him. She'd become so accustomed to his leapfrogging ahead of her that she didn't even bother to pause in her remarks when she moved from one room to another. "But more importantly, if I ever do, it'll be my call to make, not yours."

"Okay, then," he said soberly. "Sounds reasonable enough. I don't get to decide all on my own about somethin' that involves you."

"Exactly." That was easier than she'd anticipated. At the very least she'd expected another lecture on safety and experience—her safety, his experience. She pulled a box of granola down from the pantry shelf and poured some into a small bowl. She hadn't eaten any breakfast before heading off to Yaphank, and her stomach was grousing about it.

"I assume the same rules apply to you as well," Zeke

said. "You don't get to decide all by your lonesome about somethin' that involves me."

"That's only fair," she agreed warily. She had the sense that he was leading her along a lovely garden path and straight into a trap that suited his agenda. But before she could figure out what that might be, he disappeared. She was sure he wasn't finished with her, not by a long shot, but maybe she'd at least get to eat breakfast in peace.

She went to the refrigerator for milk and was pouring it over her cereal when Hobo emerged from beneath the table, one of his favorite places to snooze. He'd been sleeping so soundly that he hadn't even heard her come home. That was fine with her. It meant he was fully comfortable with his strange, new family. He stretched, a long luxurious stretch, first with his front legs, then with the back ones. His lips peeled back in a comical yawn as he ambled over to her to say "hello" and see if he could coax her into giving him some goodies.

She offered him a granola cluster that he sniffed thoroughly before finally accepting. "We can't eat filet mignon all the time," she chided him as she carried her bowl to the table. He followed, settling down beside her in case she was feeling generous. She was only a few spoonfuls into her breakfast when Zeke popped into the chair across the table, her sketch pad floating a few inches above his hands. He'd opened it to her most recent sketch, the woman she'd drawn from Eloise's description.

"You ought to practice what you preach, darlin'," he said with the satisfaction of the cat that had nabbed the canary and thought it was particularly tasty.

"How did you find that?" Rory asked, indignation trumping guilt for the moment. Staying out of her bedroom was one of the bylaws he'd agreed to when they'd first worked out their living arrangements. "I left it in my bedroom."

"Let's see," he said, inclining his head as if he were

considering her words. "Nope, I'm pretty certain that's not the right reaction. Given the circumstances, I was expectin' somethin' more along the lines of an apology."

"Any apologizing had better start with you." She knew she wouldn't win any awards for diplomacy, but she couldn't help herself. If he'd broken his promise, their relationship, even their partnership, had to be reexamined. "If you've been abiding by our agreement, how did you know where it was?"

"I happened to see you walk into the house with it the other day. You took it straight into your bedroom. Far as I know you've always left it in the study. So I was curious. But I didn't follow you in there. When I give my word, I don't take liberties with it." His tone had sharpened to a steely edge. "This was the first time I've been in your bedroom since I met you. And seein' as how you were down here, I knew I wouldn't be intrudin' on your privacy up there. In fact, I had trouble even findin' the damn pad, precisely because I didn't see where you hid it."

He'd slammed the ball squarely into Rory's court, and she found herself unable to fire it back. Although she didn't like being bested in any match, she believed he was telling the truth. If she'd learned anything about the marshal over the past six months, it was that he lived by a strict, if sometimes odd, moral code. If she expected the truth from him, she had to live by it as well. She wasn't going to cut herself any slack.

"I didn't show it to you because I knew we'd just wind up arguing about it," she said. Not much of an excuse given that here they were arguing about it anyway.

"You've been visitin' with Eloise, haven't you?" He sounded like a cop grilling a suspect.

"Yes, not that it's any of your business. You don't have veto power over my relationships." Why was he bent on making this one molehill into a mountain range? A startling possibility popped into her head. "You know who the woman in the sketch is, don't you?" she said. That was why he'd immediately associated the drawing with Eloise—Eloise, who seemed able to see into the future and the past.

It was Zeke's turn to backpedal. "Whether I do or not ain't the point here. A man's got the right to keep some thin's private."

Rory's imagination kicked into overdrive. Who was this woman who aroused such emotion in him? And was she the reason he felt threatened by Eloise? Stop it, she chastised herself. Everyone *did* have the right to some secrets. She should let it go. If and when he wanted to tell her, he would. Fine advice. Now if she could just follow it.

She looked across the table at him, ramrod straight in his chair, jaw set hard with determination. She cast about for a way to break the tension between them, but came up empty. Well, almost empty. She could try a peace offering. Something sincere that didn't involve dropping to her knees and begging forgiveness, since to her way of thinking she hadn't actually done anything that required that sort of apology. As long as they were talking about rights, a girl had a right to some dignity too.

"Okay," she said, "I agree. You do have a right to secrets. In recognition of that, I'll try to keep my distance from Eloise. But you need to understand that's not quite as easy as it might sound, since she's the one who keeps initiating things. So if I happen to see her, I'll do my best to stop her from saying anything related to you." There—no scraping or groveling involved.

Zeke seemed to understand that this was her best offer. His posture relaxed and a smile hitched up the corners of his mouth. "Mighty obliged, darlin'," he said. "I knew you'd come around to my way of thinkin' if I gave you enough rope to play it out."

So much for diplomacy and compromise. Although she'd

been trying to defuse the situation in as equitable a way as possible, he'd been busy "handling" her the way he would a wild horse he was trying to break. Well, she knew exactly what he could do with his chauvinistic, condescending attitude. But he vanished before she could share that bit of wisdom.

# 1878

## Denver, Colorado

Marshal Drummond rode into Denver a full ten days after leaving Albuquerque behind. Since there were no tracks to point him in Trask's direction, he'd had to make do with experience and instinct. The way he figured it, Trask might well be a man without a conscience or a heart, but he was hardly a man without a brain. Aware that the law would be on his trail, and presumably without a hidey-hole nearby, the best place for him to take cover would be in a big city. Denver was the closest one that fit the bill.

The ride had been hard on the marshal, who had not fully recovered from his grim bout with death. The aching and throbbing of his body had worsened with each day he spent in the saddle, each night he lay upon the hard ground. By the sixth day, a peculiar numbness had set in, as if his mind had determined there was nothing to be gained by reminding him of his distress. On several occasions, he went hungry rather than lose time looking for a farmhouse where he might buy a meal. As long as his horse had oats and grass, he could hang on. He hadn't owned much of an appetite of late anyway. And in spite of the endless hours with only the chestnut for company, he didn't allow himself to wonder what he'd do if he couldn't pick up the killer's trail. Failure was simply not to be contemplated.

Upon reaching Denver, Drummond immediately made the rounds of the city's stables. A man planning to lay low for a while would need to board his horse. At each stable he pulled out the picture of Trask. He hit pay dirt at the third one.

It was the blacksmith's apprentice, Tom, a scrawny youth with a long stalk of a neck and hooded eyes, who recognized Trask. "That's the guy; that's definitely the guy who sold us the buckskin two, three weeks back," he said, passing the picture to his boss.

"You're certain about that?" Drummond asked, afraid to believe things might finally be turning in his favor.

The blacksmith, who introduced himself as O'Malley, looked at the picture and nodded. "That's him all right—a nasty son of a bitch if I ever met one. I came close to throwing him out of here."

"Sounds about right," Drummond said. "He didn't happen to say why he was sellin' the horse or where he might be headed?"

"No sir, Marshal. He didn't volunteer nothin', and I didn't say more to him than was necessary for conductin' our business. But I can tell you the horse was sound enough. Just in need of some rest and food. That Trask had pretty much run him into the ground."

"What's he wanted for anyway?" the apprentice asked, his eyes glittery with excitement.

"Murder," Drummond told him solemnly, "and other things you don't want to know."

Tom opened his mouth as if he was about to dispute that assumption, but he closed it again without saying a word.

Drummond refolded the picture and tucked it back in his pocket. "Either of you seen Trask around town since that day?"

"I seen him the very next day over at the Lucky Lady," Tom piped up eagerly.

"I ain't seen him at all," O'Malley said, turning to glare at his apprentice. "Your mama and your aunt Jean'll tan your hide good, boy, if they find out you were hangin' round a saloon."

"I wasn't, Uncle Will. I was just passin' by there is all." His voice had taken on a high, nervous warble. "You ain't gonna tell them, are you?"

"Much obliged for the help," Drummond interrupted, since he didn't have time to wait for the family drama to rattle on to its conclusion.

"More than welcome," O'Malley said without taking his eyes off his nephew. "I hope you find him."

As Drummond led the chestnut outside he heard the blacksmith resume lecturing the boy in louder, more graphic terms. The odds were good that Tom wouldn't be sneaking into another saloon until he came of age.

Before mounting the chestnut, the marshal took a moment to decide on his next move. He tried to think himself into Trask's boots. He might have sold the horse intending to buy another, one less likely to be identified with him, or he might be planning to travel by train. Denver provided several different options in that regard. He could take the Denver and Pacific Railroad link to Cheyenne and pick up the main line of the Union Pacific to head either farther west or east to Chicago. Or he might hop on the Kansas Pacific and ride it out to Saint Louis.

If it had been up to the marshal, he'd have chosen to stay on horseback, but Trask hadn't asked his opinion. In any case, as his first order of business, Drummond had to find out whether Trask was still hunkered down somewhere in

Denver or had already left for parts unknown. With no quick way to check through the entire city for him, the train depot seemed like the most efficient option. Drummond stopped a man on a passing buckboard and asked to be directed there.

The depot was a small, wooden structure that no one had seen fit to paint. It was the same grimy color as the rails that ran past it and the locomotives that rode upon them. Drummond tied the chestnut to the hitching post and mounted the few steps to the narrow porch that ran the length of the building. Three men and a woman were waiting on benches provided for that purpose, with their travel bags at their feet. They were all dressed in their Sunday finest, in stark contrast to their current surroundings. Under normal circumstances, the marshal would have been ashamed of his appearance. Both he and his clothing were in dire need of soap and water. But as his manners were as yet unsullied, he nodded to the men as he walked past them, and gave the lady a perfunctory tip of his hat.

He walked inside the depot, where there were two more benches to accommodate passengers waiting for a train in inclement weather, a pot-bellied stove that wouldn't be fired up until summer had run its course and a wooden counter presided over by the ticket agent. The agent, who'd doffed his trademark jacket and cap to work in his shirtsleeves, was busy with a customer. When it was Drummond's turn, he identified himself and handed the agent the well-creased picture of John Trask, along with a brief explanation of why he was looking for him.

"That fella was in here," the agent said, thumping the picture with his finger. "Most definitely. Had a chip on his shoulder the size of a two-by-four. Struck me as strange too. He asked a bushelful of questions, but wouldn't say where he wanted to go. Got downright angry when I pressed him on it. It wasn't like I was trying to be nosey, you understand.

It's just a whole lot easier to recommend train routes if I know where a person's headed. Dealing with the public you'd think I'd seen it all by now, but people keep right on amazing me. And never in a good way."

"Did he wind up buying a ticket?" Drummond asked, scarcely able to hide his impatience with the agent's chummy, "down-home" style.

"Yes he did. Bought himself a trip to Cheyenne, as I recollect."

"Do you recall the date?"

The agent chewed on his lower lip while he thought about it. "I make it a couple, three weeks ago."

Drummond wasn't happy to hear that. Not only were the time and distance between him and Trask growing, but the killer had taken the train to Cheyenne, where the Union Pacific would offer him many more options. It wasn't even a matter of where the rail line ended. Trask could leave the train at any stop along the way.

The marshal bought a one-way ticket to Cheyenne and thanked the agent for his help. He untethered his horse, pulled himself into the saddle with some difficulty and headed back to O'Malley's. He and the blacksmith worked out a simple deal. He paid a month's board in advance for the care of the chestnut. If he didn't return by the end of that time, O'Malley could assume ownership of the horse and tack.

The marshal ran his hand along the horse's neck and withers and made him a silent promise to do his damndest to come back for him. Then he walked out of the smithy alone, his saddlebag slung over his shoulder. He'd thought his heart was already too shattered to break anymore, but he was wrong.

# Chapter 18

Rory was awakened by the garbage truck instead of her alarm clock, which she'd apparently forgotten to set. The day was off to a great start. She was barely conscious, and she was already running late. Hobo, who was stretched out beside her, opened one bleary eye, then closed it again and snuggled deeper into the covers.

"Yeah, yeah, I get it," she said to him as she dragged herself out of bed. "You've got a better life than I do. You really shouldn't gloat though; it doesn't become you." She grabbed her robe from the closet and double-timed it into the bathroom.

She was scheduled to meet with Dorothy Johnson at 9:30 in Northport, which gave her less than an hour to shower, dress and drive the fifteen minutes there. In spite of Dorothy's age and the foot she'd fractured in the flood, she wasn't lying around taking it easy. Since her driving foot was just fine, her days were as busy as ever. On that particular morning, she was fitting Rory in after her appointment at the nail salon and before her quilting class.

Rory was drying her hair and reading the news crawl on the mini television Mac had installed to the right of the bathroom mirror when a loud thud against the door startled her. The dryer flew out of her hand, tumbling onto the tile floor, where the plastic casing cracked in two and the motor went ominously silent. Another thud, this one accompanied by a flickering of the bathroom lights. Too little, too late. She'd realized who was making the noise even as the dryer was busy obeying the law of gravity. Aside from her, Zeke was the only member of her household who could approximate a knock by using his energy to throw something against the door. Hobo generally scratched at closed doors or howled to gain entrance. If it wasn't Zeke, she had more to worry about than wet hair and a moribund dryer.

"Mornin'. Do you have a minute?" The marshal's voice, casual and upbeat, floated through the door. He'd clearly left yesterday's argument behind.

Although Rory wasn't aware of any desire on her part to reprise last night's drama either, the image staring back at her from the mirror was wearing a harried "What do you want?" expression that would surely start things off on the wrong foot. She unknotted her brow and slapped on a smile before opening the door.

"Hi," she said, unplugging the dryer and retrieving its remains.

"My apologies if I caused that thingamajig to break," Zeke said, managing to look both rueful and pleased at the same time. As far as Rory could tell he'd never met a machine he liked or trusted.

She set the pieces on the counter with a shrug. "It was probably ready to retire anyway." She was glad her hair was short enough to dry quickly on its own, since April was back to doing its best impression of winter.

"So what's up?" she asked, turning back to the mirror to apply a quick swipe of mascara to her lashes.

"We've got some catchin' up to do. We never went over Dobson's visit and we oughta get that out of the way before we meet up with Dorothy."

There'd been so much going on the past few days that Rory had set the director's visit to simmer on a back burner of her mind and then forgotten it was even there. "I guess we should, but . . ." She stopped before the words "that's hardly an emergency" spilled out of her mouth. Apparently she was more annoyed about the broken hair dryer than she'd thought. Patience and diplomacy, she told herself. Patience and diplomacy.

"But what?"

He clearly wasn't going to let her off the hook. "But . . . we'll have time to talk about it in the car," she said, doing a quick ad-lib. Since she'd already brushed her teeth and destroyed her hair dryer, there was no longer any need for her to remain in the bathroom. She went over to the doorway, which Zeke was still blocking. "I'd better get dressed, or we'll miss the meeting with Dorothy altogether," she said, waiting for him to take the hint and move aside.

"That's a fine idea," he said, without budging.

"Excuse me."

"Oh, why, yes, ma'am." He stepped back with a bow and a gallant sweep of his hand. Rory couldn't tell if he was mocking her or just trying to be a gentleman. In the interest of harmony, she decided she didn't need to know.

"I don't much care for the man," Zeke said from the passenger seat. They were driving into Northport along Woodbine Avenue, the winding, one-lane road that overlooked the Long Island Sound. Grand Victorian homes with magnificent water views straddled the hills on the east side of the road. Smaller houses with more stalwart occupants crouched over the Sound on the west side, the angle down to them so precipitous that navigating it required stairs. Cars were out of the question. They had to be left on the apron of level ground at the side of the road.

Although the marshal had initiated the discussion about Stuart Dobson as soon as they'd pulled out of the driveway, he'd been having a hard time staying focused since they'd turned onto Woodbine. Having lived his entire life in a place where a lake was the largest body of water around, he seemed mesmerized by the proximity of the Atlantic, including this tranquil strait of water leading to it.

"I don't like Dobson either," Rory said, trying to reel Zeke back in. "But he isn't running for Miss Congeniality. Bottom line—do you think he did it?"

"Miss who?"

"Sorry." There were still times she forgot the marshal wasn't from the here and now. "I just mean he doesn't have to be likeable to be innocent."

"I never said he did."

Rory stopped herself from trying to explain her explanation. Sometimes they seemed to be speaking different languages and it was simply best to let the subject go.

"In answer to your question," Zeke resumed, "Dobson's not the one. Why would a killer with half a workin' brain up and pay a visit on the investigator? Put himself under that kind of scrutiny?"

"To make me think he isn't guilty."

Zeke shook his head. "I might buy that if he hadn't been so angry from the get-go. No, I think he's miffed 'cause you're messin' with his troupe. He's protectin' his interests. He can't go on bein' king if he has no subjects."

"And I suppose Brian must have wanted to stay in Dobson's good graces in order to get the better roles," she said musing out loud.

"Which means no scams, no blackmail. Dobson might be the one person in the troupe who didn't have a motive to kill him. So, as much as we don't like him, we've got to move on. You never get where you're goin' by constantly sniffin' around the same tree."

"By the way," Rory said, "you shouldn't have put that ball where he could trip on it."

"Yeah, I know," Zeke said with a grin. "I just couldn't resist."

They'd reached the intersection where Woodbine crossed the northern end of Main Street. As Rory turned onto Main, she checked for nearby cars and pedestrians. Fortunately, the town was quiet on weekdays, especially before the warm weather took hold. With no potential witnesses around, she told Zeke it was time for him to vanish, which he did, on cue and without argument. Rory wondered if it qualified as a miracle.

She pulled into one of the angled parking spaces a few doors down from the little storefront diner where Dorothy had suggested they meet. Inside, Rory found her waiting in one of the booths, adding milk to her coffee. Her chin-length brown hair seemed to be in the throes of indecision, some of it curling toward her face, some away. Her only makeup was an overly bright swath of blush on her plump cheeks, which added to her generally round appearance. From what Rory could tell from her brief encounters with Dorothy in the past, the older woman had surrendered to, if not welcomed, the additional pounds menopause offered.

Rory slid into the booth across from her, and by the time they'd exchanged their "hellos" and "how are yous," the waitress appeared to take their order. Rory asked for coffee, orange juice and an English muffin, since there hadn't been time for breakfast at home. Dorothy said that sounded good and ordered a carrot muffin, which apparently sounded even better.

"Now, what can I do for you?" she asked. "You were rather vague on the phone."

"I guess you've heard that Brian's mother asked me to look into the circumstances surrounding his death?"

"Yes, I couldn't help but hear—you know, the old grapevine. How's it going?"

"Investigations are kind of funny that way. You can't always tell how they're going until they're over."

"Sounds a lot like acting." She laughed. "No matter how much work you do beforehand, there's no way to be sure how it will turn out until the curtain comes down opening night. Can I be of any help?"

"Just making the time to see me today is great. What I'm looking for are any insights you might have into Brian and his relationships with the other Players who were there the day he died."

"Such a horrible day," Dorothy said with a little shudder. "It still doesn't seem completely real to me. I guess when your time is up, it's up. What else can you say when an old lady like me makes it out in almost one piece while a strong, young man like Brian drowns?"

"Then you think Brian's death was a matter of fate, not murder?"

"I know Clarissa thinks he was murdered, but doesn't a flash flood sound more like fate to you? Not that the two have to be mutually exclusive, I suppose," Dorothy said, pausing as if to consider her own words. "I mean what if fate sent the flood that made the murder possible?"

The waitress arrived with their breakfast, and Rory waited until she'd set everything down and walked away before speaking. "That's certainly one way of looking at it." She added milk to her coffee and spread strawberry jam on her English muffin. "But getting back to basics, how would you say Brian got along with the rest of the troupe?"

Dorothy had cut her carrot muffin in half and was

spreading each side with orange marmalade. She took a bite and chewed thoughtfully for a few moments. "I don't think I have the kind of insights into Brian that you're hoping to hear," she said after swallowing. "I had very little personal interaction with him."

"Whatever you can tell me is probably more than I know."

"Well, he could be . . . what's the word . . . charismatic, that's it. Like the cult leaders you hear about on the news from time to time. I think it was easy to be drawn in by him."

"Slick?" Rory offered, quoting the others she'd interviewed.

Working on another mouthful, Dorothy just nodded.

"Do you think all the Players were taken with him?"

Dorothy sipped her coffee. "To one degree or another. Unfortunately, for a few it was hook, line and sinker." Her lips tipped up in a nostalgic smile. "My late husband liked that expression, used it all the time. I guess that's because he loved to fish. Isn't it strange the things that stay with you after you lose someone?"

Rory could certainly have empathized if she'd had the time for that. But the half hour was flying by, and soon Dorothy would be off to her quilting class.

"Charlie, that was my husband, he always wanted me to go fishing with him," Dorothy said with a soft chuckle. "But the very first time I did, the boat capsized. It's funny now in the retelling, but it wasn't at all funny back then, because I'm not much of a swimmer. It's like another time when we were up in Montreal. . . ."

Rory was waiting for the right moment to interrupt, but Dorothy was on a roll, barely coming up for air. One story segued into another. She seemed to be enjoying her memories so much that Rory hated to spoil her fun. She promised herself she'd get the conversation back on track at the end of the current story no matter what. But she never had the opportunity. She was reaching for her coffee cup when her hand somehow clipped the glass of orange juice. It toppled over, splashing juice across the table and onto her lap. She quickly slid out of the booth, but the damage was done. The lap of her jeans was soaked through. She excused herself and hurried off to the ladies' room to try to clean up the mess.

As soon as the bathroom door closed behind her, the fluorescent lights blinked and Zeke appeared, arms folded over his chest like a principal about to lecture a delinquent student.

Although words were piling up in her mouth, Rory didn't say anything until she'd checked the two stalls to make sure they were empty. "What the hell do you think you're doing? You can't just pop up in a ladies' room. What if someone else was in here?"

"I checked it out myself," he said, "before I—"

"Before you knocked over the juice," she said, the truth dawning on her. "I didn't think my hand was close enough to have done it. Good job! Look at me—I'm dripping wet!" Her voice was getting louder by the second, and she didn't even try to rein it in.

"What was going on out there?" Zeke asked, clearly trying to contain his own irritation. "How much longer were you goin' to let her ramble on like that? This is an investigation, not a tea party."

"I was just about to stop her when you butted in. Talk about wasting time." She pulled a handful of paper towels out of the dispenser beside the sink and started blotting at her jeans.

"I didn't mean for that to happen," he said, finally sounding a bit contrite. "I was aimin' to knock the little jam container on to you to get your attention, but I used too much power. I didn't exactly have time to practice, you know."

Rory wasn't in any mood for lame excuses. She balled

up the wet towels, threw them into the wastebasket, then pulled down another bunch. The juice had soaked through the jeans into her underwear, making her even more uncomfortable. "We'll talk about this later," she snapped, tossing away the rest of the towels and storming out of the bathroom directly into Dorothy, who was about to walk in.

"Is everything okay in there?" the older woman asked, craning her neck to see over Rory's shoulder as the door swung closed behind her.

Rory held her breath for a second, praying Dorothy hadn't caught a glimpse of the marshal. When the concern on the older woman's face didn't change to shock, Rory knew she'd dodged the bullet. A man in the ladies' room would be hard enough to explain, much less a man straight out of the nineteenth century, complete with badge and gun. Zeke hadn't bothered to change into modern clothing, having assumed he'd be staying out of sight.

"I couldn't help but overhear—it sounded like you were yelling at someone. Is there a man in there?"

"No, no, everything's fine. I was on the phone. I accidentally had it on speaker at one point, that's probably what you heard. A repairman was supposed to come later today to fix my TV, and he called to say he can't be there until tomorrow. I guess I lost my temper."

Dorothy didn't seem completely convinced. "Well, . . . as long as everything's okay," she murmured. "I'll just be a minute. Too much coffee this morning." She limped into the restroom leaning on her cane, her left foot still encased in an orthopedic boot.

When Rory returned to the table, the spill had already been cleaned up. She sat down and finished half of her English muffin while she waited for Dorothy to return. When the actress hobbled back, Rory glanced at her watch. Only ten minutes left.

"To get back to Brian," she said as soon as Dorothy

settled herself. "Did you have the feeling he was going to be trouble from the start?"

"No, and I'm embarrassed to admit that," Dorothy said sheepishly. "I've always considered myself to be a good judge of character. But like everyone else in the troupe, I thought Brian was an all-around great guy in the beginning. He was charming, well-mannered, always quick with a compliment; he'd bring in treats for everyone, roses for all the ladies on Valentine's Day and so forth. But then I started to hear about some of the things he was pulling on the others."

"That's when you stopped baking him cookies?" Rory asked bluntly, hoping to catch an unvarnished reaction.

Dorothy's brows bunched together like little fists. "Who told you about that?" she asked sharply, surprise and irritation seasoning her tone. Rory had never seen this side of the troupe matriarch before, but then she barely knew the woman. When you watched actors perform, it was easy to fall under the assumption that you knew them, knew their character, their weaknesses and strengths, even their moral code. A risky assumption if you were an investigator working on a murder case.

"Forgive me," Dorothy sighed. "That didn't come out at all how I meant it. It's just that I don't like people telling tales or sticking their noses into my business. But we are only talking about cookies here. My daughter tells me I need to lighten up. She's probably right."

"Did Brian ever try to involve you in a scam or anything shady?" Rory asked. The clock was ticking, and she didn't have the time to nudge the conversation back onto the right track in a more subtle fashion.

Dorothy didn't seem to mind. "No, I don't have the kind of money that would have interested him, and he certainly wasn't after my body," she added with a self-deprecating laugh. "Even in my prime, I wasn't the type to catch the eye of a man like him. And I was probably better off for it." She paused for a moment and looked up at the clock hanging on the wall behind the counter. "Oops. I hope you'll excuse me, Rory," she said as she waved her hand, trying to catch the waitress's eye. "If I don't leave now, I'll be late for my class."

"That's okay—you go ahead," Rory told her. "Breakfast is on me." As soon as she heard her own words, she started laughing. "Literally as well as figuratively, you might say."

Dorothy, who was sliding out of the booth, dissolved into laughter too. It was the kind of full, well-used laughter that Rory thought of as jolly. The actress rose to her feet, holding onto the table until she found her balance with the boot and cane. "Thanks for breakfast, and give me a call if you have any more questions," she said, still chuckling as she headed to the door.

# Chapter 19

Clarissa Carpenter had gone with friends to an upstate spa for some R&R after the stress of settling her son's affairs. It was only for a few days, but from Rory's perspective, it was the epitome of bad timing. Of course, Clarissa had no way of knowing that the investigation was about to uncover the big, fifty-thousand-dollar question.

Rory had considered calling her cell, but since the information they needed wasn't going to vanish, and there was nothing Clarissa could accomplish while she was away, there was no point in interrupting her vacation. Instead, Rory left a message on her home phone. With her usual "get it done yesterday" ethic, Clarissa called back within minutes of arriving home and listening to her voice mail.

"I thought I'd heard it all when it came to Brian," she said after Rory laid out the theory of blackmail to explain the sudden infusion of funds in his account. "But even dead and gone, he's still managing to surprise me."

She didn't sound at all surprised to Rory. Her tone was

businesslike, devoid of emotional distress, the words a simple statement of fact. Rory struggled with her response. It seemed like she should offer a comment, something supportive that wasn't trite or sappy. While she was digging around in her etiquette file, Clarissa took charge.

"We have to find out who gave Brian that money."

"As his next of kin, you're the only one who can access his records," Rory said, glad to be moving on.

"But I've already closed out all his accounts."

"No problem. Banks are required to keep records for years after an account is closed. According to the statement we saw, the fifty thousand was deposited in the form of a check. All we need is a copy of that check to tell us who gave him the money and we may just have the name of his killer."

"I'll be at the bank when it opens tomorrow."

Rory's eyes popped open at five a.m. with no intentions of closing again anytime soon. After fifteen minutes of concentrated effort she gave up and accepted the fact that she wasn't going to fall back to sleep. She crawled out of bed in need of a strong cup of coffee. If she had to be awake, she should at least feel awake.

Hobo followed her downstairs and went straight to the back door to be let out. Either he was feeling her restlessness or his bladder was demanding attention. By the time he returned, she was sipping her coffee and trying to decide what to do with this unexpected, and largely unwelcome, bonus chunk of time. Watching an old Clark Gable movie was a heavy favorite, but paying the bills before finance charges were tacked on won in the end. Having fewer options to consider, Hobo curled into a tight circle and promptly fell back asleep.

After emptying her checking account, Rory cleaned the

house and did the laundry. When she looked at her watch, it was 8:45—another fifteen minutes before the bank would even open. She peered out the living-room window. The street was wet, but from what she could see, it didn't appear to still be raining. She'd treat Hobo to a nice long walk. She pulled a Windbreaker over her sweatshirt and jeans, hooked Hobo's leash to his collar and tucked her cell phone into her pocket.

As soon as they stepped outside Rory realized that the view from the window had been deceiving. The air was so laden with moisture that it actually seemed to be raining in slow motion, the droplets of water moseying through the air as if they lacked the energy or ambition to do the job properly. But since rain of any speed was still wet, it was only a matter of time before it worked its mischief. Before they'd reached the end of the third block Rory's hair was plastered to her head and Hobo was a bedraggled mess. Every few steps he looked up at her with eyes that clearly begged for a return to sanity.

Wet and miserable herself, Rory gave in and was heading home when Clarissa finally called. She sounded winded, her words jammed together between quick intakes of air. Rory had to ask her to slow down and repeat what she was saying.

"Brett," she said, enunciating more carefully. "The check was signed by Brett Campbell."

B ack in the house, she toweled herself and Hobo as dry as she could, given that both of them had limited patience with such activities. Then she changed into dry clothing. Her hair was once again on its own, since she hadn't yet replaced the defunct dryer.

On a whim, she went from room to room calling Zeke's name in the hope that one place in the house might be closer to the plane he inhabited than another. No response.

Apparently his dead zone wasn't as quirky as the ones that plagued cell-phone systems. They really had to work out a way for her to contact him, if that was even possible. Since the last room in her grand tour happened to be the study, she sank into the chair behind her desk and tried to decide what to do next.

As much as she wanted to tell someone about the amazing turn of events in the case, with Zeke out of range, there wasn't anyone she *could* tell. Leah didn't know any of the pertinent details about the case or the people involved in it, and during a workday she definitely didn't have the time to be brought up to speed. The rest of Rory's friends were busy with careers of their own or young families or both. Their socializing had been whittled down to postings on Facebook and the occasional phone call. Getting together was a biannual event. The only person in the loop was her aunt Helene, and Rory knew it wasn't a good idea to let on how close she was to solving the case. Her aunt not only loved counting chickens before they hatched, but was also known for helping them incubate. Rory couldn't take the chance that she might say the wrong thing to the wrong person. On the other hand, she needed to speak to Helene to gather some background information on Brett before interviewing him. Since he was now the star suspect, she wanted to be as prepared as possible. That would have to satisfy her for now.

"He's a sweet boy," Helene said when Rory called and asked about Brett. "And easy on the eyes."

Rory laughed. "Aunt Helene, don't tell me you're turning into a cougar."

"Wouldn't that be fun? If only I weren't all bark and no bite," she added with a sigh. "Seriously, though, I think Brett's a gifted actor. He has great presence on the stage. But offstage, he's kind of shy."

"Did he have any issues with Brian?" Rory asked, grabbing a pen and legal pad from the top of the desk.

"None that I'm aware of." Helene paused for a moment as if the hard drive in her head had spit out another byte for her to consider. "But now that I think about it, he did seem to be steering clear of Brian lately. I don't know if that was based on intuition or because bad blood had developed between them. Brett is certainly from the opposite end of the personality spectrum."

"Do you know what Brett does for a living?"

"Here's the thing," Helene said. "In the spirit of full disclosure, you should be aware that most of what I know about Brett I got from Jessica. He's probably closer to her than to anyone else in the troupe. Now, it may all be 100 percent accurate, but I can't actually vouch for any of it."

"Duly noted," Rory said. She didn't like getting information through a second party, let alone a third, but she wasn't in any position to be picky. If need be, she could always try to corroborate the facts later. In a surprising about-face, she caught herself wishing Zeke would hurry up with his recharging so she could get his take on things.

"Brett works for a nonprofit animal shelter," Helene went on. "But he mostly lives off a big, juicy trust fund. His folks are loaded. The father owns a company somewhere on the Island. I forget what kind. Anyway, one of the conditions of the trust is that Brett be gainfully employed. At first, his father wanted Brett to work for him. The two of them fought about it for a couple of years. In the end, the old man sucked it up and agreed his son could work wherever he chose to as long as the work was legitimate and he lived responsibly. If not he could kiss the trust fund good-bye. Jessica thinks he was worried Brett would turn into one of those jet-setting good-for-nothings who are always popping up in the news. According to her, if the man had worked less and spent more time getting to know his son, he would have realized Brett was the least likely candidate for that kind of lifestyle."

"Wow." Rory laughed. "Here I was hoping for some crumbs and you handed me nearly the whole cake."

"Crumb cake—mmm," Helene murmured. "I can't remember the last time I had it. You know, if I leave right away, I'll have time to swing by the bakery and pick some up before my Zumba class."

After they said "good-bye," Rory spent a few minutes digesting everything she'd heard. She already knew the blackmail had been paid by Brett, and now she understood how he'd come by so much cash. What was still missing from the puzzle, however, was the nature of the secret he was trying to keep hidden.

# Chapter 20

With no way to reach Zeke, Rory decided to proceed on her own. They could discuss that decision, or more likely argue about it, when he was back in the neighborhood. Brett Campbell proved to be more accessible. When he answered the phone that evening, Rory could barely hear him above the riotous barking in the background. He excused himself and tried to quiet the dogs with only marginal success. Trying to make herself heard above the commotion, Rory felt like she was at a wedding reception where the music was amped way up. She had to shout to be heard, and even in the most amicable of settings, shouting had a tendency to come across as aggressive. Fortunately, Brett didn't take it that way. When he heard her name, he didn't sound the least bit guarded or apprehensive. In fact, she would have described him as surprisingly calm in spite of the hullabaloo raging around him.

"Oh, Rory, hi," he said. "Sorry about the noise. I brought

a couple of new dogs home with me and there's some jockeying for position going on in my little pack here."

To Rory, it sounded more like a major uprising. She would have been calling for reinforcements, dart guns and armor, but Brett seemed to be taking it all in stride. That explained a lot. For a man who refereed canine brawls and dealt with blackmail, it was clearly no big deal to talk to a PI about a case the police had officially closed. That suited Rory just fine. If he believed he had nothing to fear from her, she stood a better chance of surprising him with what she already knew and catching his unguarded reaction.

Brett agreed to see her the next night. Rory wasn't sure if she was hoping Zeke returned in time or not. Although stress often seemed to hitch a ride with him, having an extra pair of ears for this interview could be helpful. Especially now that Brett had snagged the lead in the escalating drama of Brian's demise.

Rory tucked a copy of Brett's fifty-thousand-dollar check to Brian in her handbag, along with her loaded .45. Her aunt had characterized the actor as shy, but when murder was the topic of conversation it didn't pay to take chances. How many times had she heard a killer described by friends and family as "such a nice, quiet guy"?

As she approached Brett's stately fieldstone-and-clapboard colonial at the eastern edge of Huntington, she could hear a chorus of canine vocals like the ones she'd been treated to over the phone. This time they were coming from the fenced-in backyard. At least she wouldn't have to deal with them. But when Brett opened the door, there were two more dogs flanking him, both of indeterminate lineage, no doubt the result of many generations of carefree crossbreeding. One appeared to be a border collie mix; the other looked a lot like a golden retriever. Neither of them was a breed associated with ferocity or aggression. Of course, she had no way of knowing what Brett had trained them to be.

The dogs looked at her, then back at their master, as if trying to assess her status. When Brett smiled and held the door open for her, their plumed tails echoed his welcome. Rory held out her hand for them to sniff before she gave them each a good scratch around the ears. The golden groaned with delight. Okay, maybe there wasn't any cause for concern.

"How many dogs *do* you have?" she asked, realizing belatedly that the question might have come across as rude.

"Cagney and Lacey here are the only ones that are officially mine. I got them as pups. The three you hear making such a racket out in the yard I'm just fostering until they're adopted. When dogs have lived in a shelter, they need to be reminded of proper social etiquette from time to time. Sort of like continuing-ed courses for doctors and lawyers. That way when they're adopted—the dogs, not the doctors and lawyers—they transition into their new families more easily."

Rory laughed, then scolded herself. She was there to draw out a possible killer, not to be charmed by him. Too bad, her shameless alter ego sighed. Not only was he movie-idol cute, with thick dark lashes and a sensuous mouth, but he also seemed to have a sense of humor. What a pity he was probably a murderer. Falling for one was unfortunate. Falling for a second would be a wake-up call for therapy. Wouldn't the marshal have a field day with that?

"Come on inside," Brett said, leading the way into what the architect had probably intended to be a formal living room. The available seating consisted of two brown couches that looked like they'd been snatched from the maw of a garbage truck and partially reupholstered with fur. They faced each other across a low table embellished with a crosshatch of scratch marks. Three empty dog crates were lined up along one wall, each with a thick pad and chew toy inside. Clearly none of the trust fund had been used on interior decorating.

Brett didn't try to apologize for the décor; for which Rory was grateful. If he had, she would have been in the awkward position of politely assuring him it was lovely. He gestured to one of the couches. Once she was seated, he took the couch across from her. Cagney and Lacey hopped up on either side of him.

"So I hear Clarissa thinks one of us killed her son," Brett said amiably.

"That's right, but it sounds like you're not at all worried there may be a murderer in the troupe."

"Well, I imagine I would be if I thought it was an actual possibility."

"And you don't?"

"In a flash flood like that? Not a chance."

"Even if someone wanted him dead and saw the flood as the perfect opportunity?"

At least Brett had the good sense to frown and appear to give the possibility some thought before responding. "No, no way. If you'd been there, you'd understand. It happened so fast, it was all we could do to save our own lives. There was no time to *think* about killing someone, much less to carry it out."

Well played, Rory thought. Not too much angst, not too little. If this were a play she was watching, she would have applauded. She wondered if he'd practiced in front of a mirror or if it was all raw talent.

"Then you subscribe to the theory that it was just a tragic accident?"

"An accident, yes. But I'd hardly call it 'tragic,' " Brett said, a curl of disgust snarling his upper lip.

"Was there bad blood between the two of you?" Rory

asked, feigning shock to see how much more he might reveal.

"There didn't have to be; I saw how he treated Jessica and Sophia. And from the bits and pieces of conversation I've overheard, it wasn't hard to figure out that he'd scammed Richard as well as some of the other Players. You don't have to be sprayed by a skunk to know he's not someone you want to hang out with."

Rory had to admit that Brett was making a believable pitch for his innocence. Of course, he wasn't aware of the devastating evidence Rory had in her handbag. And she wasn't quite ready to pull it out yet.

"Let's say the situation in the canyon hadn't been quite so critical and there'd been enough time for Brian to be murdered," she proposed. "Who would have your vote as the killer?"

Brett issued a low whistle. "That's quite a question."

Rory shrugged. "I'm on the outside; you're on the inside. I'd just like to get your perspective. No big deal. I'm not asking you to sign an affidavit."

Brett sat up straighter, his body and face more rigid. Cagney and Lacey seemed to feel the shift in his attitude. Their ears pricked forward, and they stared at Rory as if to put her on notice. "There's no way I'm going to point a finger at any of my colleagues," Brett said tightly. "Not even in the guise of an intellectual game."

Rory was impressed. If he was guilty, he'd just walked away from an opportunity to lay the blame elsewhere. Murderers weren't generally that altruistic. At least now she knew how far she could push him before he pushed back. Or set the dogs on her. Maybe it was time for a little fence-mending.

"Fair enough," she said. "I guess I'd feel the same way if I were in your shoes."

Brett relaxed and sat back against the cushions. The dogs relaxed as well.

"The funny thing is that I'd initially shut the door on the murder theory myself and mostly for the reasons you cited. But after listening to Clarissa . . . well, she did manage to pry that door open a bit. According to her, Brian had more enemies than friends—real enemies who would have loved to see him dead."

"That doesn't surprise me," Brett said. "But wanting Brian dead isn't exactly in the same ballpark as killing him."

"And yet it can be. Sometimes the distance between the 'wanting' and the 'doing' is only one quick step."

He shrugged as if that statistic held no interest for him. "I guess you'd know more about that in your line of work."

"Which is why I have to investigate every red flag that pops up."

"Sure, I get it."

"I'm glad you understand," she said opening her handbag and withdrawing the copy of the check. She left the bag partially open on her lap, the .45 inches from her hand should she need it.

"Are you saying you found a red flag by my name?" Brett asked, concern finally apparent on his face.

"I just have some questions, if you don't mind."

"What kind of questions?"

The kind that require answers, she thought. It was amazing how often she heard that line. "For example, did Brian ever work for you?"

"Work for me?" Brett asked, clearly puzzled by the question, which was Rory's intention. "No, why?"

"Did you ever lend him money?"

"No."

"Or invest in one of his scams?"

"No." The actor's irritation was beginning to show. "What are you getting at?"

"Well, if he didn't work for you, borrow money from you or scam you, then I have to assume the fifty-thousand-dollar check you wrote him was a blackmail payment. And since he wasn't killed until after that payment, I also have to assume that he'd approached you for more, and you decided to put a stop to further demands."

"Wait, wait just a minute there," Brett said, he and the dogs once more on full alert. "What the hell are you talking about?"

Damn, he was good. He knew the jig was up, but he was playing indignant and innocent so well that he almost convinced her she didn't know what she knew. It was time. She unfolded the photocopied check and held it out to him.

Brett didn't reach for it, but from the distress that flashed across his features, it was clear he recognized it immediately. In the tense silence that followed, Rory hoped he wouldn't set the dogs on her. She really, really didn't want to have to shoot a dog.

"I don't expect you to understand," Brett said, standing abruptly as if his agitation was demanding some form of action. Rory and the dogs remained on their respective couches, watching and waiting as he started to pace around the couch where he'd been sitting.

Rory figured he was considering his options or building up the courage to confess. She was pulling for the confession. That was when the dogs started growling. Before she had a chance to worry about their intentions, she felt a tap on her shoulder. Zeke was back in town. For a split second, the marshal actually blinked into view, parts of him anyway. His face was hanging in the air wearing a jaunty expression, and floating in the air beneath it were several assorted limbs. In spite of the songwriter's claim, this was one instance when the thigh bone was definitely not connected to the hip bone, or any other bone for that matter.

Brett rounded the couch on his second lap in time to see the pieces of Zeke vanish. He stopped short, his face draining of color as if he'd seen a ghost. He rubbed his eyes with his fists, and when he opened them again, he was clearly glad to find only Rory and the dogs in the room. Cagney and Lacey, with their superior senses, didn't share his relief. Whimpering in confusion, they jumped off the couch and ran out of the room, tails tucked securely between their legs. Brett was still so focused on whether or not he'd had a hallucination that he didn't try to call them back.

"I didn't just . . . I mean, did you . . . no, no, forget it, never mind," he sputtered, trying to mold impossible thoughts into rational sentences.

Rory knew exactly what he was asking, but she didn't plan on clarifying anything. In fact, she was hoping the marshal's little faux pas might have rattled Brett enough to convince him that confession would be good for his soul.

"Is something wrong?" she asked innocently.

Brett dropped down on the couch again, his earlier agitation having clearly been run out of town by more pressing concerns about his sanity. "I don't think I've been getting enough sleep lately," he mumbled. "Where were we again?"

"You were about to explain why Brian was blackmailing you," Rory said. Hey, it was worth a shot.

"Any chance I could expect you to keep something in confidence?"

"As long as it has no legal significance." Like a motive for murder.

"It doesn't," he said finally, "but you're going to think it does. Unfortunately, you don't know me well enough to believe me when I say I didn't kill Brian. I didn't kill him even though I'm one of the people who wished him dead."

Rory weighed her next move. She didn't want to scare him off when he seemed so close to a confession of some sort. "How's this—I won't go to the authorities with what you tell me unless and until I have concrete evidence that you killed Brian. If you're innocent, that should satisfy you."

"Seriously?" He gave a bitter little laugh. "How do you

think that would play with all the innocent people sitting in jail right now? And why should I believe you if you're not prepared to believe me?"

"For starters, I'm not under suspicion for a crime of any kind. You, on the other hand, were with the victim when he drowned. That automatically makes you a suspect."

"In a case that's already closed."

"There are no statutes of limitation when it comes to murder," Rory reminded him. "Look at it this way; whether or not you tell me the whole story, I can still take this evidence to the police and let them decide if they should reopen—"

Zeke thumped her so hard on the shoulder that she almost flew off the couch. Grabbing the edge of the seat cushion, she caught herself before she wound up draped over the table. Brett was looking at her as if he thought this might be another hallucination.

"Back spasm," Rory said, adding a groan for authenticity. She reached around to massage her back. When it came to acting, she needed all the props and affectations she could come up with.

"Are you okay?" Brett asked, doubt written large on his face.

"I will be." She went on massaging and wincing at the nonexistent pain a bit longer. For the first time since the marshal had come into her life, she found herself wishing he could read her mind. What she was thinking at that moment might make even a frontiersman like him blush.

"The hell with it," Brett said. "I can't stand all these head games. I'm probably making the worst mistake of my life, but I'm going to trust you."

Rory tried not to show him how surprised she was. "My business depends on my reputation for being trustworthy and discreet," she said, as if she felt obliged to reassure him that he'd made the right decision. "And I have no intentions of putting that at risk."

Brett wiped his palms on the thighs of his jeans. "Brian found out I'm gay," he blurted, as if he were ripping a Band-Aid off a deep wound. "Then he nosed around some more and found out I come from money and have a father who still lives in the Dark Ages."

Rory didn't know what to say. But she knew better than to go with a thoughtless platitude or any other inane attempt to make him feel better. At the very least, Brett deserved the dignity of her silence.

"It's not even that I'd mind giving up the trust fund," he went on. "I don't need a lot of 'stuff' to make me happy. I would never have bought this huge house if it had been up to me. But my father insisted I have a place commensurate with *his* standing in the community." There was no way to miss the anger and sarcasm that seeped into his words when he spoke about his father. "The only reason the money matters at all to me is what it can do for the shelter animals."

Rory believed him. She believed him on a gut level. All you had to do was look at the inside of this house to know he was telling the truth about the money. All you had to do was look at how much time and energy, how much of himself he spent on the animals. But, unfortunately, none of it proved he was innocent in Brian's death. If anything, it was a bright, neon arrow pointing to one hell of a dandy motive.

# Chapter 21

"I was just tryin' to keep you from becomin' the next corpse," Zeke said, finally breaking the tense silence that had been building between them as they drove home from Brett's interview. Until that moment, Rory had been wondering why he was wasting the energy to sit there when he could have simply popped back to the house on his own.

"By launching me off the couch?" she asked. "In case you've forgotten, we mere mortals can't fly."

"It got away from me."

"Again."

"I couldn't just tap you on the shoulder like I do when I first arrive. It had to be different, stronger. And I had to get your attention fast, because the way you were baitin' Brett, you were pretty much askin' to be killed."

"And yet here I am."

"That's because I interrupted and defused the situation," Zeke said, patently pleased with himself.

Rory decided she was too tired to go a full fifteen rounds

with him. "So, you think Brett's the killer?" she asked in an effort to reboot the conversation.

Thankfully, Zeke was amenable. "Can't say for sure. Blackmail's the strongest motive we've come across so far in this case, but unless he's willin' to confess that he killed Brian, we can't prove it. We don't have a shred of genuine evidence. Just because Brett was the victim of blackmail doesn't automatically prove he's guilty of murder."

"I know," Rory said. "It's probably going to take a confession to close the case. And since the killer isn't likely to break down and confess just to make my life easier, I'm going to have to push him or her into it. So you'd better learn to show some restraint or you won't be welcome to tag along anymore." It was an empty threat that she had no way to enforce, so she was surprised when the marshal bid her good night and vanished without any attempt to plea bargain.

R ory was sitting on a small, upholstered bench in the department-store dressing room, critiquing a succession of cocktail dresses as Leah tried them on. Leah's sweater, jeans and sneakers were piled in one corner with her handbag, and there were dresses hanging from every hook in the tiny room. Rory was in charge of rehanging the ones they'd already eliminated and keeping them separate from those that were still in the running.

"This is what comes of procrastination," Rory pointed out as her friend executed a weary pirouette for her appraisal.

"No, this is what comes of not sticking to my diet," Leah replied glumly. "I was counting on wearing my navy blue dress with the bolero jacket, but when I tried it on last night I looked like a navy blue sausage in it."

"Don't despair," Rory relented in sympathy. "I'm sure there's a dress somewhere in this mall that's meant for you. But that little number you've got on is definitely not it."

"I really appreciate your coming to my rescue on a moment's notice," Leah said, shimmying out of the dress. "I hate clothes shopping alone." She handed the dress to Rory who was ready with the hanger.

"Hey, that's what friends do. Besides, you're always there for me."

Leah paused as she was about to pull a black, silk sheath over her head. "That reminds me—it looks like Brian Carpenter managed to stay below police radar after that one mail-fraud conviction. I couldn't come up with anything else on him."

"Impressive, considering the way he earned his living."

"Unfortunately, not all geniuses are saints," Leah said. "For every genius who spends his life trying to cure disease, there's another one busy inventing a new doomsday weapon." She popped her arms through the sleeves and wriggled into the dress. "Any early favorites among your suspects?"

"Conventional wisdom points to the blackmail victim as the killer, but I'm not convinced. There are also jilted lovers, an irate father, and the victim of a financial scam. And we haven't finished talking to everyone who was there."

"How about if I run their names and see if they have any priors? Someone with a general predilection for crime. That might help you narrow the field a bit."

"Sure, if you're twisting my arm—wait, that's it!"

"You're kidding—you just figured out who killed Brian?"

"No, but I think we just found your dress. Come here; let me zip that up."


It was already dark when Rory and Leah left the store and parted to go to their respective cars. As she drove home, Rory's thoughts wound back to her case and its suspects. What was it that made a person capable of killing another if the perfect opportunity came along? She knew a lot of people who'd voiced the desire to kill someone out of momentary frustration or anger. Yet she couldn't imagine any of them taking the leap from the thought to the action regardless of how golden the opportunity. Preoccupied with these thoughts, she didn't immediately notice that the car that had followed her out of the mall parking lot was still behind her when she turned off Jericho Turnpike onto the winding, single-lane road she always took home. With its minimal lighting, headlights in the rearview mirror loomed large, especially when those headlights were so close they were blinding. Their height suggested an SUV, but in the dark that was all Rory could tell. The other driver was either aggressive or drunk or quite possibly both. She would have loved to pull him over and write him up, but since she no longer carried a police shield, she didn't have that option. Instead she hit her flashers and edged over to the dirt shoulder to let him pass. But the SUV followed her onto the shoulder and came to a stop behind her. Okay, he wasn't just aggressive or drunk; he'd targeted her.

Whether he was after any young woman who appeared vulnerable or after her specifically didn't matter. He wasn't Ed McMahon, and he wasn't there to award her a million dollars whether she bought a magazine subscription or not. She opened her handbag and groped around in it until her fingers closed on the Walther PPK. She pulled it out and set it atop the bag as she ran through her options. There was no time to call for help unless Superman happened to be in the neighborhood. The viable alternatives were few. She could stop the car, and if the other driver got out of his vehicle to approach her, she could hit the gas and have maybe a thirty-second head start to try to lose him. Of course, if he wanted to shoot her, she'd be a much easier target while she was standing still. Or she could simply try to "get out of Dodge" without further ado. Her jaw clenched with equal parts tension and determination, she made her decision and gunned the engine, spinning her wheels and kicking up loose gravel and dirt as the tires sought traction. After what seemed like forever, the car rocketed forward onto the roadway, the rear end slewing to the left. She wrangled it under control without letting up on the accelerator. The SUV was on her again in seconds. Okay, maybe waiting until the driver had left his vehicle would have been the smarter move. But that was water under a good half-dozen bridges by now.

She raced ahead, taking the curves as fast as she dared. The car's lower center of gravity provided an advantage over the SUV, which could flip if it tried to match her speed on the turns. She was pinning a lot of hope on that possibility. After she'd navigated a particularly wicked curve she checked the rearview mirror. The SUV was no longer in sight. Without slowing, she strained to hear the sounds of a vehicle tumbling out of control, but apart from the distant buzz of traffic on the main roads, the night was troublingly quiet. She was beginning to think the other driver had given up when the SUV erupted from the side street she was passing. To Rory it looked like the driver took the turn on two wheels. Who the hell was he? A stuntman?

Her luck seemed to be running out. They'd reached the section of the road where there were fewer and more shallow curves. Her advantage was gone. The other driver realized it too. He pulled the SUV into the oncoming lane and came up beside her. At such close range, Rory could see that the vehicle was a deep green, but she couldn't stare at it long enough to make out more than a vague silhouette behind the wheel. She put her hand on the Walther, making sure it was still in easy reach. The feel of the cold steel under her fingers brought a strange comfort. Shooting blind wasn't a great option, but she'd use it if she had no other choice, and that moment was fast approaching.

The SUV started crowding her. She didn't have much

room to play with; the trees were too close to the edge of the road here. Any one of them could take her out at the speed she was going. They were rounding a long bend when there were suddenly headlights coming at them and the screaming of a horn when that driver realized the SUV was in its lane. Anticipating the SUV's next move, Rory slammed on her brakes. The SUV flew past her, barely missing her front fender as it swerved back into the right lane, avoiding a head-on collision by seconds.

Rory figured she had two options now. Hang a quick U-turn and try to eat up as much ground as possible before the SUV turned around, or find a place to hide. The houses in the area were set far back from the road, many on higher ground, their driveways hard to make out in the dark. Up until now the SUV had been too close for her to escape into any of them unseen.

She was about to go with the U-turn when she saw a break in the tree line a few yards ahead. She swung her car into it, hoping for the best. At that moment, the best would be a private road she could follow until she was out of sight. The worst would be a patch of dirt that went nowhere.

It proved to be the latter, an area of open ground maybe twenty yards wide and not much deeper, where the vegetation had been cleared by either disease or fire. She bumped along the rutted earth until the trees barred farther travel. It was time to stop running and take a stand. Dousing the headlights, she jumped out of the car and took up a position behind it. At least now she was the one setting the parameters of their encounter. She was the one lying in wait with a gun.

After half an hour had passed, Rory decided her assailant wasn't coming back. Maybe his close brush with death had reordered his priorities. She rose slowly from the place

where she'd been hunkered down behind the car, her legs
cramped and aching, her gun arm shaking from the strain
of holding the Walther in position for so long. Every time
she'd heard a car approach she'd tensed, readying herself
for the showdown. And every time the car drove by she'd
exhaled, not even aware she'd been holding her breath. She'd
debated calling 911, but decided she'd rather take care of
the problem on her own. Even if the police could find the
driver of the SUV, what would they charge him with—
"leaving the scene of what might have been an accident"?
Beyond that it was just a case of "he said, she said." Although
Leah could certainly be counted on to vouch for her, there
was no proof the incident had ever happened. There weren't
even the tiniest of scratches or dents on her car to corroborate her story. And she was beginning to think the driver
never intended to leave any evidence or do her any actual
harm. Whoever it was, he wasn't high on anything. His
actions had been too precise, in their own way too careful.
He'd had to be stone sober to try to run her off the road in
the dark without once grazing her car though there were
only inches between them. It occurred to her that it could
have been one of the suspects trying to scare her off, possibly the same person who'd broken into her house and given
Hobo the toy with the note. Or maybe it was all a bizarre
game that had nothing to do with the case, like a dare or a
hazing. She might never know for sure, and, at least for now,
she didn't care. She just wanted to get home.

The adrenaline that had coursed through her during the
chase had ebbed away, leaving her body as wobbly as Jell-O.
She climbed into the driver's seat and sat there without moving for a few minutes before she found the energy to turn
the key in the ignition. She drove home slowly, her heart
jumping every time she saw headlights behind her.

Hobo met her in the entryway. Although he was as happy
as ever to see her, he seemed to sense that all was not right.

He didn't try to jump up and plant his big paws on her shoulders. He just sidled up against her in the way a cat would and licked her hand with his rough tongue. Rory appreciated the low-key welcome. She knelt down and hugged him, burying her face in the dense fur at his neck and allowing herself a sigh of relief for the first time since the chase ended.

"My sweet, goofy Hobo, you were nearly orphaned again tonight," she told him, expecting the words to come out as silly hyperbole. Instead they brought an unexpected rush of tears to her eyes. Before she could blink them away, the light above her flashed, and Zeke appeared in the doorway to the living room; fate could sure be sadistic.

"Sounds like you must have had yourself quite a scare," he said, having apparently been eavesdropping before he materialized.

"It was probably more of an overreaction on my part," Rory replied, struggling to make her tone light while the tears spilled over her lower lids, sabotaging her efforts.

"I doubt that. If anything, I've always known you to *under*estimate the danger of your predicaments. So why don't you tell me what happened, and let me be the judge?"

"Yeah right—because you're so impartial." At any other time, her words would have contained a good dash of sarcasm, but tonight her voice hitched on a sob that was still hiding in her throat.

"I never claimed to be."

"Look, I'm telling you—my imagination just got the better of me."

"In what regard? Are we talkin' flyin' elephants or an attempt on your life?"

"Someone followed me out of the parking lot," she said, since he clearly wasn't going to drop the subject. Maybe she could get away with a brief overview of what happened, then plead fatigue and go up to bed. "It seemed like they wanted to run me off the road. You know, throw a scare into me." She tried for a casual shrug, but it came off forced and stiff. "It might have been some stupid kids working on a dare."

He shook his head. "I don't like it."

"I wasn't much of a fan myself. But it's over and I'm fine, so after I let Hobo out, I'm going to sleep if you don't mind."

"Would it help if I did?"

"Not in the least." She headed off to the kitchen with Hobo at her side and was surprised that Zeke wasn't there waiting for her with a dozen follow-up questions. When Hobo returned from taking care of his necessities, she locked up the house and set the alarm for the night. It was barely nine o'clock, but all she wanted to do was crawl into bed and sleep for a couple of weeks while her subconscious worked through whatever issues it had racked up during her adventure.

Hobo, who'd no doubt slept during her absence, had nothing against some additional shut-eye, especially when it involved a fluffy quilt and a human pillow. He bolted past her to the top of the stairs and led the way into the bedroom. While she shed her clothes and pulled on a nightgown, Hobo made himself comfortable on the bed. By the time Rory crawled in beside him, he was snoring and wheezing like a one-dog band during happy hour.

Rory closed her eyes, but sleep refused to come. She was still too wired. She considered going downstairs to watch some mindless TV or maybe drink some warm milk, her mother's old standby. She was trying to decide which course to take when sleep drew around her, safe and warm and quieting as if she were being cradled in someone's arms. She drifted off, weightless as a feather borne upon a breeze. From the edge of sweet oblivion she heard Hobo leap off the bed with a panicked shriek that trailed off to a whimper as he scrambled out of the room. She knew that sound . . . had heard him yelp like that before. . . . Already swaddled in sleep, she groped for the memory without success. On some deep level, she knew all was well.

# Chapter 22

When Rory awoke the next morning, she felt not only rested, but refreshed. Even the car chase of the previous night seemed less harrowing in the sunlight of the new day. She didn't immediately get out of bed. There was no place she had to be, and Hobo wasn't doing his little "Hurry—let me outside" jig. For that matter, he wasn't even in the room. Strange. He always slept in bed with her, usually hogging the covers. Then it came back to her. Just as she'd finally been falling off to sleep last night, he'd leapt off the bed screaming like he'd crossed some invisible border into *The Twilight Zone*. She was sure she'd heard that sound before, but when? The answer popped into her head as if it had been waiting for her to come looking for it. Months ago, back in the fall, when Hobo had still been terrified of Zeke, she and the marshal had been in the study working on a dognapping case when he'd come looking for her. He'd skidded on the hardwood floor and collided with the marshal. Although Hobo hadn't been injured in any way, he'd made that same horrific sound. But that couldn't have been what happened last night, because they'd been in her room, which was out of bounds for the marshal. Either something else had scared the dog, or Zeke had broken the rules again. The more she thought about it, the more convinced she was that Zeke had been there. That's what came of letting him off the hook too easily for past infractions. Of course, until last night she'd never actually been in the bedroom when he'd come snooping. So why wasn't she angrier about this more aggressive breech of conduct on his part? Maybe her brush with death last night had changed her perspective and made other issues seem trivial by comparison. Even so, Zeke had to be told he couldn't just ignore their agreement whenever it suited him. But first things first—she had to make sure Hobo was okay. She pulled on her bathrobe and hurried out of the room, where she promptly tripped over him sleeping in the hall.

R ory was still in her nightgown and robe, drinking her coffee, when the doorbell rang.

Out back Hobo had also heard the bell. He interrupted his morning rounds and raced to the fence at the side of the house to issue a fierce warning to any visitor with malice in mind.

Rory set her coffee mug on the table and went to see who could be on her doorstep at barely eight o'clock. After a quick glance through the peephole, she turned off the alarm and opened the door. Eloise was standing on the porch. Her white hair had been wrestled into something of a style, parted on one side and brushed smooth around her face. But there were already a few cowlicks poking up on the crown of her head, hinting that a general mutiny was under way. Her clothing was even color coordinated, but her face was set in a grim mask. Behind her was a stocky woman in her forties who looked like she could hurl a discus with the best of them and was, from all appearances, thoroughly uncomfortable to be there.

"Eloise, hi," Rory said cheerfully, wondering what message her neighbor was there to deliver that required such a dour expression.

Eloise didn't bother with a greeting or to introduce her companion. "I have to speak to the marshal," she said bluntly as if she were referring to an average mortal with whom she had business to discuss.

"I'm afraid he's not available right now," Rory said, holding out little hope that Eloise would be discreet with regard to Zeke's odd circumstances. When she was on a mission, she'd proven herself to be single-mindedly obtuse.

Before Eloise could say anything else, her companion stepped forward. "I am Olga Kolchek," she said with a thick Baltic accent. "I work as aide for Ms. Eloise. I'm sorry we bother you so early, but Ms. Eloise is very determined lady, and is difficult to change her mind once she is made up."

"I understand completely," Rory said after introducing herself. "It's nice to meet you."

The aide managed a smile. "So good of you, I try—"

"I needed to speak to him last night," Eloise interrupted, clearly believing her agenda took priority over basic courtesy. "But no one answered the phone when I called, and my son wouldn't let me come over here. He can be such a trial. And now they've hired this prison guard to keep tabs on me. You'd think I was a serial killer or something."

Rory thought she heard a little quaver of hurt in her voice. She didn't envy Eloise her circumstances. Struggling with the effects of a stroke would have been hard enough, but she was also dealing with a new psychic ability the stroke seemed to have kick-started. Not an easy combination at any age.

Olga was shaking her head in apology. "Most times she is being really very nice."

"I know," Rory said. She turned back to Eloise. "Why don't I take a message for the marshal?"

"No, that won't do at all. I have to talk to him." She squeezed past Rory to enter the house. Great, now what? Rory couldn't exactly grab her and push her back out the door.

"This . . . this is not possible, Ms. Eloise," Olga stammered, completely flustered. "You cannot . . . we cannot. . . ." Having apparently run out of English words with which to address the situation, Olga lapsed into her native tongue. Rory couldn't understand a word of it, but she was pretty sure it included a plea for help from a higher authority. She added her own to it, along with a sidebar to Mac in case he happened to be listening.

"I'll just sit down and wait," Eloise said, in a tone that brooked no discussion. She walked into the living room and made herself at home in the easy chair Zeke generally claimed.

Rory ushered Olga into the house, since there was no way of knowing how long her charge's sit-in might last. If it went on for too long, Rory would have to call in the Bowman cavalry to end it. She could do that right now of course, but it made more sense to try to accommodate Eloise, or the woman would be back on her doorstep as soon as she could swing it.

"Sorry, too sorry I am," the aide kept repeating as Rory showed her into the living room and offered her a seat on the couch. Then Rory excused herself and fled up the stairs.

The most pressing concern she faced was how to contact Zeke, followed immediately by how much flack she could expect to take if she did reach him. He'd been adamant about keeping Eloise out of their—wait a minute, Rory reminded herself, he was in no position to cast stones, having so recently violated one of the most basic rules of their living arrangement.

Rory stood in the middle of the study wondering how

she was going to contact him. She tried flickering the lights to see if he would respond to the same cue he gave her. Nothing. When no other method occurred to her, she called out his name as loudly as she dared with company downstairs. Again nothing. She was on the verge of abandoning her efforts when the marshal materialized in front of her.

"What's all the squawkin' about?" he grumbled. He looked more disheveled than usual, his hair in need of a comb and his cheeks in need of a well-honed razor. If Rory didn't know better she'd think he'd been roused from a conventional nap in a conventional bed.

Choosing her words carefully, she explained the current situation to him.

"It'll be my pleasure to throw that old biddy out of the house," he said, locking eyes with Rory as if to say he was damn sure she was somehow responsible for Eloise's visit. "What does she want?"

"I wish I knew, but she wouldn't let me take a message. She said she has to speak to you. Are you feeling strong enough to spend a few minutes with her in full 3-D?"

"I expect so. But she already knows I'm more than a few body parts shy of mortal, so it shouldn't be a problem if I can't hold it together."

Time to tell him about the Olga factor.

Zeke managed to look even more put-upon. "Then it'll be your job to draw her attention away if I start fallin' apart."

That seemed to be as good a plan as any, so Rory signed on, and the two of them marched back down the stairs together.

As soon as they walked into the living room, Rory realized they hadn't given this meeting enough thought. For starters, Zeke had forgotten to change out of his Wild West duds and into something a bit more updated. And then there was the issue of shaking hands. How would he avoid it when she introduced him to Olga? Rory was relieved to see that he'd already worked out that detail. He'd stopped far enough away from the two women that a handshake was not de rigueur.

"Nice to meet you, ma'am," he said to Olga in a particularly gracious manner. His scruffy appearance aside, Rory could imagine him in a dress coat, doffing his top hat and bowing with a gentlemanly flourish.

Olga beamed at him, her distress over Eloise's behavior apparently forgotten for the moment. If she noticed that Zeke's outfit looked like it had been stolen from the costume department of a film studio, she didn't mention it.

Eloise rose from the chair, her expression unchanged, and held onto the arms until she found her balance. "I'd like to speak to Ezekiel in private."

"Olga, why don't you come join me in the kitchen?" Rory offered. "There's fresh coffee if you'd like."

The aide seemed reluctant to trade Zeke for coffee, but she followed Rory into the kitchen anyway. Rory poured her a cup, to which Olga added two heaping teaspoons of sugar and as much milk as the cup could accommodate. They sat at the table, and Rory politely plied her with questions about her life in Eastern Europe, while she tried unsuccessfully to catch some of the conversation between Zeke and Eloise. Olga's answers were short and a bit disjointed, as if she too were focused on the other room.

The meeting between the psychic and the ghost lasted less than ten minutes. "I'm going," Eloise called out, her voice bright and airy, the carefree voice of a child.

"I'm coming, I'm coming." Olga pushed back from the table with such enthusiasm that the coffee sloshed over the sides of her cup. She was either eager to resume her duties or to spend more time in the marshal's company. Walking back into the living room, Rory had the answer. The aide's face literally lit up when she saw the marshal was still there. It looked like Zeke had found himself a fan. For a moment, Rory considered him from this new perspective and realized with some surprise how attractive he was. He'd probably been no more than forty when he died, and if you put aside the Old West trappings, some might say he was handsome in a rough and weathered sort of way.

"Thank you kindly, Miss Eloise," Zeke said with a dip of his head.

Rory was instantly on alert. This wasn't the same Ezekiel Drummond she'd spoken to in the study such a short time ago. How had Eloise managed to cure his black mood so quickly? And was there a way to bottle the cure?

"I'm going home for some ice cream now," Eloise informed them all as she headed for the door.

"No, no, is too much early for ice cream," Olga said. She turned to Zeke with the mooning smile of a teen gazing at a rock star. "Has been pleasure to meeting you."

Zeke did his little head dip for her, causing Olga's cheeks to turn scarlet. He waited in the living room while Rory followed the two guests to the door. They were saying their good-byes when Olga gasped, her eyes nearly popping out of their sockets. Before Rory even turned around she had a pretty good idea what had happened.

The marshal was losing cohesion; his left arm was already missing. Terrific. She practically dove in front of the two women to block their line of sight. When she glanced over her shoulder, Zeke was once again whole, but the strain of maintaining the image was written plainly on his face. It was now or never. She moved aside so that Olga could see that he was whole, that her eyes must have been playing tricks on her. As her expression turned from horror to confusion, Rory opened the door and herded them out. Not a moment too soon.

When she came back into the living room, Zeke was gone. Damn, she wanted to know what Eloise had told him. She was about to call his name when the doorbell rang again, accompanied by another round of barking from Hobo, who was still outside. What was this—drop in on Rory day?

This time the peephole revealed her aunt Helene standing on the porch with a sunny smile.

"Hi, sweetie," Helene said when Rory opened the door. She stepped inside and gave her niece a hug. "I just saw an old lady skipping down your street. And I don't mean my age; I mean *old*."

"That's Eloise Bowman. She moved in with her son's family after her stroke."

"Talk about a strange sight. If I knew how to use the camera in my new phone, I would have taken a picture."

"She's a little weird and very sweet," Rory said. Unless she's on a mission. But her aunt didn't need to know about that part.

"Listen," Helene said, "I have some hot news for you, and since I was passing by on my way to yoga, I thought I'd deliver it in person."

"Would you like some coffee?" Rory tried to remember if there was enough left in the carafe. If this trend kept up she'd have to start brewing more every morning.

Helene declined. "I have to talk and run or I'll be—are you okay?" she interrupted herself. "You're still in your nightgown."

"It's been a busy morning."

Fortunately, her aunt seemed too fixated on her own agenda to push the inquiry any further. "I was out to dinner last night with Richard Ames," she said. In response to Rory's unspoken question she added, "We dated for a while when I joined the troupe. I never told anyone about it, because we both recognized early on that the chemistry wasn't there. We still grab a bite together or see a movie from time to time. Totally platonic."

"Okay," Rory murmured, wondering where this was going.

"Anyway, last night he'd had a few glasses of wine, and I guess he needed a sympathetic ear, because he started talking about how his daughter's tuition was killing him. He's had to pull money out of his retirement account. Said he'd lost most of his other savings in some kind of investment boondoggle with Brian."

"Wow," was all Rory could manage. Richard, who'd been knocked down the suspect ladder by more qualified prospects, was suddenly scrambling back up again. When she'd interviewed him, he'd mentioned financial loss, but not the extent of it. Losing most of his savings was a bigger deal than he'd let on.

"I wasn't going to tell you," Helene said, "because he's a decent man, and I'm pretty sure he could never kill anyone. But then I decided you deserve to have all the facts. Either way I knew I wasn't going to be happy with myself." She sighed. "And I'm not." She gave Rory a peck on the cheek. "I'm off to de-stress with my yoga class."

"Look at that," Zeke said as Rory closed the front door after her. "And just when I thought Brett had knocked Richard completely out of the running."

"Where are you?" Rory turned in a full circle looking for him.

"Sorry, this is about all I can manage until I do some rechargin'."

She didn't like talking to Zeke when he was invisible. A person's body language and expressions often told her more than their words did. Besides, she never knew which way to face for this kind of conversation. But given the marshal's current condition, there was no point in complaining, so she focused on the arm chair and imagined him sitting there. "What did Eloise have to tell you that was so important?" she asked. The subject of Richard Ames's place in the suspect array could wait until later.

"She told me about your high-stakes car chase last night and that you have a tendency to go it alone instead of askin' for help. That much I could have told her myself."

"I had no choice last night," Rory said. "Even if I had called for help, it wouldn't have gotten to me in time to do any good." The last thing she needed was Eloise "tweeting" to the marshal about her every move.

"I can understand how that might happen on occasion," he allowed. "Hell, I've found myself in similar circumstances. But our concern is that you prefer to go it alone even when you don't have to."

*Their* concern? Since when had Zeke and Eloise appointed themselves her *guardians ad litem*? Zeke had made it resoundingly clear that he was opposed to the very concept of a psychic. Yet Eloise had managed to change his mind in under ten minutes.

"Well, haven't the two of you gotten cozy," she said tartly. "I seem to remember it was you who ordered me to avoid her completely."

Zeke issued an uncomfortable little chuckle in a nod to his fickle attitude. Rory would have enjoyed seeing his face at that moment, embarrassment not being a natural state for him.

"What can I say, darlin'? We came to an understandin'. It's a foolish general who doesn't know when to forge new alliances."

"Or honor existing ones," she reminded him sharply.

The marshal made no reply. He'd either used up his last reserves of energy or he'd chosen to end their dialogue before it deteriorated further. That was fine with Rory. She still hadn't brought up the issue of his rule breaking, but that was one discussion she wanted to have when she could see him face-to-face.

# 1878

## Huntington, New York

Weeks before Drummond boarded the Long Island Railroad train, he'd already had his fill of public transportation. He'd followed Trask by rail across the country from Colorado to Kansas and then on to Missouri, where the fugitive hopped an eastbound train to New Jersey. Although the marshal hated working by the railroad's schedule instead of his own, at least luck had started to turn in his favor. At most junctures, either the ticket agent or one of the porters recognized Trask from his picture and was able to tell the marshal where he was headed. As the agent in Saint Louis put it, "He ain't the sort of man you're apt to forget." Like a serpent eating its own tail, the monster that animated Trask rode so close to the surface that anyone who crossed his path remembered him, making it possible to track him over great distances. Even so, there were setbacks that cost Drummond time. And time was a precious commodity when it came to finding Trask.

When the marshal reached Saint Louis, the agent who'd

most likely sold Trask his ticket was away on vacation, and the marshal was obliged to wait a week until he returned. In New Jersey he was told that Trask had bought a ticket to Chicago, but as Drummond learned when he reached that city, Trask never used the ticket. Two more weeks wasted. Still Drummond refused to give up; failure was simply not an option. He'd become as desperate as the man he hunted.

Once he made it back to the East Coast, he picked up the fugitive's trail and followed it to Manhattan, where he spent days going from brothel to brothel, showing Trask's picture to every madam and prostitute in the city. His efforts finally paid off when he found Lucy Rheingold, a scrappy young woman with a broken nose and a missing tooth, courtesy of Trask's fist. According to the madam, who was fuming about the assault and subsequent loss of revenue while Lucy healed, Trask had demanded directions to the Long Island Railroad, which she'd given him, regretting only that they weren't directions to perdition.

Taking the same route, Drummond caught a ferry across the East River to Hunter's Point, Queens, and made his way to the Long Island Railroad terminal. The ticket agent didn't recognize Trask from his picture, but after showing it to his colleagues, he reported back to Drummond that the fugitive had indeed purchased a ticket to the North Shore town of Huntington.

Drummond climbed aboard the train, weary beyond endurance. He hadn't slept in a bed since leaving New Mexico, close to two months earlier, and he was running out of funds. Though his shoulder had healed, it ached like a rotten tooth when the weather was damp, which seemed to be the case more often than not on the coast. The three-hour trip to Huntington included changing trains several times, and on the last stretch, he fell asleep on the hard cane bench and would have missed his stop altogether if the conductor hadn't awakened him.

He stepped off the train somewhat dazed and stood for a moment blinking in the harsh sunlight, trying to get his bearings. He was buoyed to see a blacksmith shop and stable just across the street from the depot. He was going to need the use of a horse for the duration of his stay in the town. For that matter, Trask had probably found himself in the same position. So a visit to the smithy might well take care of the marshal's two most pressing problems—transportation and locating Trask.

As he walked inside the shop, he pulled the picture from his pocket, unfolding it with care, as it was starting to tear along the creases. The blacksmith, who introduced himself as O'Donnell, was a short, thin fellow with muscular arms that looked as if they'd sprouted on the wrong body. When Drummond showed him Trask's picture, he recognized him immediately.

"Something about him didn't sit quite right," O'Donnell said, "but I try to treat everyone equal. So when he asked where he could find work, I told him Winston Samuels was looking to hire. If I'd known he was a wanted man, I'd have kept my mouth shut. Anyways, I sold him a horse, and I haven't seen him since."

Drummond thanked him for the information, after which the two men worked out a mutually agreeable deal for the rental of a horse and tack. Although the dun had seen its finest days a decade ago, the marshal was so relieved to be in the saddle again that he barely noticed the animal's deficiencies.

He was about to ride away when a question made him turn back to the blacksmith. "Does Samuels have a family?"

"Not much of one. His wife died some five, six years ago of the pneumonia. Now it's just his daughter and himself."

"How old is the girl?" Drummond asked, afraid to hear the answer.

O'Donnell thought for a moment. "Let me see . . .

Claire's gotta be . . . gotta be thirteen by now," he said. "Pretty girl, apple of her father's . . ."

Before the blacksmith finished his sentence, Drummond had spun the horse around and raced off.

He had no problem finding the farm from O'Donnell's directions. The house itself was a white, two-story frame structure with a deep porch. He could see several outbuildings beyond the house as well, the largest of them clearly a stable. As there didn't appear to be anyone around, he tied his horse to a convenient cherry tree and walked up to the front door. He was about to knock when he heard a young girl scream. The sound seemed to come through the partially open window to his right.

He tried the door and found it locked. Gun in hand he stepped back far enough to come at the door with a powerful kick that tore it away from its hinges and sent it crashing onto the entryway floor. There was a moment of silence that told him the occupants in the next room had been unaware of his presence until the door went down. Making the most of that surprise meant acting quickly. His finger on the trigger, he stepped around the partial wall that separated the entryway from the room on his right.

Trask was standing at the far end of what was clearly a parlor with a gun in his hand. Claire lay in a heap to one side of him, a deep gash in her temple bleeding freely. Drummond could just make out the subtle rise and fall of her chest. This time he wasn't too late.

As soon as Trask saw the marshal, he dropped to his knees, pulling the limp girl up against his body like a shield. He pressed his gun to her temple. "You're gonna turn right around and walk out of here, Marshal," he said in a tone that was eerily calm given the circumstances. "No one has to die today. And you don't need to worry about Claire here; I plan on takin' real good care of her."

Drummond had Trask framed in his sights. He wanted

nothing more than to plant a bullet in the man and watch him die. But with the girl there, it was risky. His reputation as a marksman kept most men with a lick of sense from testing him. But it wasn't only his life he was gambling with here. There was no room for error.

"I have a better idea. Give yourself up, and I'll guarantee you live to stand trial," he said, his voice so thick with anger he hardly recognized it himself.

"That's not much of a deal." Trask's upper lip curled back from his teeth, giving him a feral look. "Here's how I see it. She comes along with me till I'm feelin' good and safe."

"You know I can't let that happen."

"'Course you can, Marshal. You can say that when you got here, me and the girl were already gone. There ain't no witnesses around to call you a liar. I'm sure you don't want another dead girl on your conscience. What is it now—five or six? I lose count."

Drummond's mouth went dry. If Trask wasn't making up that number, he'd violated and killed another girl some-where along the way. But he couldn't afford to dwell on that right now. Unless he shut and padlocked the door on his emotions, he didn't stand a chance of saving Claire. "I'm not leavin' here without you—dead or alive, it's your call."

Trask laughed. It was an ugly, high-pitched sound that raised the hair at the nape of Drummond's neck. "Big talk when I'm the one holdin' the ace in the game," Trask said.

This was it then. One chance. Take it, or watch Trask carry her off. "I'm sure we can come to some agreement that suits both of us," Drummond said, fine-tuning his aim on Trask's forehead.

"Well, ain't you the optimist."

It was now or never. Drummond went to squeeze the trigger, but something was wrong. He could no longer feel the gun in his hand. And then his legs gave way.

# Chapter 23

"Rory!" Helene's voice boomed from the stage when she saw her niece enter the little theater. Everyone turned to look, including Stuart Dobson, who was standing below the stage. But the director immediately turned his back on Rory, making no attempt to hide his antipathy for her. If any of the cast members were of a similar mind, they were discreet enough, or perhaps guilty enough, not to show it.

Helene, who had garnered the role of Fanny Brice's mother in their production of *Funny Girl*, was presently sharing the stage with Brett and Sophia. To Rory's untrained eye, it looked like they might have been blocking a scene. The rest of the actors were scattered through the first two rows, with the exception of Jessica and Dorothy, who were having what looked like a serious tête-à-tête off to one side. Everyone was in regular street clothing with scripts in hand.

When Rory had asked her aunt the best time to drop by the theater, Helene had told her to come near the end of rehearsals, most of which were held at night and generally ran until ten o'clock. At her aunt's suggestion, she'd picked up a few dozen doughnuts to tempt the actors into hanging around awhile before heading home. Coffee and tea were always there for the troupe, compliments of Dobson, which was nice as long as you didn't mind caffeine. Decaf wasn't an option in his theater.

"Please, don't let me interrupt you," Rory called out, quickly sitting in the last of the twenty rows. The burgundy seats were hand-me-downs from an old theater that was being razed. Although they'd no doubt been splendid at one time, they were now swaybacked, the velveteen upholstery worn and stained, and they creaked and squeaked like a house of horrors in spite of frequent applications of WD-40. Their one redeemable feature was that they'd been free to whoever wanted to cart them away. It was hard to argue with a deal like that.

Rory had come down to the theater hoping to catch the interaction among the Players when they weren't repeating lines someone else had written. She'd never worked a case that offered the unique advantage of having all the suspects gather together on a regular basis—a suspect zoo where she could come and observe the exhibits whenever she pleased. Okay, that was a stretch. Stuart Dobson was sure to ban her from the premises if she made a nuisance of herself. And as far as that went, she'd already racked up a couple of demerits in his esteem. She'd have to tread lightly around him. Very lightly.

Unfortunately, she hadn't paid enough attention to the actors' relationships and attitudes when she'd traveled to Arizona with them. She'd been too preoccupied with researching Zeke's death. Even after the flash flood, her concern had been focused on her aunt; she'd had no reason to believe Brian had been murdered. When she'd said as much to Zeke at the beginning of their investigation, he'd wagged his head as if he had a dunce for a pupil.

"It's what you don't know that'll get you killed," he'd said. "You should always be observin' your surroundin's, the people as well as the places. You never know when some gunslinger's goin' to come up behind you, and if you've been payin' attention to your whereabouts, you'll know all your options. Saved my life on more than one occasion."

Rory had been about to point out that there weren't many gunslingers around these days when she'd realized that wasn't actually true. It was just the terminology that had changed. Had she taken his advice to heart, she might have suspected earlier on last night that she was being followed. Instead of turning off the main road, she would have driven to the nearest police precinct and avoided the cat-and-mouse game with the SUV.

She set the boxes from the doughnut shop on the seat beside her, thinking this was one time when Zeke would have been a great asset. She couldn't be everywhere at once, but he had the ability to bop around the room and listen in on conversations without anyone being the wiser. He was still away though, busy recharging himself. After his first such absence, Rory had conjured up a picture of him being pampered at a retreat for ailing spirits. Images of him having a mani-pedi, a facial and a massage were always good for a private laugh. But he'd already been gone for two days, and she was missing him. Well, maybe "missing" was too strong a word, but she couldn't think of another that was quite as accurate. She missed his input on the case, missed running theories by him, even missed his unique take on things. She'd put aside her irritation over his new alliance with Eloise. After all, it wasn't technically his fault. Eloise had lured him with the bait of information. If Rory had been in his position, would she have walked away from information she might otherwise be denied? If she wanted to be honest with herself, the answer was "not likely."

Fifteen minutes after Rory arrived at the theater, Dobson

called an end to the rehearsal with a quick pep talk and an admonishment for everyone to be on time the next night. Helene, who was still onstage, took that opportunity to announce that her niece had brought doughnuts. Everyone seemed to perk up at that prospect. Taking her cue, Rory picked up the boxes and headed toward the front of the theater, where she was greeted with varying degrees of enthusiasm. She'd met most of the Players, if only briefly, after one performance or another. She'd naturally become better acquainted with those who'd been on the trip, but some of them seemed noticeably cooler to her now that she was looking for a killer among them.

The coffee and tea were set up on a shaky, old bridge table off to the right, in the walkway between the stage and the first row of seats. Rory set the doughnuts down beside the cups and stepped back as the cast members flocked around to grab their favorites. Dobson was the only holdout. He made his way around the troupe to reach Rory. She'd just finished embracing her aunt and was standing alone waiting for the troupe to disperse a bit so she could start "working the room."

"Are you wearing your PI hat tonight or your niece hat?" he inquired sardonically.

Rory had a hard time trying to remain pleasant when the director's tone had already set off another salvo in their ongoing hostilities. "A little of each," she said, pulling a smile out of her bag of tricks.

"Let me just remind you that you're on my turf here, and I won't have you creating more tension among my actors." Dobson was clearly enjoying his "king of the realm" status.

"Understood," she said sweetly, thinking how grand it would be to watch him being arrested and hauled off to jail. Too bad he was the least likely suspect in the troupe.

With nothing more to say, Dobson stalked off to meet with his set designer backstage. Grateful to be rid of him,

Rory looked around, "observing her whereabouts," as Zeke would have put it. The Players were drifting away from the table and into small groups, chatting and eating their doughnuts.

Sophia was in a tight knot with Jessica and Brett a few feet from the table. Rory was surprised to see them all being lighthearted and sociable together. Was it possible the two women had found a common bond after Brian dumped Sophia? And if they'd become united in their anger against him, had one plus one added up to murder? Rory decided it was time for her to have a doughnut. She passed as close to the trio as she could without bumping into them. From the few words she caught, they seemed to be talking about other productions of *Funny Girl* they'd seen. Since she wanted to listen in a while longer, she poured herself a cup of coffee and made a production of adding the right amount of milk and sugar. Then she took her time looking over the few remaining doughnuts. She wasn't actually hungry, but she selected a glazed one and nibbled on it while she heard their conversation move from the musical to pop-culture icons and then to recent headlines in the news. Nothing interesting so far. If she stayed there eating alone and in slow motion, someone was going to notice and wonder why she'd bothered to stop by at all.

Where to next? Helene was talking to Adam Caspian and three of the Players who weren't with them in Arizona. Given that she had a limited amount of time before everyone headed home, Rory needed to make the best use of every minute. Since Adam was the only potential suspect in that group, he would have to wait. Instead, she turned her attention to Greg and Amy Renato, who were laughing about something Richard Ames had said. Since Rory knew little about the young, married couple, this seemed like a good time to remedy that. Sometimes a casual meeting like this loosened people's tongues, and they said things they would never reveal in a more formal setting. She ambled over to them as if she had no particular agenda in mind.

They all greeted her warmly. "You've won my husband's loyalty forever," Amy said. "Or at least until someone else brings in doughnuts."

Greg swallowed the last bite of a custard-filled one. "Thank you sooo much," he said, hamming it up. "All the food in our house is healthy and boring. I know it's because she wants me to live forever, but I'm just not convinced it's worth it." That bought a round of laughter, and after it faded, Amy asked how the investigation was going.

"Making progress," Rory said. Judging by their faces, they were all interested in her answer, but not heavily invested in it. She'd already decided she'd have to push the conversation in the right direction if she wanted to learn anything of value tonight.

"You know," she added lightly, "from what I can tell, you and Greg may be the only ones who *didn't* have a motive to kill Brian." Her statement didn't appear to trouble the Renatos in the least, but she could swear she saw Richard blanch a bit. Of course, she'd just called him a suspect to his face.

"I imagine, as motives go, there are a wide range of them," he said, "some more pernicious than others."

To Rory he sounded like he was trying to defend himself. She shook her head. "You'd be surprised. Vengeance, it turns out, is a very personal thing, and everyone has a different threshold. One person might only be compelled to take a life for a life, while another will kill over a broken heart or financial ruin." She watched Richard carefully, but he was prepared this time, and his face told her nothing more.

"If we managed to stay out of Brian's web, all the credit goes to my wife," Greg said proudly. "She has this sixth sense about people, and the day that man joined the troupe, she told me to steer clear of him, that he was nothing but trouble."

"I'm afraid my fan club here tends to exaggerate things," Amy said. "I'm far from always right."

Rory would have liked to take Amy aside right then and there to ask who she'd finger as the killer. Of course, it would be purely academic, since a sixth sense was hardly enough to indict, let alone convict, someone. "Maybe you should go into the PI business," she suggested.

Amy laughed. "No thanks, I'll stick with teaching. Fifth graders are about as much danger as I can handle."

Rory felt a tap on her shoulder. Zeke was finally back in town. Another tap, this time harder and accompanied by a woman's voice. "Excuse me?"

Rory turned around to find Dorothy Johnson standing there. "I just wanted to thank you for the surprise doughnuts, dear. Such a thoughtful thing to do." She leaned in to touch her cheek to Rory's. "Time for this old lady to be getting home. You take care. Night all."

After Dorothy left, the rest of the impromptu party started to break up, some of the actors grumbling about having to get up early in the morning for work. With the exception of Stuart Dobson, everyone made sure to thank Rory for the doughnuts; several voiced the hope they'd see her opening night.

"You couldn't keep me away," Rory assured them as she and Helene cleaned up and tossed the empty doughnut boxes into the garbage. But the more important question, she thought, was which member of the cast would not be there when the curtain rose on opening night?

# Chapter 24

Zeke was standing near the living room window when Rory and Hobo came in the front door. "I was about to go lookin' for you," he said.

Rory unhooked Hobo's leash from his collar, and the dog trotted off to the kitchen. A moment later she heard him slurping up water from his bowl. They'd taken a long walk to enjoy the first truly mild day of the month. The air had finally lost its bite and lay as gently against the skin as a baby's breath. Hobo had been so pleased with the weather that he'd strutted beside her with all the nobility of a dog trailing a long pedigree.

"Marshal, we have to talk," Rory said as she also headed to the kitchen. Zeke was leaning against the center island when she reached the sink. She ran the cold water and filled up a glass from the cabinet. The walk had left her as thirsty as the dog.

"Sounds serious," he said.

Rory drained her glass before speaking. "It is."

"Tell the hangman I'm ready," Zeke said with a wink.

Rory leaned her back against the edge of the sink so that they were facing one another with only three feet between them. "You were in my bedroom a couple of nights ago."

"Yes," he said although it hadn't been a question. His directness bought him some points in her regard but not nearly enough to table the subject.

"I thought I could trust you." It was an effort to keep her tone and temper even. She'd purposely waited a couple of days to broach the issue in the hope that time would mellow her anger so they could have a discussion instead of an argument.

"You *can* trust me."

"I'm afraid I have a problem believing that now."

"Look," he said, "I could tell you it was an impulsive mistake, but that wouldn't be true. I knew damn well what I was doin', thought hard about it, and I knew you'd be madder than a bear in a circus wagon."

Rory shook her head, temporarily at a loss for words. "Then why . . . why in hell would you do it?" she sputtered finally.

"You needed the comfort of another soul," he said without melodrama.

"In your estimation."

"In my estimation."

"That's not good enough," she said. "You don't get to decide what's best for me."

He looked her directly in the eye. "If I'd asked permission to be there, what would you have said?"

She took a minute to consider her answer, wanting to be truthful with herself as well as with him. "I'm not sure. That night was difficult; I might have opted for the company."

She saw the skepticism flash across his face, but he didn't try to argue the point. "Then you have my apologies," he said stiffly. "It won't happen again."

With a start, Rory realized there was nothing more he could say. It was up to her to either accept the apology or pack her things and move out. Although that had once been a much easier option, the past year had made it gut-wrenching. She loved the house, and in spite of the difficulties in living with the marshal, she loved her life there. Case closed, at least for now.

"I appreciate your honesty," she said, "and I'm going to take you at your word. But my patience has its limits."

Zeke nodded. "It's been my experience that everythin' does."

Rory had no idea what he meant by that, but she suspected it might lead down a road from which there was no returning, so she let it go.

"You might want to check that there answerin' machine," Zeke said as he slowly sifted away into the ether.


J essica arrived at precisely two o'clock. The message she'd left on Rory's voice mail was a simple "Please call me," along with her phone number. When Rory called her back, she'd been no more forthcoming. She'd requested a meeting but refused to say why.

From her office, Rory heard the car pull up, followed by the staccato tapping of stilettos crossing the driveway. She opened the door before Jessica could knock. Their greeting was restrained and somewhat awkward, since their last time alone together hadn't ended under the best of circumstances. Rory was tempted to ask how the dental appointment had gone, but common sense prevailed and she kept her mouth shut.

The actress's arm was still in a cast, but other than that she looked as flawless as ever in black leggings and an emerald green tunic that skimmed her body and set her red hair on fire. Rory wondered if she had a professional makeup artist and hairstylist on retainer—or chained up in her basement.

Jessica was about to take a seat on the couch but abruptly changed her mind and chose the armchair instead. Rory didn't understand why until she noticed a few strands of Hobo's hair on the couch. She almost apologized but decided she'd rather start their conversation from a position of strength. And allergies aside, a little dog fur never hurt anyone.

"So how can I help you?" she asked once the actress had settled herself.

Jessica took a deep breath and squared her shoulders as if she were about to launch into a lengthy soliloquy. "I've been troubled by our last conversation," she said. "I was in a hurry that day and I hadn't been expecting you. As a result I may have come across as . . . difficult. I'd like to correct that impression."

Rory had imagined half a dozen reasons why the actress might want to speak to her, but that hadn't been one of them.

"I know ex-lovers are traditionally suspects in a murder investigation. I've seen it so often in screenplays that it's actually become trite."

Rory didn't bother to point out that, trite or not, in real life ex-lovers were still committing murder. Apparently Jessica kept up on current events by way of screenplay plots.

"Anyway, I was thinking about the case, trying to figure out who could have killed Brian, but it was impossible. I mean, the troupe is like a second family to me, so it's hard to imagine one of them being a killer. And that's when it dawned on me that I could help you narrow your list of suspects."

Rory's interest scooted up a notch. "Okay, you've got my attention."

"I have a witness who had me in sight the entire time we were in that godforsaken canyon. If I had killed Brian, she would have seen me do it."

Rory was skeptical. It was hard to put much stock in an observation by someone who was stoked by adrenaline and literally struggling not to drown.

"Well, aren't you going to ask me the witness's name?" Jessica asked impatiently, as if she'd already forgotten that she wanted to correct a bad impression.

Rory realized she wasn't playing the role of the PI the way the actress had scripted it in her mind. "Well, sure, of course." She tried to pump some enthusiasm into her words. "Who is it?"

"Dorothy Johnson," Jessica said, as if she were announcing an Oscar winner.

"Dorothy?" Rory had a memory flash of Jessica and Dorothy seated off to the side of the theater, their heads together, deep in conversation.

Jessica seemed irritated that her news hadn't immediately brought her a round of applause or a chorus of thank-yous. "Yes, Dorothy," she said tossing her head so that her long hair danced around her shoulders. No doubt a winning technique with men.

"You're saying she had you in sight the whole time you were in the flood waters?"

"Yes. Why are you having such a problem with that?"

"A person in that kind of situation isn't generally a reliable witness," Rory said, barely managing to contain her own temper with this diva. "They're way too busy struggling to stay alive to be keeping tabs on someone else."

"Well, I don't know what to tell you. Maybe you should speak to Dorothy, because that's what she said to me." Jessica was becoming huffier with each word.

"I will. I most definitely will," Rory assured her. In fact, she intended to make that call the minute the actress left. "Was there anything else you wanted to discuss?"

Jessica stood up abruptly, her posture stiff and formal. "Isn't this enough? I thought you'd be thrilled to eliminate me from your list."

"You've certainly given me something to think about," Rory said with as much sincerity as she could muster. She knew it wasn't close to what Jessica had hoped to hear, but then she wasn't in the business of coddling suspects with bruised egos.

Jessica left with a frosty good-bye, their relationship worse than it had been when she'd arrived. Rory sat down at her desk and dialed Dorothy's number.

Rory's second meeting with Dorothy took place in the older woman's home, a neat, little Cape Cod in East Northport. The house had a cozy, country feel that seemed a lot like Dorothy herself. As soon as Rory stepped inside, the smell of cinnamon wrapped itself around her.

"I thought some coffee cake would be nice," Dorothy said when Rory commented on the lovely aroma. "I was up early, and you know what they say about idle hands."

Rory didn't know what they say, but she nodded as if she did. No point in wasting time when there were more pressing questions to pursue. She followed Dorothy into the kitchen, where the table was set for two, the cake starring as centerpiece.

Dorothy poured the coffee and cut the cinnamon ring, placing a large piece on Rory's plate and a much smaller piece on her own. "I had to start cutting back," she said with a sigh. "Lately, I gain weight by just being in the same room with cake. I still cheat a little from time to time though," she added in a whisper, as if the calorie police had the room bugged.

Rory cut off a forkful of cake, thinking that if it tasted half as good as it smelled, she'd be hooked for life. The moment it hit her tongue she knew she was in trouble. "I'm not leaving here without this recipe," she said.

Dorothy preened as if she'd just won first prize at the county fair. "Why, thank you, dear. Most folks do seem to enjoy it."

Rory took another few bites before she forced herself to put the fork down. There was work to be done. "I saw Jessica yesterday," she said to get the conversation rolling.

Dorothy speared a piece of cake and popped it into her mouth. "Yes, she mentioned she was going to see you."

"She says you can attest to the fact that she couldn't possibly have killed Brian, since you had her in sight throughout that whole, terrible ordeal."

Dorothy took a sip of her coffee. "That's right. I did."

"But that first surge of water must have knocked everyone right off their feet," Rory pointed out.

"Well, yes, I suppose I may have lost track of her for ten, fifteen seconds. Hardly enough time for her to get to Brian and murder him."

Jessica's alibi was starting to leak like a sieve.

"Surely in all the confusion, with the water rising so fast, everyone screaming and being thrown against the canyon walls, you must have lost sight of her for longer than that."

"No, I've gone over and over it in my head. Now, don't get me wrong; I'm not looking for sainthood here. I was mainly focused on keeping myself alive—but it happens that I also had her in sight. I know she didn't kill Brian."

"Then you also had Brian in view the whole time?" Rory asked to see if she could trip her up.

She gave Rory an odd look. "Of course not, or I'd know for sure if he'd actually been killed and who killed him, now wouldn't I?"

Rory couldn't help but smile. "Yes, I imagine you would."

"I may be the oldest member of the troupe, dear, but I'm no fool."

"Sorry. It's my job to throw a few curves and see what you'll swing at."

"Apology accepted."

Rory paused to drink her coffee. "Did Jessica ask you to vouch for her?" she asked casually, as if they were just two women chitchatting with nothing at stake.

"Yes. She was worried that her history with Brian made her a prime suspect. But she didn't ask me to lie for her," Dorothy added quickly. "I would never have agreed to that."

"Would you say the two of you are pretty close?"

Dorothy nodded. "As unlikely as that may seem. She's young and glamorous, and I've got more than twenty years on her. If memory serves, I've also never been glamorous. But then we're not the type of friends who go clubbing together, if that's the right word. Anyway, I think she sees me as something of a mother figure." She cut herself another sliver of cake. "You're definitely going to have to take this home with you. I have no won't power at all."

"I'll be more than happy to help you out," Rory said with a laugh. "One last question, and then I'll get out of your way. If you were in a courtroom under oath, would you be willing to state that Jessica could not possibly have murdered Brian?"

Dorothy looked her straight in the eye. "Yes, without reservation."

A few minutes later, Rory was on her way home with the remainder of the cinnamon cake wrapped in aluminum foil, a promise from Dorothy to e-mail the recipe, and one less suspect on her list.

Rory was in her backyard raking up the last of the leaves she'd missed in the fall when Zeke popped in to say "hello." She'd immediately put him to work using his energy to push the leaves from the farthest corners of the yard toward the pile she was creating. A leaf blower without the noise and noxious fumes. If only there was a way to patent the technique and manufacture the product. Hobo was also hard at work chasing squirrels and doing his best to follow them up into the trees. Pure Americana. Rory wondered if Rockwell would have appreciated the scene.

"Do you think Dorothy's covering for her?" Zeke asked as he worked his way back to her. His voice was loose and easy as if he'd put the bedroom incident behind him. Rory had decided to go that route as well. She'd had her say, and there was nothing to be gained by hanging on to her anger.

"No, I think she believes what she told me. The question is—how reliable are perception and memory when a person is in a life-and-death struggle?"

"I say we drop Jessica to the bottom of the list," Zeke said, "but we don't outright eliminate her."

Rory nodded. The bottom of the list was becoming crowded now that Jessica had joined Adam and Sophia Caspian there. "I was thinking along the same lines as far as Dorothy's concerned," she said. The more the merrier. "I mean why would she be so willing to help eliminate one of the suspects unless she had nothing to worry about herself? If she were guilty she'd be thinking, 'The more suspects to hide among, the better.'"

"Plus, she's got no motive as far as we know, and I'm downright positive she doesn't have the skills to have broken in here or tried to run you off the road."

Rory was laughing at the thought of Dorothy sneaking into her house when she saw Hobo barreling toward them at ramming speed. "Incoming," she yelled seconds before he pounced on the mound of leaves as if he were trying to bring down a lion.

Zeke barely managed to blink away in time to avert a collision. He popped back into view several yards away.

"That's one seriously crazy mutt," he said with a grin that seemed to stretch his mustache from ear to ear.

As if to support that theory Hobo flipped onto his back to wriggle around in the leaves with his legs dancing in the air.

# Chapter 25

Rory's eyes flew open. One minute she was sound asleep, and the next she was wide awake, adrenaline kicking her heart into high gear. Zero to sixty in less than three seconds. But she didn't have a clue as to why. The digital clock on the nightstand read 2:20. The house was silent and dark, the only light coming from the tiny night-light in the hall between her bedroom and the bathroom. She was still trying to puzzle out what had pulled her from her dreams when Hobo started barking somewhere downstairs, providing her with a eureka moment. If this was his encore, his opening act must have awakened her. But having resolved that question, she was faced with a tougher one. What had set him to barking in the middle of the night?

It was possible he had an upset tummy and needed to be let out. He was big on eating grass along with other, more exotic delicacies that could be found in the backyard. Rory was pushing her feet into flip-flops that doubled as slippers when the doorbell rang, reverberating through the house like a gunshot. Hobo took it as a cue to ramp up his own rhetoric. Okay, then, it probably wasn't a digestive issue after all.

She found him stationed at the front door, his nose pressed to the doorjamb as if he were trying to get a better whiff of whoever was on the other side. She flipped on the light in the entryway as well as the outdoor light and put her eye to the peephole. She jumped back in surprise when she saw another eye staring back at her. Hobo, who appeared to have finished his olfactory assessment of the visitor, was now merrily wagging his tail.

"Who is it?" Rory called out, reassured by his recommendation.

"It's Eloise," came the impatient reply.

Rory opened the door, wondering how her elderly neighbor had managed to sneak out of her son's house again. Eloise stepped inside wearing a Windbreaker over her pajamas and sneakers on her otherwise bare feet.

"What are you doing here in the middle of the night?" Rory asked. "If Doug wakes up and realizes you're gone, he'll be frantic."

Eloise brushed away that concern with a wave of her hand. "I don't know how I managed to have such a neurotic child."

"Regardless," Rory said, in no mood to debate nature versus nurture. "You should be home in bed like everyone else."

"Yes, well tell that to the powers that be."

"What does that mean?" She was pretty sure she knew the answer, but she didn't want to risk planting any new ideas in Eloise's head.

"It means I can't get any sleep with all the chatter coming at me from the other side."

"Is it something they want you to tell me?" Rory asked,

thinking that whoever "they" were, they could at least take
into account the fact that mortals slept at night.

"Of course. Why else would I be climbing out of windows and ringing your doorbell at such a crazy hour?" In
her own bizarre way, Eloise sounded utterly sane.

Rory didn't have any response to that. She hated to be a
tattletale, but she'd have to tell Doug how his mother kept
escaping, preferably before she fell and killed herself.

"Abner Jensen doesn't have much time left," Eloise
announced with all the gravity of a journalist delivering bad
news. "It appears to be cancer, though that wasn't entirely
clear."

Rory had been planning to go back to Tucson to talk to
him, but it seemed she might have to make that trip a lot
sooner than she'd anticipated. When Abner died, any information he had about the Jensen family would die with him.
And although the odds weren't great, he might just know
something that would lead her to the name of Zeke's killer.

"Did they tell you how much time he has?"

Eloise shook her head, a smile starting to chip away at
the tension in her face. "Can I have ice cream now?" she
asked brightly.

Rory was about to remind her what time it was, then
decided it would just be easier to give her some ice cream
before calling Doug to take her home. Hobo followed the
women into the kitchen with a jaunty gait as if he sensed a
snack in the offing.

Rory settled Eloise at the table and scooped up some
cherry vanilla for her. She was giving Hobo a little in his
dish when Zeke appeared. There was no warning flicker of
lights, no gradual fade-in. One moment he wasn't there and
the next he was, arms crossed and brows inching toward a
frown. He hadn't bothered switching his Western garb for
modern clothing, either because Eloise already knew he

didn't come from the here and now or because he'd been in too much of a hurry.

Eloise didn't seem to care that he'd joined them. She kept right on spooning ice cream into her mouth, her eyes dreamy with pleasure. Hobo had set his big head in her lap hoping to finagle a bit more for himself.

"Well, someone was in such a hurry to get here he forgot his manners," Rory remarked as she put the ice cream back in the freezer. "Afraid Eloise was going to tell me something you don't want me to know, Marshal?"

Zeke dialed his expression up to cordial. "It came to my attention we had company," he said, "so I thought I'd be sociable and stop in."

"What's the deal with you two anyway?" The question had been nagging at Rory since he and Eloise had had their little tête-à-tête.

Zeke shrugged. "We just recognized that we have some common interests."

"Would one of those common interests happen to be me?"

"You are not the center of the universe, my dear Aurora," he said with a chuckle.

Rory knew the jab was meant to derail her from pursuing the question, so it had little effect on her. But she didn't know what to make of him calling her Aurora again, unless it was simply another ploy to distract her.

Zeke popped into the chair beside Eloise, who'd just finished her ice cream. She set the bowl on the floor for Hobo to lick, which he did with gusto. "What brings you by tonight, Miss Eloise?" Zeke asked, sounding like Rhett Butler in Wyatt Earp duds.

"There's nothing better than ice cream," she said, licking her lips in imitation of the dog.

He tried a different tack. "Did you and Rory have a nice talk?"

"I like Rory. She buys good flavors. Jean only buys chocolate and strawberry."

"Surely you didn't come here in the middle of the night just for ice cream." A hint of irritation had crept into his voice.

Eloise turned to Rory as if the marshal's words hadn't even registered. "Would you call Douglas and ask him to come take me home now?" She yawned and rubbed her eyes like a child who was ready for a bedtime story.

"Eloise," Zeke said sternly, "I asked why you came over here tonight."

The abrupt change in his tone made Rory wonder how he'd treated suspects and uncooperative witnesses when he'd worn a real badge, back in the days before criminals had more rights than the law-abiding public.

Eloise finally turned to him with a shy smile. "There's no need to be afraid of what's coming, Marshal Drummond," she said softly. "I promise—cross my heart."

Rory saw Zeke's face twist into a scowl. So much for their collaborative effort, she thought, happier about its demise than she probably ought to be. In spite of Zeke's denial, she was sure she'd been the common ground in their short-lived truce. Although their intentions may have been noble, she didn't need two of them trying to keep her out of harm's way.

Zeke looked as if he wanted to grab Eloise and shake some sense into her. Before he could attempt any version of that scenario, Rory plucked the phone off the wall and dialed the Bowman household, sorry she was about to disturb their peaceful night too.


Rory was on her way home from the pet store with a thirty-pound bag of Hobo's favorite kibble and a red Frisbee. She was looking forward to throwing it for him. With his natural exuberance, she could picture him leaping into the air to catch the toy, his shaggy fur blowing every which way. She was a few blocks from her house, doing the local speed limit of thirty, when a dark green SUV came barreling around a curve at her, hogging the center of the road. She pulled her wheel sharply to the right, barely avoiding a collision with the SUV, and then slammed on her brakes as she headed straight for an up close and personal with one of the stately, old oak trees that lined the road. She brought the car to a screeching stop inches from the tree trunk, memories of her last wild ride flashing through her mind. She was a little shaky and a whole lot of angry. It had happened so fast she didn't see the SUV's license plate, but she did catch a decent glimpse of the other driver. The woman behind the wheel had been staring straight ahead as if she had such important matters on her mind that she hadn't noticed she'd run Rory off the road.

By the time Rory pulled into her driveway, her heart rate and blood pressure had fallen back into the normal range, and she'd given herself a rational pep talk. In spite of the fact that this SUV was the same color as the first one that had chased her and tried to run her off the road, the two incidents couldn't be related. This driver hadn't been following her; she'd been going in the opposite direction. It was simply one more case in a growing epidemic of drivers who believed that everyone else on the road should make way for them.

She lugged the bag of kibble, her handbag and the Frisbee to the front door, wondering why Zeke rarely showed up when there was heavy lifting to be done. She set the kibble down on the porch and unlocked the door.

Hobo and the marshal were in the entry waiting for her. Hobo welcomed her with his usual fanfare, but Zeke looked grim. "We've had another visit from the dog-toy fairy," he said holding out his palm. There was a small stuffed pig riding the air above it.

Rory didn't say anything. The color draining from her face, she dropped the Frisbee and her handbag on the floor and raced up the stairs, leaving both the dog and the marshal bewildered.

When she didn't return after a couple of minutes, Zeke popped up to the second floor hallway to look for her, followed closely by Hobo, who took the stairs two at a time with the new red Frisbee in his mouth. They found her sitting on the edge of the bed with her sketch pad and pencil. Hobo went in without hesitation and lay down at her feet, where he proceeded to gnaw on the plastic disk. Zeke stayed on his side of the doorway. Rory was so absorbed in what she was doing that she didn't notice him standing there.

"Looks like you had a sudden urge to do some sketchin'," he remarked by way of announcing himself.

"Sorry," Rory said without looking up, "I need to get this on paper before I forget any of the details."

Five minutes later she turned the pad around so he could see it. The woman she'd drawn appeared to be in her thirties. She had sharp features, a strong jaw and short hair that was clearly a lifestyle choice rather than an aesthetic one, given that it did nothing to enhance her appearance.

"Who is she?" Zeke asked.

"The woman who ran me off the road a few minutes ago. I figured she was just another crazy driver until you told me about Hobo's new gift. That's when I realized she was probably racing away from the scene of her second break-in here."

"Do you think she's the one who followed you the other night?"

Rory shook her head. "Initially I didn't, but now . . . It was so dark then I could barely see that the SUV was green. I couldn't make out the brand or model, let alone what the driver looked like." She detached the sketch from the pad and rolled it up before joining the marshal in the hall. "I'm going to make a copy of this and give it to Leah to run against the police database. Maybe we'll get lucky. But first I want to take a good look at that pig." She started down the stairs, Hobo and his Frisbee at her heels.

When they reached the living room, Zeke was waiting. "There's a note sewn onto it like last time," he said lobbing the toy to her. Hobo tried to snag it out of the air, but Rory grabbed it first, promising he could have it back soon. This time the lettering on the added label was larger and easier to read since the quote was shorter: "Pretty is as pretty does."

"Nothing newsworthy there," she said. "The writer is still trying to point us in Jessica's or Sophia's direction. For now, the messenger is more interesting than the message."

"With her expertise at breakin' and enterin', this can't be the messenger's first job," Zeke observed.

"That's what I'm counting on. If she has a rap sheet, we'll find her. Then it should be easy enough to convince her it's in her best interests to give up her employer." Sketch in hand, Rory grabbed her purse from the entry floor where she'd dropped it. On her way out, she tossed the pig to Hobo, who immediately got down to the business of disemboweling it.

"No problem," Leah said as she walked Rory back to her car at the Suffolk County Police Headquarters in Yaphank. "I'll come in early tomorrow and run the sketch when there aren't so many prying eyes around. But you do realize you have a perfectly legitimate reason for requesting it? Someone's tried to run you off the road twice since you've been investigating this case."

"But I'd have to file a report, and I want to avoid that."

"I know—you don't want the police looking over your

shoulder. You want to do things your way," Leah parroted, having learned the routine by rote. "I'm afraid one day I'm going to be saying 'I told you so.' I just hope you're still alive to hear it."

# Chapter 26

"Are you sure?" Rory asked, fully aware of how stupid the question was but unwilling to make peace with the answer. "I was so certain we finally had a break in the case." She'd been cleaning the last of winter's debris out of the flower beds in the front yard when Leah called.

"That's why I ran the sketch twice. Of course, that doesn't mean she's innocent; it just—"

" . . . Means she hasn't been caught committing a crime yet." Rory completed her sentence. There was no doubt in her mind that the first attempt to run her off the road had been premeditated. But even if the second time was accidental, there was a good chance it was connected to the second break-in at her house. The woman she'd drawn was guilty. She felt it in her gut. But guilty of exactly what?

They talked for another minute; then Rory clicked off the call and looked up at Zeke, who'd been leaning against the house watching her work. Since he was in view of anyone walking or driving by, he'd changed into what he called his "public duds." Given time and his well-honed observational skills, he'd learned what type of apparel was called for in most situations. That day he'd imagined himself into jeans and a white Polo shirt. Rory thought he looked like the real deal, even if his hair could have used a good stylist. Now if he could just keep his body intact.

"I take it she couldn't find a match," he said.

"No." She pulled a matted pile of leaves from between two pink azaleas that were on the verge of blossoming. "How much easier life would be if the damn trees would just hold on to their leaves." She threw the pile of them into the garbage can she'd lined with a plastic bag for that purpose.

"I've been thinkin' about it," Zeke said.

"The leaves?"

"You know how I keep sayin' the intruder is way too good to be an amateur?" he went on, ignoring her attempt at humor. "I think that's the point we need to be focusin' on."

"Meaning?" Rory brushed off her hands and stood up.

"I'm willin' to bet my spurs our intruder's in law enforcement of some kind."

"A cop?"

"Or the FBI. Maybe even the CIA."

"Moonlighting with her own agenda," Rory murmured, rolling the idea around in her mind. "The trouble is, asking Leah to check the police personnel records for a match is one thing, but I don't have any pull with the clandestine services."

"Okay, that's not all bad news. Let's see if Leah can help us," Zeke said. "A starvin' man never throws out an apple that's only half rotten."

Rory smiled. "You paint a lovely picture. Ever consider going into the greeting-card business?"

* * *

Spurred by Eloise's prognosis for Abner Jensen, Rory started making plans to fly to Tucson. Her first order of business was to call the Jensen home, where she spoke to a woman who didn't bother to identify herself. In a clipped, no-nonsense tone she informed Rory that Abner wasn't having a good day and then only grudgingly agreed to take a message for him.

It took Rory a moment to come up with one that was succinct and would still make sense to the man, since he had no idea who she was or what she wanted. "I'm doing research on Tucson's history," she said after making a point of introducing herself, "and since Mr. Jensen's family has lived there for so many generations, I was hoping I could stop by and have a little chat with him on the subject." Not bad as explanations went and completely truthful, which wasn't often the case when working on the marshal's behalf.

"I'll let him know," the woman said, "but I can't make any promises. He's quite ill, and it's hard to say in advance when he might be feeling up to company."

That wasn't the answer Rory had hoped to hear. "Of course, I understand. I'll call again when I'm in town." She left her cell number with the woman in case there was any change in Abner's condition.

She was surprised to find a reasonably priced flight, but because she was booking it so few days in advance, she was stuck with a middle seat. If she'd been willing to wait a couple of weeks she could have had a much-coveted aisle seat. Of course, Abner might well be dead by then, which made her decision easier. As her uncle Mac liked to say, "Sometimes you're the bug; sometimes you're the windshield."

She arranged to bundle Hobo off to her parents again,

which seemed to suit all concerned. Her father promised to teach his "granddog" the finer points of Frisbee playing during her absence. Since Rory couldn't say she was going out west to do more research for her resident ghost, she'd also recycled the cover story for her trip. She was going back to finish the visit with her college friend.

Since she was still working for Clarissa, she felt obliged to let her know she was taking a few days off to attend to personal matters but could still be reached by phone.

At the eleventh hour, it occurred to Rory that she'd made provisions for everyone but Zeke. She certainly didn't want him showing up at the Jensen house and sabotaging her mission.

Although he should have been thrilled that Abner Jensen was still alive and might be able to shed some light on the question of his killer, the marshal had been dead set against her plan to interview him. There was clearly some information he didn't want her to uncover even if it meant never finding out the killer's name. That, of course, made the matter irresistible to Rory. But if she wanted free rein when she talked to Abner, she had to make the trip alone.

Since the only fail-safe solution was to deplete Zeke's energy reserves, she demanded a lengthy practice session with him out in public. It happened to be a reasonable request given that his last few appearances had been somewhat less than tidy. Fortunately, Zeke was in an accommodating state of mind. They spent the day before her secret trip running errands together. The bad news was that several people at the supermarket and dry cleaners were going to be hustling off to the optometrist or opting for long-term psychotherapy. The good news was that the marshal could barely croak "good-bye" before he limped off to recharge. That should buy her several days of ghost-free interference. Now, if Abner Jensen would just cooperate and hang in there a little longer.

# Chapter 27

After landing in Tucson, Rory rented a car and drove to the same chain hotel where she'd booked a room on the previous trip. By the time she checked in she felt as if she'd been traveling forever. And since Arizona doesn't observe daylight saving time, she was dealing with a three-hour time difference as well.

Although she was hungry and nearly asleep on her feet, she pulled her phone out of her handbag and dialed Abner's house as soon as she was alone in her room. It rang five times. She was about to end the call when the same woman she'd spoken to previously picked it up. She sounded breathless and annoyed.

"Have I called at a bad time?" Rory asked after identifying herself.

"There never seems to be a good time anymore," the woman said with a heavy sigh. "I'm trying to do three things at once, and the damn phone hasn't stopped ringing since it woke me up this morning."

Under any other circumstances, Rory would have politely apologized for the interruption and called back later in the week. But the reality was that she'd flown across the country and she had little more than forty-eight hours before she had to turn around and make that same trip home. If she had to deal with a disgruntled relative, aide, housekeeper or whoever this woman was, so be it. Abner Jensen might well be her last chance to get at the truth behind who'd killed the marshal, and she intended to speak to him while he still resided on this side of the veil.

"I'm really sorry to bother you, Ms. . . ." Rory said, trying to coax a name out of the woman.

"Hathaway. Lydia Hathaway," she supplied grudgingly, as if she suspected Rory was actually a solicitor who wanted to sell her vinyl siding or a cleaner chimney.

"Hi, Lydia," Rory said sweetly, hoping to wheedle her way into the woman's good graces. "I just got into town, and I was wondering if Mr. Jensen is feeling any better?"

"He's better than I am," Lydia said. "He ate his breakfast without too much fuss and he's not complaining for the moment. I suppose I should be grateful. I guess you're calling because you still want to see him?"

"Very much so," Rory replied, investing her words with as much sincerity as possible.

"I suppose you can stop by for a little while as long as you don't get him all riled up." She sounded as if she'd rather undergo a root canal without the benefit of Novocain than handle a "riled-up" Abner.

"Of course," Rory promised. Although she had no idea what might rile the elderly man, she didn't ask Lydia to elaborate. The less she knew, the easier it would be to excuse herself if she unwittingly crossed some arbitrary line in the sand.

They agreed on two o'clock. That gave Rory time to change out of her jeans and sweater and into lightweight chinos and a short-sleeved shirt, which were better suited to early May in the desert southwest. Since the trip was a short one, she'd brought only a carry-on with essentials. At the last minute, and based solely on a hunch, she'd thrown in the picture of the woman Eloise had insisted she sketch, the woman Zeke had seemed to recognize. It was a long shot, but maybe Abner could shed some light on who she was. Rory removed the travel tube holding the sketch from her suitcase and tucked it into her oversized handbag. The next item on her agenda was to scout out some food to appease her empty stomach.

Armed with caffeine, a GPS and Lydia's directions, Rory found her way to the Presidio, where the oldest homes in Tucson stood. According to the travel guide she'd picked up on her first trip there, the Jensen house dated back to the last half of the nineteenth century and had remained in their family from the day it was built to the present. Since Abner had bequeathed the house and its contents to the historical society, Rory assumed the family line ended with him.

Even if she wasn't going to the house specifically to talk to its owner, she would have been interested in visiting a place where so many generations of one family had lived. What treasures might one find stored away in the attic of such a house, assuming, of course, it had an attic. But the fact was that she did have a discrete and singular purpose in going there, and she didn't need to remind herself to stay focused on it. Although she'd initially been reluctant to take on the search for Zeke's killer, somewhere along the way, when she wasn't paying attention, the need to know had become hers too, as if it were contagious, a pathogen that had worked its way into her bones.

When she reached Abner's neighborhood, she was glad to see that on-street parking was permitted. There was even an available spot right on his block. His house was a two-story adobe Victorian, an interesting combination that Rory had never encountered before. The low railings that ran the length of the front porch, as well as the trim around the windows and door, were all painted green, with smaller architectural embellishments in orange. To Rory's untrained eye, the house looked to be in good repair for its age, no doubt a function of family pride.

She climbed the few steps to the porch and rang the bell. After what seemed like ten minutes, but was more likely less than two, the door was opened by a woman in her seventies wearing a navy velour sweat suit. Her white hair was neatly coiffed, and there was a light swath of blue eye shadow across her eyelids. She greeted Rory with a pleasant enough "hello," but her expression was stern, as if her features were locked in permafrost.

"Come in," she said stepping back to leave room for her in the narrow entry.

"Thanks so much for letting me visit," Rory said, raising her voice in competition with the television that was blasting in the next room. "I'll keep our conversation as brief as possible."

"I'd appreciate that," Lydia said, leading her into what would've been called the parlor back when the house was built.

The interior of the house was clean but dated, little or nothing having been done to spruce it up since the fifties. Of course, even that era was modern in comparison to the age of the house. Looking around, Rory felt a tug of disappointment and realized she'd imagined finding the house decorated as it had been back when the original Jensen family lived there. Now that she thought about it, this wasn't a museum; it was a house in which real people had lived for generations.

When she and Lydia walked into the parlor, Abner didn't immediately look up from the TV program he was watching. He was sitting on a tufted velveteen sofa that had probably once been a vibrant red but was now faded and worn to an uneven dusty rose that matched the flowers on the wallpaper. There was an oxygen canister on the floor beside him, and a clear, thin tube snaked its way up from the canister across his chest and into his nostrils.

"You have company," Lydia yelled, as if she were trying to get the attention of someone across the street. No response. She plucked the remote from Abner's hand and turned off the television. "You have company," she repeated only a little more softly.

Abner finally turned toward them, his watery blue eyes as faded as the room. "Why'd you go and turn off my program?" he demanded in a thin, wobbly voice.

Lydia ignored his question. "He's deaf and won't wear his hearing aids," she explained in a quiet aside to Rory. "He's had three pair and complained about every set of them. So I've given up. I'm not throwing any more money down the drain."

So Lydia was in control of the finances, which meant she wasn't an aide or other employee. And since Rory had already noted that she wasn't wearing a wedding band, that left two options—relative or good friend. In either case, Lydia had taken on a huge burden in caring for the elderly man, and Rory's respect for her instantly quadrupled.

She stepped forward and extended her hand to Abner. "Hello, Mr. Jensen," she said, raising her voice the way Lydia had. "I'm Rory. It's so nice to meet you."

Abner gave her hand a surprisingly firm shake. "Please excuse me for not standing up."

She smiled brightly and assured him that wasn't a problem.

Lydia was busy pushing a leather hassock across the hardwood floor to her. "If you don't sit close to him, his answers won't have much to do with your questions."

"Thank you, that's perfect," Rory said taking a seat. She'd been wondering if she'd have to squeeze in next to Abner, who was planted in the middle of the small couch.

"If you need me, I'll be in the kitchen," Lydia told her. Then she looked Abner sharply in the eye. "Now, you behave yourself," she warned him, before marching out of the room.

"Celibacy," Abner grumbled. "There's much to be said for it."

Rory couldn't help laughing at the remark. "I'm sorry," she said as if she were addressing an auditorium without benefit of a microphone. "I just didn't expect you to say anything like that."

"I'm chock-full of clever and pithy things," he said cracking a smile. "But I'm afraid my dear Lydia's funny bone has dried up and withered away."

"Dear Lydia"—so she was more than just a friend after all. Maybe a longtime girlfriend and lover. Rory had a hard time picturing them in such a relationship, and since it was really none of her business, she immediately stopped trying.

"Would you mind if I asked you some questions about your family?" she asked, thinking it was a miracle Lydia wasn't permanently hoarse from constantly straining her vocal cords.

"Ask away," Abner said, using his palm to smooth down an imaginary cowlick among the few white hairs still clinging to the back of his head. He seemed thoroughly pleased to be the center of attention. He was sitting up straighter, his body no longer sagging against the soft cushions of the couch. Even his face had come alive with expression when she'd started talking to him.

"Do you know much about the Jensens who built this house?" Rory began.

"Less than I should, I'm ashamed to say. Family history never interested me much. But it intrigued my mother no end . . ."—Abner paused to catch his breath—"God rest her soul."

"Can I get you some water?" Rory asked, concerned about the grayish cast to his skin. "Should I get Lydia?"

He shook his head. "I just . . . need to pace . . . myself."

Rory waited a nervous couple of minutes and was relieved when she saw his face pinking up again.

"My mother was always telling me and my father," he resumed in a halting manner, "about every little thing she dug up about the 'first people.' That's what she called them. I don't think my father paid any more attention than I did. What I do remember is that the Jensens settled here in Tucson, and somewhere along the line, they built this house next to their general store. I think there were three children. One of them, a girl I believe, was kidnapped and murdered. A terrible tragedy in any era."

Rory was starting to worry that she'd come all this way only to find out what she already knew. No, she scolded herself. Giving up was unacceptable. Abner's memory might just need some more priming. "Do you recall hearing about a federal marshal by the name of Ezekiel Drummond in relation to the girl's death?"

Abner closed his eyes as he shuffled through the files of his memory. When he didn't open them for a while, Rory wondered if he'd fallen asleep. She was debating the best way to go about waking him without giving him a heart attack when he looked up at her again.

"I do believe I've heard that name," he said, "but I can't quite put my finger on it. Just a second." He called out for Lydia.

She came running into the room, wiping her hands on the apron she was now wearing. "What's the matter?" she asked, her brow creased with concern.

"Nothing's the matter," Abner said irritably. "If something was the matter, I probably wouldn't be able to yell for you."

Lydia shook her head and sighed as if this was an exchange they engaged in far too often. "Then what's so important that you had to interrupt me when I'm trying to make your favorite stew?"

"Remember that diary you found in the attic some years back?"

"Of course."

Rory's heart tripped into overdrive. A diary was more than she could have hoped for if she'd freed a genie from a lamp.

"Do you recall if it mentioned a federal marshal by the name of Ezekiel Drummond?" he asked.

"As a matter of fact, it did. It would be hard to forget a name like that. Why?"

"Rory here was just asking about him."

Rory realized she'd been holding her breath. If she wasn't careful she'd wind up needing a hit or two from Abner's oxygen tank. "What do you remember reading about him?" she asked, trying not to sound too deranged with excitement.

Lydia shrugged. "Just that he was after the man who killed their daughter and some other young girls. To be honest, as diaries go, it was pretty dull stuff. I skimmed through most of it."

"Do you still have it?" Rory thought she might actually cry if she found out it had been discarded.

"Of course, but the better question is where did I put it? I know I didn't take it back into the attic. It was horrible up there, and I have no intention of ever going up there again. I was almost bitten by a brown recluse spider." She shuddered at the memory. "Just give me a moment—it'll come to me."

Rory was willing to give Lydia all the moments she needed between now and her flight home. Who was she kidding? She'd pay the cancellation fee and change her flight if that's what it took to get her hands on that diary.

For ten endless minutes, Abner worked at his breathing, and Rory tried not to fidget while they waited for Lydia to have a breakthrough. Rory was about to suggest they start searching through the house for it when Lydia's face brightened, and she came as close to smiling as Rory had yet seen her. "I've got it," she declared triumphantly as she headed out of the room.

She returned holding a plastic storage bag with what looked like a thin writing tablet inside it. "It's very fragile, so I put it in the bag to help preserve it." She handed the bag to Rory. "I'm afraid we can't let you take it out of the house. Abner's determined to give all of these old things to the historical society."

"It's the least I can do," he said, "since I don't have any heirs to keep the family name going." He seemed genuinely apologetic about this failure.

"Is it okay if I stay to read it?" Rory asked, to be polite, even though it was clearly the only option they'd left her.

"Well, I don't see any other way around it," Lydia said. Not the most gracious invitation but one that Rory quickly accepted.

"I think you'll be better off sitting in the dining room," Lydia added a bit more hospitably. "That way Abner can watch his programs, and you won't have your ears blasted off."

Rory, who would have been willing to sit on a bed of nails at a drum recital in order to read the diary, gladly followed her hostess across the entry hall into the formal dining room, where sliding pocket doors helped drown out the worst of the TV noise.

"Can I get you some water?" Lydia inquired.

She was really rolling out the red carpet. Rory thanked her but declined. She was taking a seat on one of the ornate dining room chairs, eager to get started, when she noticed the portrait of a young woman on the wall across from her. Her heart quickened with recognition. The woman's hair and clothing, even the style of the painting, were clearly from an earlier era.

"Excuse me," she said, stopping Lydia who was on her way back to the kitchen. "Who's the woman in that painting?"

"That's Katherine Jensen. She and Frank were the first owners. I'm sorry, but I have to check on the stew." She was gone from the room before she finished speaking.

Rory opened her purse and took out the tube containing the sketch. When she unrolled it, she was amazed by how well it captured the woman in the painting. There was only one way that could have happened. Eloise had seen Katherine Jensen in some way, in some form. There was simply no other explanation for it. Had Katherine contacted Eloise because she wanted Rory to come here and find the diary? That sounded six shades of crazy even to Rory, who was a card-carrying member of the "I believe in ghosts" club. Surely departed souls had better things to do than co-opting old ladies and sticking their metaphorical noses into mortal affairs. Rory shook her head as if to clear her mind. Regardless of how or why she'd come to be in this house, the most important thing now was the diary that lay on the table in front of her.

Her palms were clammy with nervous anticipation as she opened the plastic bag and withdrew the tablet. Lydia was right; it was terribly fragile. The dry, Sonoran weather had taken its toll. A piece of the cardboard cover flaked off in her hand as she turned to the first page. Since she didn't know where in the diary she would find references to Zeke and since she couldn't just go flipping through the pages without causing major damage to them, she decided to start reading from the beginning. Although the writing had faded badly with time, Katherine's penmanship was impeccable. Rory had no trouble deciphering her words.

# Chapter 28

Rory boarded the plane for home with a feeling of accomplishment and several pages from the diary that Lydia had almost graciously copied for her on Abner's combination printer/copier/fax machine. She'd also been given copies of three letters that she'd found tucked into the back of the journal. Zeke was going to be thrilled. Or he would be after he got over his anger at having been duped into staying home. Only one thing niggled at her. Whatever information he'd wanted to keep from her was still a mystery. She hadn't discovered anything scandalous. There was nothing that even painted him in a bad light, other than a mother's understandable frustration with a law enforcement system that had failed to protect her child.

Aside from that, when Rory had left Abner's house that day, she'd had everything she'd come for, and since it had taken only one afternoon, she'd been left with a free day to enjoy like a real vacation. She'd been out hiking in Sabino Canyon early the next morning when Leah called.

"Sorry to be the bearer of bad tidings again," she'd said. "The woman you sketched in the SUV remains a mystery. In spite of her talent for breaking and entering, she hasn't made the criminal database, and she's not a comrade in arms. I know that isn't what you wanted to hear, but I have to admit I'm kind of glad. Contrary to conventional wisdom, there *is* such a thing as bad publicity, at least when it comes to the police."

Rory had stepped to the side of the trail to allow other hikers to pass more easily. "Hey, I'm completely with you on that. I just had to check all the possibilities."

"Could the sketch be somewhat off, because you didn't get a good enough look at her?" Leah asked.

"I could swear I did."

"Listen, you were trying to avoid a collision. That's not the best scenario for a cool-headed, objective memory of a face that flashed by you in a second."

"You've got a point," Rory grumbled, "but that doesn't get me any closer to figuring out who she is and what she has to do with my case."

"Those questions will still be around when you get home," Leah said, "so you may as well enjoy the rest of your time out there. Otherwise, that woman, whoever she is, will be guilty of stealing your vacation on top of everything else."

Rory knew she was right, but it had been difficult to let go of the disappointment. She'd resumed her hike, channeling her frustration into a faster pace that left her tee shirt clinging to her body in sweaty patches.

Back at the hotel, she'd showered and changed her clothes, then treated herself to a ridiculous lunch consisting of a chocolate-ice-cream soda and salty, greasy french fries, which made her feel a whole lot better. Her uncle Mac had introduced her to that guilty pleasure when she was nine years old. They'd made a pact back then not to tell her mother, and to the best of Rory's knowledge, her mother was still in the dark about their snacking habits.

After that she'd spent the rest of the afternoon relaxing in the shade of a palm tree at the hotel pool, questions about the mystery woman temporarily deep-sixed beneath a sugary, fat-filled high. She couldn't remember the last time she'd felt so marvelously unfettered. No one was expecting anything of her—no family members, no Way Off Broadway Players, no deceased marshal, no Hobo. Although, to be honest, she was beginning to miss the dog.

By the time she'd settled into another middle seat for the flight home, she was feeling mellow enough not to care that she was wedged in between two oversize men. She even managed to fall asleep for a few minutes. But her "mellow" ended abruptly when she was awakened by a tap on her shoulder. Judging by the reactions of the two men, she realized she must have jumped up from her seat as if she'd been poked with a cattle prod.

"Didn't mean to scare you, miss," said the man in the window seat. "I just need to get out to the bathroom."

Rory tried to gather her wits as she stood up and followed the man in the aisle seat out of the row. She was still half expecting to see Zeke, or parts of him, floating nearby. But since none of the passengers looked like they'd seen a ghost, her heart slipped out of her throat and back into her chest, where it belonged.

Once she and her seatmates were reinstalled in their designated places, she withdrew the journal pages from her handbag. There were a lot of entries in the diary that she hadn't asked Lydia to copy for her. Since they weren't pertinent to Zeke's quest, there was no need for him to see them. They'd been difficult enough for her to read, and that was with a buffer of more than a hundred and thirty years and no direct connection to the family.

In those pages, Katherine Jensen had described the way they'd struggled with the loss of Betsy. Her husband, Frank, devoured by an angry sadness, worked late every night until sleep felled him at his desk, where she would find him in the morning. Their sons put up a brave front in public rather than risk being ridiculed by the other boys, but Katherine heard their breathless sobs during the night. Then there was her own exquisite pain, which hollowed her out, leaving a deep numbness in its wake, so that for a long time, she could hardly feel anything at all.

Remembering her words was enough to make tears spring up in Rory's eyes again. She clenched her jaw and blinked them away before anyone could notice. The last thing she wanted to do was draw the stares and curiosity of an airplane full of people. She quickly unfolded the less emotional entries she had with her and got busy reading them for the second time.

*July 9th*

*A stranger came into the store today asking for Frank. He had a hard look to him, the kind of look that makes gentle folks shrink back. I can't imagine why such a man would know my husband by name. Before I could excuse myself to find Frank, he came out of the storeroom carrying a twenty-pound sack of flour. Upon seeing me in conversation with the stranger, he dropped the sack on the floor and made straight for us. I don't know how to describe the expression on his face. It was both grim and pleased, and I would be happy not to ever see it again. He called the man Hargrave but made no attempt to introduce him to me, which I find peculiar, because my Frank has always been the politest of men. He led this Hargrave back to the storeroom and shut the door*

*behind them. They came out less than ten minutes later,
and Hargrave walked past me and out of the store without so much as a "thank you, ma'am" or "good day."*

*July 10th*

*Frank told me that he has contracted with Hargrave to
find John Trask, so that he may be brought to justice for
taking the life of our daughter, Betsy. Although I understand and share his desire to see Trask punished, it will
not bring Betsy back. I don't like the idea of Frank dealing with a man of such low principles. I fear that no
good will come of their association.*

*July 11th*

*I was setting out the new bolts of material in the store
this morning when I overheard Frank speaking in a
hushed voice with his brother Max. He was telling Max
that he'd instructed the gunman to kill Marshal Drummond as well. He said it cost double for the marshal as
he's a lawman. I could scarcely credit what I was hearing. This does not sound at all like the Frank Jensen I
married. As soon as we were alone, I questioned Frank
about it, and he did not deny any of it. When I tried to
reason with him, he told me to stick to women's business
and leave men's business to him.*

*July 25th*

*Two weeks have passed, and to the best of my knowl-
edge, Frank has not heard anything from his hired gun.
Perhaps this is why he is so impatient and irritable with
the children and me. I know what troubles him, but the
boys have no idea. Noah has told me that he misses the*

*father he once had. I try to comfort him. Nothing is the same anymore.*

*August 5th*

*Frank is of the opinion that something has gone amiss with Hargrave. He asks everyone, especially strangers who stop into the store on their journeys, if they've heard of a gunfighter meeting his end. So far no one has.*

*August 6th*

*When Frank is not busy at the store, he comes home and paces from room to room, locked in his own thoughts and misery. I have tried talking to him, but he tells me to let him be. I feel like I'm losing another part of my family.*

*August 10th*

*Frank is gone. He woke me before dawn to tell me he was leaving. He said he must find out what became of Hargrave. If all went according to plan, the gunman would have returned for the rest of his money. If he needed more time, he was supposed to send word about his progress. They'd shaken hands on the deal. I didn't point out that a handshake with a hired gun was not likely to be worth much. Frank already knows this, but he has clearly chosen to ignore it. When I told him I don't know how I will manage the children, the house and the store by myself, he said he had faith in me. There was nothing more for me to say. I could tell by the emptiness in his voice that he had already left.*

As Rory read the copied letters, she had the uncomfortable sense that someone else was reading along with her.

She glanced to her left and met the startled eyes of the man in the aisle seat. He gave her a sheepish smile before quickly looking the other way. She refolded the pages and stowed them back in her handbag. She really shouldn't be expecting privacy in an airplane, where people were crammed together like sardines in a high-altitude tin can. Reading the letters again would have to wait until she was home. She plucked the airline magazine from the seat pocket in front of her but found it hard to concentrate on the articles about great places to visit and expensive items to buy. The diary and letters were still uppermost in her mind, as they had been from the moment she'd first read them. One question in particular refused to be silenced or ignored. Why had Frank Jensen hired Hargrave to kill the marshal too?

# Chapter 29

"I don't take kindly to bein' deceived," Zeke said, his eyebrows lowering like dark clouds before an advancing storm. He was standing in the hallway outside Rory's bedroom, watching her unpack. His hair looked more disheveled than usual, as if he hadn't taken the time to "comb" it in his rush to confront her.

"I never lied to you," she said calmly as she slid two tee shirts into the top dresser drawer.

"But you did trick me, so own up to it. Don't go playin' semantics with me."

Rory looked up at him, realizing a second too late that her expression was a dead giveaway.

"Surprised I know a word like that?" he asked with the sly smile of the cat who'd just caught the mouse pilfering cheese. "It's never wise to underestimate me, darlin', in any respect."

"Look, I just needed to get away," she said in a cajoling tone, "and I figured if I mixed a little business with pleasure

I could deduct the trip as a business expense." It was a good thing she could think fast on her feet. The excuse even sounded genuine to her.

"No, you're not gettin' off that easy," Zeke said apparently not buying any of it. "The truth is, you didn't want me gettin' in your way out there. I believe in callin' a pig a pig if it wallows in mud and oinks."

Rory started to shake her head.

"Don't you try denyin' it. It's past time for some straight talk here."

"Okay," she said. If he was insisting on the bare-naked truth, she would give it to him. She walked over to the doorway, stopping inches from him, the threshold between the bedroom and the hall lying between them like a disputed boundary between hostile nations. "You've been so paranoid about keeping some secret or other from me that I thought you'd prevent me from finding out anything, including the name of your killer." She was speaking in a calm, reasonable voice, hoping to keep the tension between them from escalating. "I can't work in handcuffs or with blinders on."

Zeke didn't have an immediate comeback for her. Judging by his unsettled expression, he seemed to be wrangling with her accusation, trying to decide what response would best serve him.

"Why are you so concerned that I'll find out this secret of yours?" she went on. "Everyone has something they're not proud of. How awful could it be?"

"Why do you feel the need to stick your nose into business that ain't yours?" he countered.

"Your life became my business when you insisted I find out who killed you," Rory reminded him, her tone sharpening in spite of her efforts at détente.

"Well then, I'm takin' you off the case."

"Too late. I already have the answer," she shot back. "And as it happens, that's all I found out. So it seems your big secret went to the grave with you." Damn, this wasn't at all how she'd imagined telling him that in spite of all odds, she'd found out who'd killed him. Talk about blowing a presentation.

The news seemed to hit Zeke like a round from a .45, his image wavering under the impact. "What . . . what are you saying?" he asked, stumbling over his words. "You know . . . you know for honest and true who shot me?"

"Yes." Rory had never seen the marshal quite so off balance before, and she had to admit that she was probably enjoying his discomfort more than she should. But he was the one who'd insisted she continue the search her uncle Mac had started, and now that she'd succeeded, he was acting like a pro surfer pulled under by a wave he hadn't seen coming.

"Do you plan on sharin' that information with me anytime soon?" he asked once he'd regained some of his composure.

"I think you should read it for yourself so that you get the context and all." Rory had come to that conclusion during the flight home. News of this magnitude needed to be couched in the proper terms.

"Why can't you just give me the answer without all the fanfare?"

"Humor me, please."

"Fine," he grumbled, "but I'm not a patient man."

"Gee, I never would have guessed that on my own." She wriggled past him and took the stairs down to the bench in the entryway, where she'd left her handbag.

When she walked into the kitchen, the marshal was pacing around the center island as if he'd been waiting untold hours for her to arrive. Hobo, who'd been passed out under the table after the excitement of her homecoming, was now pacing at Zeke's heels like a mutant shadow. The dog looked up at Rory with a baffled expression that clearly asked why the marshal and he were going in circles.

Since Rory couldn't offer an explanation he would understand, she shook her head and smiled in commiseration. The marshal was often an enigma to her too. She set her handbag on the table and pulled out the photocopies of the diary and letters. As soon as she put the thin stack of them at Zeke's usual seat, he abandoned his pacing and his faithful shadow to pop into his chair. Hobo lay down beside the island as if prepared to follow should the marshal choose to continue his strange journey.

Rory took a seat beside Zeke in case he became too excited or overwrought to turn the pages without flinging them across the room. Apparently of the same mind, Zeke didn't even try to turn them himself. Instead, he gave a little nod as he finished reading each page. Although he didn't make any comments while going through the diary entries, when he reached the one about Frank hiring Hargrave, she noticed his jaw tighten. It wasn't until he started reading the letters that Rory was able to see waves of emotion pulling at his face.

*August 22, 1878*

*My dearest Katherine,*

*I have been gone for nearly two weeks, and I already miss you and our boys desperately. Please be assured that I would never have left if there had been any other way. I discovered today that Hargrave's body was found in an abandoned barn in the New Mexico Territory, half a day's ride from Albuquerque. He'd been shot to death, but no one seems to know by whose gun. I must assume that Hargrave found either Trask or Drummond and was in the end outgunned. I am left with one last choice in this matter. I can look for these men myself, or I can give up and come home. Please trust that I have* searched my heart well before deciding to continue on. Were I to come home now with this business left unfinished, I would not be able to live with myself, and over time you and the children would also find it impossible to live with me.

Your devoted husband,
Frank

August 28, 1878

My dearest Katherine,

Time has lost all meaning for me. I sleep when my eyes will no longer stay open. I eat when there is time and food available. I count myself lucky that there have been enough sightings of Trask and Drummond to make tracking them possible. It came as something of a surprise to me that the marshal had left his jurisdiction and is hunting Trask too. I wonder if guilt pushes him, or if he is driven only by the habit of his profession. In any case it makes my work easier. I will write again when I can.

Your loving husband,
Frank

September 7, 1878

My dearest Katherine,

I had to leave my horse in Colorado and continue by train to New York City and then onto the Long Island. At a farmhouse in a town called Huntington, I finally caught up with both Trask and Drummond. As fate *would have it, I came upon them in a rather dramatic standoff. The marshal had his revolver on Trask, who was holding a young woman at gunpoint. I did not allow myself to think about what I was about to do for fear that my resolve might come undone. There is no need for you to know the details of what transpired there. Suffice it to say that I sent the marshal to his reckoning and wounded Trask, although he managed to get away on horseback. Once I saw that the girl was in no grave danger, I took off after him and tracked him to another town, where he had stopped to seek medical attention. At the first opportunity, I dispatched him to what I can only believe is his eternal damnation.*

*I send this letter to you as I am about to board the train to make my way home. I ache to see you and the boys again even as I wrestle with the knowledge that I have become a killer myself. Yet for me that is an easier pain to live with than the pain of letting our Betsy's death go unpunished. I will not try to justify my actions by claiming that I did it to save other young girls from the same fate, because this was not an act of altruism. It is important to me that there be no lies between us.*

*Please embrace our boys for me and tell them I will be home before too much longer.*

> *Your loving husband,*
> *Frank*

Zeke vanished from his chair the instant he finished reading the third letter. Before Rory could ask if he was okay. Before even offering her a "thank you."

"You're welcome," she called out to him and then was immediately sorry for the sarcasm in her tone. She wasn't being fair. She shouldn't be putting etiquette before compassion. Big deal if he hadn't rushed right out and sent her a thank-you bouquet. The guy deserved a break. He'd waited for more than a hundred years to find out the truth about his death. It was understandable if he needed some time alone to absorb it all. She was always criticizing Zeke for his lack of patience, and now it seemed she could use a few lessons in that gentle art herself. Where had she misplaced her much-vaunted sensitivity for that matter? By the time Rory finished scolding herself, she felt positively wretched. Apologizing would make her feel better, but without Zeke, there was no one to apologize to. She'd just have to keep busy until he was ready to return.

In that spirit, she headed back upstairs to finish unpacking her things. Hobo trotted past her and had already made himself comfortable on her pillow when she reached the bedroom. He remained asleep there even after she'd put away the suitcase and gone into the study to deal with what was sure to be a ridiculous amount of e-mail that had accumulated while she was gone. She was waiting for the computer to boot up when she noticed the sheet of paper lying in the printer tray. It turned out to be from a Pennsylvania newspaper dated April 2, 2003, and it contained several short articles and a photograph. Either Zeke had printed the page for her to see, or Hobo had recently grown an opposable thumb and an interest in detective work. Her money was on the marshal.

She was immediately drawn to the headline, "Suicide Linked to Scam." But when she started reading the article, the very first line made her stop short.

*York, Pennsylvania: Police have named Thomas Kent a person of interest in the Ponzi-like scheme that may have led to the suicide death of Jill Harrison.*

"Thomas Kent"—the name rang a bell in Rory's mind, though she couldn't quite place it. She assumed that since

Zeke had left the printout for her, the article had to be related to Brian's death, but she couldn't see the connection. She held the paper directly under the desk lamp to get a better look at the small photograph. It showed two women in their late thirties or early forties decked out in evening clothes. The caption beneath the photo read, "Jill Harrison with her sister Paula Imperiali in happier times." Rory stared at the picture more puzzled than ever. Although she'd never heard either woman's name before, she immediately recognized the woman identified as Paula.

# Chapter 30

Paula Imperiali's face had been etched into Rory's mind when she came barreling down the center of the road, forcing Rory onto the shoulder. She was the woman Rory had sketched and asked Leah to run through the police database. No matter how much some women teased their hair or how much mascara and lipstick they applied, they never really looked any different. Paula, with her sharp features and utilitarian haircut, was clearly one of them.

Rory sat back in her chair, thoughts swirling madly around in her head like lights from a disco ball. She wished Zeke was there so she could ask him how he'd found the article and if he'd printed it out only because he too had recognized Paula from the sketch. Since Rory had no idea when Zeke might return, she did a Google search that turned up several women who shared the name "Paula Imperiali." But with only a name to go by, even Google wasn't much help in narrowing the field. In the best of all possible worlds, one of the Paulas would have been listed as a skilled break-in

artist and stunt driver. That not being the case, Rory set
aside the article and her questions until Zeke was "back in
town" and resigned herself to tackling the fifty-two e-mails
waiting in her inbox.

She'd made it through a quarter of the e-mails when she
remembered why the name "Thomas Kent" was familiar
to her. It was one of the aliases Brian had used as he'd hop-
scotched across the country, leaving misery in his wake.
Zeke had suggested doing Google searches of the names on
all the false IDs to see if he could round up any useful clues,
but until now the results had been dismal. While Rory was
away in Tucson, he'd obviously hit pay dirt with the "Thomas
Kent" pseudonym. It occurred to her that she might be able
to follow up on the trail Zeke had left her. If she could learn
more about these sisters, she might find a clue to the con
man's killer. She logged out of her e-mail account and found
her way to the newspaper from which Zeke had printed the
article. Then she checked the obituaries for that day. No
mention of Jill Harrison. Rory checked the previous day's
obits and found it there. According to the short memorial
column, Jill had lived a normal, unremarkable life and had
been well loved by family and friends, who were all devastated by her loss. She was survived by her husband, Daniel;
her son, Ryan; her sister, Paula Imperiali; and her mother,
Dorothy Johnson.

Rory had to read the name twice to make sure she hadn't
misread it the first time. Helene had never mentioned that
her colleague had lost a child. Of course, Helene had joined
the troupe less than a year ago, and it was entirely possible
that Dorothy was a private sort of person who chose to keep
her pain a private matter. But it did help explain why she
kept so busy. Less time to think about the unthinkable.

Rory sat back in her chair as the weight of this new information settled upon her shoulders like a coat of lead. A disturbing image of the elderly woman being led off to prison in handcuffs and shackles ran through her mind. As difficult as it was to accept, Dorothy had the best motive of all for killing Brian. Not to mention a broken foot that could have occurred in the commission of the assault. But Brian outclassed her in age and weight and testosterone. Any physical match between them would have made the battle of David and Goliath look like a bout sanctioned by the most reputable boxing associations. If her daughter Paula had been on the trip, it would have been easier to believe that *she'd* been the one who'd slammed Brian's head into the rocky canyon wall, knocking him unconscious to drown in the flood waters. But Paula's part in the crime seemed limited to trying to scare Rory off the case and breaking into her house to leave messages directing her attention to other suspects. If the murder had happened under different circumstances, Dorothy might have had the time to enlist someone else's help, but premeditation wasn't possible given the nature of a flash flood.

In any case, all of this was pure conjecture. Dorothy and Paula were the only ones with the answers, and Rory needed to find a way to question the two women. She knew where to find Dorothy, but Paula proved to be another story. Even her phone number was unlisted. Rory toyed briefly with the idea of getting Leah involved. Very briefly, because once the police knew what she'd discovered, they'd take over completely. What was the point of doing all the legwork in an investigation if you didn't get to actually take down the bad guys? There had to be a shrink somewhere who would agree that Rory deserved to have "closure" in her work. Of course, Leah would brush that off as so much psychobabble. And Zeke could be counted on to deliver a stern, make that outraged, lecture on her foolhardy, strong-headed impulsiveness. Rory decided it was probably a good thing he wasn't around right now.

A fter a restless night of listening to Hobo snort and snore his way through an entire symphony of noises, Rory was exhausted, but she'd come up with a plan of action. She brewed a pot of strong coffee and let the dog out to take care of his necessities. Then, coffee in hand and Hobo underfoot, she went up to the study to create a mysterious note of her own. It was short and to the point, and with any luck it would produce the desired result.

*I know what you did, Dorothy, and why you did it. I also know what Paula's been up to. Bright and early tomorrow, I'm going to enlighten the police.*

Rory hit "print," and the machine spat out the note. She plucked it off the printer tray, folded it and slipped it into an envelope, which she addressed to Dorothy, leaving no return address. She didn't need a stamp, since she intended to deliver it herself.

She dressed in jeans and a short-sleeved tee shirt, since the weatherman called for warming temperatures, and set about putting her plan into action. Her .45 nested in her handbag, along with two pair of plastic cuffs, just in case. She'd promised her conscience, which had begun to resemble Zeke in her mind, that she'd call the police if things started to get out of hand. Of course, she'd never been a particularly good judge of that moment just before the scales tipped against her.

At nine o'clock she called Dorothy's home, drumming her fingers on the kitchen counter as she listened to the phone ring. When Dorothy finally picked it up, she was breathing hard.

"Am I speaking to Mrs. Johnson?" Rory asked in the deepest voice she could affect.

"Yes. What can I do for you?" Dorothy sounded rushed.

"We're conducting a poll of TV viewers' preferences. It will only take about twenty minutes, if you'd—"

"No, no. I'm sorry." Rushed and flustered. "I'm already late for rehearsal." She hung up before Rory could say anything else, which was fine with her. She'd found out what she needed to know. Dorothy was at home but would be leaving momentarily for an early rehearsal.

Rory drove to East Northport, stopping around the corner from Dorothy's house. To be sure nothing else had happened to delay the actress's departure, she keyed Dorothy's number into her cell. This time the phone rang until the voice mail picked up. Rory didn't leave a message. Everything she had to say was in the note she was about to deliver.

She pulled to the curb beside Dorothy's mailbox, tucked the letter inside it and was on her way home in less than a minute. She'd originally planned to stake out the house all day and into the night if necessary until Dorothy returned, found the letter, and Paula showed up in response to what Rory assumed would be her mother's frantic call. At least that was how Rory had envisioned the scenario playing out. But since Dorothy had mentioned she was on her way to rehearsal, Rory and her bladder had been granted a reprieve. Dorothy would be gone for hours. For a better idea of just how many, Rory placed a call to the theater.

"Stuart Dobson." With just the few syllables of his name, the troupe's director managed to convey his irritation with whoever had the audacity to interrupt his work.

Rory would gladly have called her aunt Helene's cell instead, but she knew that Dobson forbade all cell phone use during rehearsals. Except, of course, his own.

"Hello," Rory said, going for the flat, robotic voice of a thoroughly bored secretary chewing a thick wad of gum.

"What time was it you wanted our cleaning crew to be there?"

"Cleaning crew? What are you talking about?" Dobson's irritation was growing thicker by the second.

"I've got a work order here with your address."

"I didn't arrange for any cleaning crew."

"Are you the owner of the premises?"

"No, I'm a tenant."

"I guess your landlord made the arrangements," she said, adding a good dash of testiness to her tone. Dobson always brought out the worst in her. "So when do you want the crew there?"

"Fine," Dobson snapped. "Two. And not a minute sooner." He ended the call.

Rory was sure he would have loved having an old fashioned phone at that moment, one with a receiver he could have slammed down in anger.

Figuring travel time from Bay Shore to East Northport, Dorothy wouldn't be home until two thirty, at which point she'd look through the mail, read the anonymous note and immediately place a panicked call to her daughter. Although Rory had no idea how far away Paula lived, it was reasonable to assume that she wouldn't make it to her mother's side much before three. Rory planned to be there first. That way she and Dorothy would have time for a nice, private chat before Paula arrived.

# Chapter 31

O n her ride home after dropping off the letter, Rory called Clarissa to update her on the progress in her son's case. Ordinarily, she would have waited to make that call after the day's events played out, but she wanted to confirm something Clarissa had said when she'd hired her.

"I was going to give you a call today," Clarissa said after they'd exchanged pleasantries.

"I'm sorry I wasn't in touch sooner," Rory apologized, "but I didn't have much to report back until now."

"That sounds promising."

"As you'd anticipated, almost everyone on the trip with your son had a good motive to kill him. It was only yesterday that we had a significant breakthrough." Rory went on to explain what she and Zeke had discovered.

"You're certain it was this woman Dorothy Johnson?" Clarissa asked, the reservation in her voice hard to miss.

"I know it doesn't seem possible that an elderly woman

could take on your son and win, but you have to remember the circumstances were unique and chaotic."

Clarissa still didn't seem convinced. Not that Rory could blame her. She'd had difficulty accepting the unlikely scenario herself. It would be a lot easier to sell her client on the idea when she had all the facts and, more importantly, a confession.

"I expect to interview Dorothy later today," she said, "and I'll be in touch afterward. But I do have a question for you."

"Sure, anything if it will help."

"When we first spoke, you said you had no interest in asking the police to reopen the case or in prosecuting anyone. Do you still feel that way?"

Clarissa didn't pause to consider her answer, and when she spoke, there was no reluctance in her voice. "Nothing's changed. If Brian had lived, he would have hurt and defrauded more innocent people. Regardless of who killed him or for what reason, the case will remain closed. It's just my heart that needs the answers. Why do you ask?"

"I can't explain it all now, but if I need a bargaining chip that fact might be useful."

Reiterating that she would call Clarissa back later, Rory thanked her and said good-bye.

With several hours to kill before she went back to Dorothy's house at one thirty, Rory spent the time catching up on paperwork for her smaller cases, paying bills, balancing her checkbook, more or less, and playing Frisbee with Hobo until they were both out of breath. Then they shared a tuna sandwich and a couple of Oreos—she had the chocolate wafers, Hobo had the creamy centers.

When she looked at her watch she was surprised to see that it was not yet one o'clock. Time seemed to be marching one step forward, two steps back.

For the fourth time, she checked to make sure her .45 was in her handbag, along with her digital recorder in case she was lucky enough to get a confession from one or both of her suspects. There was nothing left to be done. She sat down to read the newspaper, but couldn't make it through a single article. Although she could generally count on the TV for some mindless distraction, she couldn't find a program to hold her attention. She finally gave up and wandered restlessly from room to room.

What exactly was she hoping to find? As she passed through the kitchen on her third lap, it hit her—she was looking for Zeke. She imagined him leaning back in his chair at the table, dirty boots crossed casually on the glass surface, his mouth twitching with amusement or grim with a scowl. She could imagine him in every room of the house, haunting her more with his absence than he had with his presence.

Surely a day was enough time to come to terms with the name of his killer. Rory still didn't understand why knowing who'd pulled the trigger was so important to him anyway. When so much time had passed, knowing changed nothing. And then, with a peculiar tug in her chest, she realized she was wrong. He'd said it so often that she'd stopped paying attention to the words. "I'm not going anywhere until I know the name of the coward who shot me in the back."

Now, thanks to her efforts, he knew. Rory fell back against the refrigerator as if she'd had the wind knocked out of her. Was it possible he'd left the moment he had his answer? Had he rushed straight toward the light or whatever signpost led the way out of his self-imposed limbo? No, she refused to believe that. It wasn't at all like Zeke. No way would he have left without at least saying "good-bye." Unless maybe she didn't know him as well as she thought she did. She was arguing both sides of the issue and getting nowhere. But since no one else knew about Zeke, there was no one she could go to for another, more objective opinion. No one except Eloise. And Rory had no doubt that if Eloise had important information to convey, she would have already come knocking on the door.

There was a time early on in Rory's strange relationship with the marshal when the prospect of never seeing him again might have actually lifted her spirits. That time had long passed though, because the thought of his permanent absence was dragging at her heart. To counteract her melancholy, she made a mental list of all his irritating ways, his caveman view of women, his too easily wounded pride, his disgust with modern values. She told herself that life would be easier without him and that her business would do just fine without his services. And she almost managed to convince herself it was true. She was so locked in this internal dialogue that she jumped when the telephone rang.

"This is Eloise," said the voice on the other end of the line. Speak of the devil.

"Hi," Rory replied. It wasn't her neighbor's "little girl without a care" voice. It was her "I'm on a mission" voice, which generally didn't bode well.

"You need to be very careful, or something terrible is going to happen."

The last time Eloise had been so cryptic, Brian had drowned in the flood. But before Rory could ask for more details, there was a click on the line followed by dead air.

Rory started to call her back but stopped before she'd punched in all the numbers. Eloise had always been as forthcoming as she was able to be. If she didn't say more, it was because she didn't have more to say. Great—that sounded like one of Zeke's pronouncements. She tried to relax the little knot of anxiety that was tightening in her chest by assuring herself that if she were careful, everything would be fine. Isn't that what Eloise had implied? Rory just wished the warning had been less ambiguous.

She glanced at her watch. In spite of how busy her mind

was, the hands on the watch were still barely inching their way around the dial. She felt like a hare living on snail time.

Ironically, when one thirty finally rolled around, it took her by complete surprise. Someone was messing with the space-time continuum, she thought as she grabbed her handbag, and there was no Captain Kirk around to put it right.

# Chapter 32

W hen Rory reached Dorothy's block, she did another quick drive-by of the actress's house to assess the situation. She recognized her pale blue Kia in the driveway. Okay, she was home, and there was no second car there, which meant Paula had not yet arrived.

Rory parked farther down the street so as not to give Paula a heads-up that someone else had beaten her there. The more unexpected Rory was, the more control she'd have over how the meeting played out. And given Eloise's dire warning, "caution" was the watchword of the day.

Before ringing Dorothy's bell, Rory turned on the recorder. When the actress asked who was there, she cheerfully called out her name.

"Rory?" Dorothy sounded perplexed as she opened the door. "What are you doing here?"

It was a good bet she'd read the mystery note, because the Dorothy that Rory had known up until then had always been a model of politeness. She would never have been so abrupt and unwelcoming unless she'd recently been thrown for a double-wide loop. Dorothy's eyes were flitting all over the place. They lit briefly on Rory again before jumping past her to scour the street as if she were expecting someone else. Rory had a pretty good idea who that might be.

"Dorothy," she said firmly to reel in the older woman's attention. "I need to talk to you about something. May I come in for a minute?"

"Come in?" Dorothy repeated as if it were a concept she couldn't quite wrap her mind around.

"It's important or I wouldn't bother you."

Dorothy's eyes focused briefly on Rory. "No, no this isn't a good time. It's not a good time at all." Then her gaze darted back to the street again.

"We really do have to talk," Rory said crossing the threshold into the house and effectively forcing Dorothy to step back out of the way.

"But I'm waiting for—" she started to protest.

"I know, you're waiting for Paula."

Dorothy looked at her as if she'd just pulled a rabbit out of a hat along with its extended family. "How did you know?"

"Come sit down, and I'll explain everything," Rory said more gently. She closed the door and took hold of the actress's forearm to help her into the living room, since she hadn't taken her cane when she'd gone to answer the bell.

Dorothy allowed herself to be led to the sofa, with its bright country plaid and softly ruffled skirt. Rory took the matching armchair to her right and set her handbag on her lap, unzipped to provide better access to her gun, even though she didn't think she'd need it, and better clarity for the recorder.

"First of all," she said with complete sincerity, "I want to tell you how terribly sorry I was to learn that you'd lost your daughter Jill. No mother should ever have to lose a child. It doesn't matter if they're five or forty-five."

Tears instantly sprang up in Dorothy's eyes. She shook her head, clearly too choked up to speak. Rory was sorry she'd had to broach such a difficult subject, but since it might well be the reason Brian was dead, she'd had no choice. While she waited patiently for Dorothy to regain her composure, she did an in-depth study of her cuticles, which looked as if they could benefit from some moisturizing the next time she had nothing to do. After a minute or two, Dorothy plucked a tissue from the decorative box on the end table between the couch and armchair and loudly blew her nose.

"Thank you for your kind words," she whispered, as if her throat was too constricted with emotion to permit the passage of a louder sound.

"Until the other day, I had no idea what you'd been through or that Jill had been one of Brian's victims," Rory said, proceeding gently.

Dorothy exhaled a shaky sigh. "She and Daniel—that's her husband—lost most of what they'd worked so hard to save for the past twenty years, and Jill took complete responsibility for it. You see, Daniel teaches high school music there in York. He's a great guy and a talented musician, but he never had much of a head for finance. Jill always took care of that stuff. She was good at it too. She invested in the market and built up a nice portfolio, from what she told me. Then Brian came to town with his tricks and promises. Back then he was using the name Thomas Kent."

"How awful," Rory said, trying to imagine how deep Jill's despair must have been for her to take her own life. Brian had essentially loaded the gun, handed it to her and dared her to pull the trigger. "Did you know who Brian was when he joined the troupe?" Rory asked.

Dorothy shook her head. "I'd never met him before, and when he joined the troupe he was using the name Preston so I had no way to put the two together."

"Then how did you figure out who he was?"

"My daughter Paula did. She'd met him once when she was in York visiting her sister. Then when she came to see our last play, there he was on stage right smack in front of her."

"It must have been a terrible shock for you to find out you'd been working so closely with the man who'd brought such tragedy into your life."

Dorothy sighed again. "You have no idea."

"How were you able to stay with the troupe after that?" Rory knew she was close to crossing the line between merely nosy and downright obnoxious, but she didn't have the luxury of time to get at the answers she needed. And so far, Dorothy didn't appear offended by her questions. In fact, she seemed strangely willing to uncork the story that was bottled up inside her.

"It wasn't easy being around him every day, but Paula and I had a plan. I'd do my best to draw him out and keep tabs on him until she could gather enough evidence to put him away for the rest of his miserable life."

"Didn't she go to the police?" Rory asked, knowing full well that she hadn't but hoping the answer might clear up the question of where Paula had come by her lock-picking, alarm-thwarting, stunt-driving ways.

"Paula's with the FBI," Dorothy said, a note of pride poking through her sadness.

So Zeke was right. And FBI training would account for a lot. It would even explain why someone with a patent disregard for certain laws hadn't turned up as a frequent flyer when Leah ran her sketch through the police database.

"Even so," Dorothy went on, "she was having a hard time backtracking on Brian's trail and getting enough evidence to put him away for more than a few years." The actress leaned in closer to Rory. "She was getting so frustrated, she even hinted she might take matters into her own hands."

By "matters," Rory assumed the actress meant "justice."

She wondered if Paula had ever "taken matters into her own hands" on previous occasions and if that was why Eloise had issued her warning.

"If anything happened to Paula, I don't know what I'd do." Dorothy's voice cracked and tears flooded her eyes again.

Rory pulled out another tissue for her. "When the flash flood came, it must have seemed like perfect timing," she said, like a friend commiserating with her.

Dorothy was nodding and sniffling, but instead of using the tissue to blot her eyes or blow her nose, she was kneading it between her fingers like worry beads.

"I haven't known you for very long," Rory said softly, "but I've always been good at reading people." Okay, with the exception of falling for the man who'd murdered Mac nearly a year ago. But Dorothy didn't need to know about that. "And I can tell you're a moral person. You live your life always doing what's right. Then one day, life deals you an awful blow, a blow that almost does you in. And you start wondering why there's no justice in this world." She paused to shake her head. "I can't even imagine what it's been like for you." She'd expected this interview to be difficult, but she'd had no idea just how difficult. A sizeable part of her wanted to stop right there. To move to the couch beside the older woman, draw her into a hug and tell her she understood and that she would keep her secret safe. But Rory had been hired to find out the truth about Brian's death. She'd spent hours debating how best to approach Dorothy in order to elicit a confession. It came down to two basic options. She could come right out and accuse Dorothy of murder. But such a direct approach often ignited a person's defenses and resulted in a stubborn refusal to capitulate. Or she could try to slide in under the actress's radar with understanding and compassion. Rory had opted for the latter. At the time, it had seemed more humane. Now, she wasn't so sure. In any case, it was too late to start rethinking her strategy.

Dorothy was biting her lower lip; the tissue lay shredded in her lap.

Rory swallowed around a growing lump in her own throat, gave herself a quick pep talk and pushed on. "It's pretty rare, but sometimes fate offers up an opportunity to right a wrong, you know, square things a bit."

Dorothy's head bobbed up and down. Whether she knew where Rory was heading or not, she'd clearly bought a ticket for the ride.

Outside, someone slammed a car door shut. Rory had been on high alert for that very sound. Paula had no reason to proceed by stealth, no reason to suspect that anyone was there with her mother. Mired in emotion, Dorothy didn't even react to the sound.

"A saint would have had trouble ignoring an opportunity like that," Rory said with authority, as if she'd recently taken a poll of saints on that very topic. As she talked she slid her hand inside her pocketbook, where her fingers curled around the grip of the .45. Since Dorothy was staring off into space, probably stuck in the memory loop of what had happened during the flood, Rory managed to withdraw the gun and hide it between the bag and her body so that neither Dorothy nor Paula would be able to see it. "I know if I had been in your shoes, I would have looked at the flood as that kind of cosmic opportunity."

Dorothy stopped nodding, but she didn't try to deny anything. She looked at Rory a bit bewildered, as if she were surprised to find herself in a place she didn't remember heading to.

"I imagine the rushing water knocked you off your feet at first, but then you must have found something to hold on to; maybe there was a rock or a ledge?" Rory prompted, to move the story along. Time was almost up for their private chat.

"A ledge," Dorothy said, picking up the narrative in a

weak monotone. "And a second later the water swept Brian right to me. He was floundering, trying to find something to hold on to. That's when I kicked him. Not hard. I didn't think it was hard enough to do much damage, but his head must have hit the canyon wall." Her shoulders heaved with a quiet sob, and tears began to stream down her cheeks. "I'm not even sorry he's dead." She made a few halfhearted attempts to wipe the tears away with her hands, but when they kept coming, she gave up, leaving them to run down her face and puddle on her shirt.

Rory was glad the recorder was taking down the actress's confession, because she'd had to shift most of her attention to listening for footsteps or any sound that would tell her if Paula was coming in the front door, which was close to where they were sitting, or the back door, through the kitchen. Although Rory had no intentions of using the recording against the actress, she thought it might come in handy when she was negotiating with Paula. Of course, that was based on the premise that words, not bullets, would be flying.

She finally heard the sound of the back door lock being engaged and opened, followed by the creaking of the old hinges. She trained her eyes on the doorway where the hall led from the kitchen into the living room. Paula would be appearing there any moment. Rory tightened her hand around the gun thinking, not for the first time, that waiting in a highly charged situation deserved its very own ring in Dante's version of Hell.

# Chapter 33

Dorothy had stopped talking, although she didn't appear to have heard her daughter enter the house. She was once again staring off into space.

"You probably didn't even care if you drowned in the flood," Rory said without taking her eyes off the doorway. She needed to keep Dorothy talking so she could record as much of the confession as possible before they were interrupted.

"I didn't care," Dorothy echoed her words. "And it would have been easier that way . . . so much easier." She'd started rocking back and forth like a small child trying to comfort herself. "So much easier."

"Don't say another word," Paula commanded. She was framed in the doorway holding a forty-caliber Glock, standard issue for an FBI agent. Her dramatic entrance had roused Dorothy out of her nearly hypnotic stupor. She jumped at the sound of her daughter's voice. "Paula!" She admonished her, clutching at the tear-drenched shirt over her heart, "You scared me half to death."

"I was trying to stop you from confessing to a crime you didn't commit," Paula snapped in a "you've got to be kidding me" tone of voice. "You should be thanking me instead of complaining."

"Oh no, I didn't mean to complain, dear, but . . ." Dorothy was squirming in her seat as she looked from her daughter to Rory and back again. She seemed distressed to be having a family argument in front of company.

Paula advanced into the room. "McCain's not a cop," she said ignoring her mother's discomfort. "She's just a busybody for hire. You don't have to talk to her. Hell, you didn't even have to let her in the house."

While Paula went on trying to set her mother's priorities straight, Rory was working on some priorities of her own. Her most pressing concern was the question of how far Paula would go to keep her mother out of prison. She'd clearly been okay with breaking and entering and trying to run Rory off the road. And even though murder was a very different sort of offense, she'd indicated that she might resort to it with Brian. So Rory had to assume it was still an option in the agent's arsenal.

"Hi, Paula. I don't believe we've met before," Rory said in a polite, conversational tone. "But I guess your mother must have mentioned my name." When a situation started off with guns drawn, it was generally a good idea to try to defuse things.

Paula's eyes narrowed. "You're not here on a social visit, so cut the crap right now." Apparently she'd played hooky during "Defusing 101." "You should be ashamed of yourself for trying to entrap a helpless old lady."

"Old?" Dorothy sounded hurt. Maybe she did need help prioritizing.

"Entrap?" Rory repeated. Neither of them was going to win any awards for originality.

"I heard you, McCain. You were leading her, putting

words in her mouth. If I hadn't arrived when I did, you would have wheedled a phony confession out of her."

"Are you sure it would have been phony?" Rory asked, still trying to be civil. "I don't know how much your mother told you, but it's pretty obvious she's been carrying a heavy burden since the flood. That doesn't happen without good reason."

"The trauma of the flood left her memory muddled. She's confused wishing for Brian's death with the ridiculous notion that she was responsible for it."

Rory wondered if Paula believed her version of the story or was just good at thinking on her feet. Thinking on her feet won by a landslide. Functioning in crisis mode was surely an important requisite for an FBI agent.

"The Navajo medical examiner determined Brian's death was an accident," Paula went on. "The case is closed, and there isn't one decent reason to reopen it."

"A confession might be one," Rory suggested, fully aware that she was now the one ratcheting up the rhetoric. Although Clarissa had made it clear she had no intentions of prosecuting anyone, Paula didn't know that.

"In spite of how clever you obviously think you are, there is no confession," she said, "and there's never going to be one. I'll see to that."

"Then you must be planning to kill your mother along with me, because it's pretty obvious that she wants to unburden her soul. Sooner or later she's going to find someone who's willing to listen and take her seriously."

"Girls, girls," Dorothy said, finding her voice again. "There's no need for all this nastiness." She sounded like a parent trying to make peace between siblings.

Paula looked at her mother as if she'd suddenly grown a second head. Although Rory found the remark equally bizarre, she kept her eyes on Paula and the Glock.

"Why don't I put up some water?" Dorothy went on,

starting to rise from the couch. "We can talk about this in a civilized manner over a cup of tea. I made some lovely carrot muffins—"

"Sit down," Paula commanded. "And shut up."

Dorothy looked stricken. She opened her mouth as if to protest, then thought better of it and remained silent.

"I can manage my mother," Paula said, turning back to Rory. "You're the only problem I have to resolve."

If there was ever a time for negotiating, this was it. "I may have a solution to your dilemma," Rory said a lot more calmly than she felt. Now that push had actually come to shove and possibly murder, her idea didn't seem quite as foolproof as it had minutes earlier when she'd learned Paula was with the FBI. But it was all she had.

"I'll walk away from the case claiming I found no evidence that Brian's death was anything more than an accident."

Paula was eyeing her warily. "And the quid pro quo?"

"You immediately tender your resignation to the FBI. Use whatever excuse you like—family issues, medical problems. I don't care."

The agent gave a derisive laugh. "And why would I do that?"

Rory decided she needed to put herself on an equal footing with her adversary. She pushed her handbag away so that Paula could see the .45 she was holding and slowly rose to her feet. It was easy to see by Paula's expression that she hadn't expected this turn of events. Her emotional involvement in the situation had obviously taken a toll on her FBI cool.

"I thought you might prefer resigning to being fired," Rory replied. "The bureau isn't going to look favorably on an agent who's used her position and training to commit crimes against an innocent citizen. Can you imagine the field day the media would have with the story?"

"That's quite an accusation," Paula said, managing to

sound as if she still had the upper hand, "but you don't have a shred of proof."

"I saw you leaving my house after your second *visit,* and I gave the police a sketch of you." Technically, Rory hadn't seen her exiting the premises, but Paula didn't know that. "To my way of thinking, you belong in prison more than your mother does. But hey, I'm trying to be generous here. I'm giving you a chance to save her and yourself."

For the first time in their encounter Paula was at a loss for words. Rory could almost see the wheels spinning in her head as she tried to decide on her next move. From Rory's perspective, the agent had two options: the one Rory had proposed or the one she herself had alluded to—eliminating the problem by eliminating Rory.

Holding the gun in firing position, Rory's arm was beginning to tire. Another minute or two and it would start to visibly shake. Paula's arm still looked rock steady. She had a lot more practice in situations of this kind.

"If I agree to resign," Paula said finally, "you leave my mother alone and you don't bring any charges against either of us, now or in the future."

Rory stifled a sigh of relief. "As long as you leave me and mine alone as well," she said.

"If you renege on any part of this agreement, I'll bring you down, McCain. I will haunt you for the rest of your life."

Rory felt like saying, Bring it on, girl—I've been haunted by the best. But given the circumstances she said simply, "We're agreed then."

Paula lowered her gun. "Get the hell out of here."

The muscles in her right arm screaming in distress, Rory gratefully lowered her weapon too. But she kept a close eye on the agent as she picked up her handbag and withdrew to the front door. "The irony in all of this," Rory said as she opened the door, "is that I might never have discovered your mother was the killer if you hadn't been trying to scare me off the case. You might want to consider that when you're busy blaming me for forcing you out of a job." She walked out, closing the door behind her. If Paula had anything to say in reply, she wasn't interested in hearing it.

With the confrontation over and the danger past, a triumphant high started pumping through Rory's veins like fine wine, exhilarating and heady. She had to restrain herself from skipping down the street like Eloise. Way to go, McCain, she congratulated herself, since there was no one else there to do it. Too bad the marshal hadn't been there to witness her victory. The thought put an immediate damper on her spirits. She still couldn't believe the ingrate had left without so much as a good-bye. Well, she wasn't going to let his lack of courtesy ruin a great day. She opened the car door and slid behind the wheel. What she needed was an upbeat tune to restore her good mood. She turned the key in the ignition and was hunting for the right song when a familiar voice said, "Well done, Aurora. Well done."

# Chapter 34

When Zeke popped into the passenger seat a second later, Rory didn't know whether to welcome him back or tell him to take a permanent hike. She was leaning toward the hike.

"How long were you there watching?" she asked.

Zeke's cheeks hitched up in a broad grin. "Darn near the whole time."

His response bothered Rory on a couple of levels. "What happened to letting me know you were nearby?" she demanded.

"Well, darlin', I didn't want to interrupt. You appeared to have Dorothy under your spell, and you were doin' just grand."

Rory was finding it hard to stay angry when he was praising her. Compliments were not his forte. But she wasn't ready to be sweet-talked out of her irritation. "As I recall, interrupting never bothered you before."

"I'm tryin' to be more thoughtful." His eyes twinkled, challenging her to find fault with that argument.

"Did it ever occur to you that I might not want to be surreptitiously observed?" she asked, neatly sidestepping the trap.

Zeke chewed on the question for a minute. "Can't say it did," he admitted. "But it's not like you were doin' somethin' private."

"Think about how you'd feel if the tables were turned. Let's say you were out rounding up a couple of cattle rustlers, and you found out that some ghost was hanging around watching you as entertainment."

Zeke's smile vanished "Some ghost?" He sounded insulted.

Rory realized that her choice of words had been less than diplomatic and that she'd probably picked them for precisely that reason—payback for letting her think he'd moved on without so much as a backward glance.

"You're avoiding the issue," she said, no apology on her agenda. "How would you feel if you were in my shoes?"

"I suppose I might take exception," he allowed. "But I wasn't watchin' you for my amusement. I was there for backup in case things started goin' bad."

And there was the second reason she was annoyed. "So you expected me to blow it and need to be rescued."

"Now don't go puttin' words in my mouth."

"Am I wrong?"

"I know you're capable of pretty much anythin' you set your mind to. I was just there in case. . . . like an extra wheel on a Conestoga wagon that's headin' through Indian territory."

Rory almost cracked a smile in spite of herself.

"But if you feel so strongly about it," he went on, "I'll refrain from observin' unbeknownst in the future. Does that suit you?"

"Yes, thank you," she said finally letting go of her pique.

It had been too good a day to spoil by holding on to her anger. In a calmer state of mind, she put the car into drive and pulled away from the curb. On the ride home, they fell into talking about the particulars of the investigation, where they'd been right and where they'd been completely off track, and how the right bit of information could untangle the most complex case. By the time Rory swung into her driveway, her spirits were once again high. And, as always, Hobo's delighted greeting added to her good mood.

Dropping her purse on the bench near the stairs and kicking off her shoes, Rory headed toward the kitchen for some celebratory ice cream. Both Hobo and the marshal were waiting when she got there, Zeke at the table and Hobo at the refrigerator like a sentry guarding the royal jewels.

"Am I that predictable?" she asked, plucking a pint of butter pecan from the freezer.

Zeke laughed. Hobo just licked his chops.

"Yeah, well you're pretty predictable yourselves," she groused good-naturedly. When she pulled the lid off the ice cream, she decided there was no point in dirtying a bowl. She could eat what was left directly from the container. It always tasted better that way anyhow. She took her seat across from Zeke. Hobo sat beside her, still as a statue except for the trickling of some anticipatory drool.

Rory was raising the third spoonful to her mouth when a remark Zeke had made in the car popped into her mind, demanding her attention. She let the spoon fall back into the container. "When we were in the car before, you used the phrase 'in the future.' How did you mean that?"

"After today, from now on," Zeke said, his brow furrowing. "Is there some other future I don't know about?"

"But I found out who killed you."

"My apologies," he said smoothly and without a trace of sarcasm. "I guess I never thanked you properly. I know you went to a lot of trouble on my account."

Rory shook her head. "I thought you'd be moving on from here now that you have the answer."

"Oh, about that . . ." he said, looking as if he'd rather have all his teeth pulled out than continue the discussion.

"I don't get it; I thought you'd want to leave." Although their relationship had had its rough patches—okay, more rough patches than an eighteen-hole golf course after a tornado—she'd be happy to have him stay on as her partner. What she couldn't fathom was why he would choose to continue existing in limbo.

"I'm afraid it's a mite more complicated than that," Zeke said finally.

"But you said—"

"I know," he cut her off. "I'm pretty clear on what I said. Only it wasn't the whole story." He sounded as if he too were haunted, and by far darker demons than she'd ever known.

"Okay," she said, "then what *is* the whole story?" She figured two treks out to Arizona had at least earned her the right to the truth.

"How about you just trust me when I say you're better off not knowin'."

"Not this time. You asked me to find out who killed you, and I was willing to do it, because I thought I'd be helping you move on. I did my part, and I deserve some answers."

"I'm sorry you feel that way, but if there are things about my life I don't want to talk about—that's *my* call."

Rory heard the defensive anger rising in his voice as if he were circling his wagons and loading his rifle for a showdown at the O.K. Corral.

"I'm not your enemy, Marshal," she said hoping to disarm him.

"That's funny, because right now it sure feels like you are."

"Hey, hold on there," she said, trying to tamp down her

own fire. "You're the one who drew me into this. And Mac before me."

"It was the only way to get you and your uncle to stop pushing me to follow the blasted light!" Zeke snapped. "The two of you were cut from the same cloth. I never knew me a more tenacious pair."

"Then having the name of your killer doesn't really matter?" Rory asked, bewilderment infiltrating her anger.

"Of course it matters, just not enough to make me change my present circumstances."

"What is so awful that you can't bring yourself to tell me? Even if it's something monstrous, something despicable, what exactly could I do to you? You're already as dead as you're ever going to be."

"You could leave," he said, looking her straight in the eye. "And that would be worse than death."

Rory had long believed that selling the house was her only bargaining chip in their relationship, but until now Zeke had never admitted as much. She was grateful for his honesty, but she wasn't ready to let him off the hook until he'd answered the rest of her questions. He was no fool, so he had to realize he'd just given her the right caliber ammunition to go gunning for those answers. Either he was hoping she wouldn't use it, or on some level he wanted to be forced into unburdening himself.

"If we're going to keep living and working together," she said, "you're going to have to come clean—no more dark secrets. I need a show of faith. Trust me enough to tell me, or tomorrow I call a real estate agent and put this place up for sale." There; she'd given him a simple choice. If he refused, he would lose her. No gray areas. She didn't like having to back him into a corner to get at the truth, but it was the only option he'd left her. Of course, she would wind up losing Mac's house as a result, but she didn't allow herself to dwell on that part of the gamble. All Zeke had to do was open up to her, and she'd stay. She couldn't imagine anything he could have done that was hateful enough to make her run away in horror.

Zeke wagged his head and issued a deeply troubled sigh. "You're goin' to ride this horse into the ground, ain't you?"

"You'd do the same."

"I expect so." He was silent for a long while.

Rory struggled to be patient.

"I'm in no hurry to leave here," he began finally. "Never have been. Sure, I wanted to know who shot me, needed to know, but that wasn't goin' to change anythin'. You said so yourself enough times." He looked beaten, all the fight and bluster gone out of him. "You want to know why I'm still here, Aurora? Well, it's because I won't be goin' to a good place when I leave—heaven, or whatever you want to call it. That's not where I'm headed."

"That's crazy. Of course you are. You more than most people," she said, completely baffled by his concern. "You were a federal marshal. You upheld the law. You spent your life catching bad guys."

"I have the blood of at least five innocent children on my hands," he said bluntly, the words sounding as if he'd wrenched them straight from his gut. "And likely others I don't know about."

"That doesn't make sense," she said. "Trask killed those children. You tracked him all the way across the country to bring him to justice."

"When you read Katherine's diary, didn't you wonder why her husband hired someone to kill me? And when that didn't work, why he left his home and family to find me and finish the job himself?"

"Yes, but I figured he was so distraught over his daughter's death that he blamed you for not catching Trask before he reached Tucson."

"He blamed me, and rightly so, because I *did* nab Trask before he got to Tucson." Zeke hung his head as if he couldn't bear to look her in the eye a moment longer. "I was full of myself over it too. We rode into town just after nightfall, and I took him straightaway to the jail. The sheriff was off somewhere; only the deputy was on duty. I could tell the man had been drinkin'. He reeked of the whiskey, and he could barely stand upright. I knew I shouldn't trust him to watch my prisoner. Trask was too smart, too wily by half for the deputy even when he was sober. But I was tired and hungry, and I hadn't seen the woman I was keepin' company with for better than a month. So I sold myself a bill of goods dirt cheap—what was I worried about? It was a sturdy jail cell, and far as I knew, the deputy never actually lost a prisoner. And off I went to meet my lady friend. And while I was thus engaged, Trask conned the deputy into unlockin' the door. At least that's how the deputy told it the next morning when I found him sleepin' off his drunk in the cell. That would have been bad enough, but before Trask left town, he broke into the Jensen house right there beside their general store and snatched little Betsy out of her bed."

"But—"

"No, darlin', there's just no way around it. Believe you me, I'd have found it if there were. I'm as responsible for that child's death as if I'd strangled her myself. Her and all the others he killed after that."

Rory understood now why he'd refused to tell her. He believed unequivocally that he'd been Trask's accomplice in killing those children. And for all she knew, back at that time he might have been hanged for his part in their deaths, if not by the law than by vigilante justice. He'd been punishing himself for over a century, the pain becoming part and parcel of who he was. She wished she had the means to ease his suffering. Surely in the balance of things a hundred-odd years should be considered time served.

"You're only human," she said softly. "We all make mistakes in judgment. And as awful as this was, you never meant for it to happen. Remorse has to count for something."

"Remorse I have," he said looking up at her again, "and plenty of it, but I'm not of a mind to test your theory just yet. So if you can bear to stay on here with me now that you know everythin', I'd be much obliged. And I'll do my level best to be of help in your work."

Rory found herself stumbling over her words. "Of course you can stay; I mean, of course I'll stay," she amended with an awkward laugh.

Zeke closed his eyes for a moment, and Rory swore she felt the intensity of his relief like a shock wave breaking and rolling off him.

Hobo chose that moment to lay his shaggy head in her lap and whimper out of empathy or because he hadn't yet been offered any ice cream. The latter was easy enough to remedy. She stuck two fingers into the container and let him lap off the melting ice cream with one slurp of his long tongue, bringing an unexpected smile to Zeke's face.

She smiled back at him. "How could I ever break up the Three Musketeers?"

"The three who?" Zeke chuckled, clearly ready to leave the painful discussion behind.

Rory was well into an explanation of Dumas's story when a sharp rap at the back door made them all jump. Hobo ran to the door barking ferociously as if ashamed that he hadn't alerted them to the trespasser sooner. "That's what comes of being fixated on the ice cream," she scolded him with a laugh as she peeked outside.

"It's Eloise," she said, turning to Zeke who was in the process of vanishing. "You can stick around."

"That's okay," he said as he faded away, "I'll let you two ladies chat."

"Coward," she called after him, wishing she could also

disappear. When she opened the door, Eloise stepped inside without so much as a "hello." She was wearing blue pajama bottoms, a festive, red-ruffled blouse and her serious face. Oh no, Rory groaned to herself, adrenaline already pumping. What now?

Eloise scratched absently at Hobo's head as she looked around the kitchen, her gaze sweeping over the ice cream container as if it held no particular interest. Serious mode squared. "Where's your sketch pad?" she demanded, focusing on Rory again.

"Upstairs, why?" After her interview with Dorothy, her standoff with Paula and her discussion with Zeke, the last thing she needed was a psychic with a pressing agenda.

"Well, go get it," Eloise said impatiently shooing her out of the room. "We don't have all day, you know. Someone's been murdered."

What is the only word in the English
language that ends in -*mt*?

# BOOKS CAN BE
# DECEIVING

-A Library Lover's Mystery-

## JENN MCKINLAY

Answering tricky reference questions like this one
is more than enough excitement for recently single
librarian Lindsey Norris. That is, until someone in
her cozy new hometown of Briar Creek, Connecti-
cut, commits murder, and the most pressing question is whodunit . . .

"A sparkling setting, lovely characters, books, knitting,
and chowder . . . What more could any reader ask?"
—Lorna Barrett, *New York Times* bestselling author

facebook.com/TheCrimeSceneBooks
penguin.com
jennmckinlay.com

M981T0911

M959T0911

# Contents

# Acknowledgments

*To the people of ox country, whose words and images fill these pages.*

In acknowledging the essential contribution of those who allowed us to quote from interviews, it is important to note that we have freely placed their words next to photographs that best illustrate their story. More often than not, persons shown in the photographs are not those being quoted.

\* \*

In a project where so many people were photographed, where so many people answered questions, where assistance and friendliness were offered again and again, it is difficult to select those few who deserve a special mention. The following are some of the people who made this book possible. They answered innumerable questions; they allowed us to tape–record interviews; they invited us onto their land and into their homes. A special thank–you to:

Teresa Bezanson, Emilie Bolivar–Hayward, Leo Bolivar, Katie Creaser, Harry Eisnor, Frank Gammon, Graham Hayward, Granville Hayward, Drew Hiltz, Maxwell Hiltz, Percy Jollymore, Jerry Jordan, Peg Jordan, Donald Joudrey, Lloyd Joudrey, Gerald Langille, Harley Levy, Hazel Levy, Robie Levy, Roy Levy, Bazel Lohnes , Clayton Lohnes, Doris Lohnes, Gordon Lohnes, Merrill McCarthy, Bazil Meisner, Toby Mosher, Keith Nodding, Neil Oickle, Earl Seamone, Claude Silver, Douglas Slauenwhite, St. Claire Tufts, Arthur Young, Henry Young, Lois Young, Leone Wilkie, Hilda Zinck

In addition to those listed above, we wish to thank as many of the other persons who are also featured in the photographs as we can. Also appearing in the photographs are:

Ted Bezanson, Allison Corkum, Leo Eisnor, Robert Hall, Jay Hiltz, Donald Hirtle, George Joudrey, William Joudrey, Delbert McDow, Basil Mansfield, Allisha Merry, Matthew Merry, Earl Nauss, Michael Reeves, Steven Russell, Gordon Simmons, Robert States, Freeman Swinmar, Junior Tufts, Marcus Tufts, Stewart Veinot, Wendell Wagner, Avery Zwicker, Bernard Zwicker

Words of appreciation are also due to several people who supported and assisted us throughout this project: our friends and family members, Clark Biesele, Eric Hayes, Joan and Rachel James, Richard Plander, Earl Rutledge, and Sarah Solley; at Nimbus Publishing, Dorothy Blythe; and at GDA, Steven Slipp.

It has been our pleasure to come to know many people who preserve a place for oxen in their lives. To everyone in this warm–hearted community, we extend our friendship and gratitude.

Frances Anderson
Terry James

# Preface

**I**F YOU HAVE EVER HEARD THE sound of ox–bells, you are likely to remember them forever. Here where I live in southwestern Nova Scotia, there are thousands of people who can simply close their eyes and hear that melodious jangling that accompanied them through much of their early years. It's a playful noise that suggests a gentler time when machines did not dominate the soundscape of our farms and woodlands. And it's a sound that frustrates me, as a photographer, because it cannot be translated into the silver halides and color dyes of my medium. Yet, inwardly I smile when I recall the day this sound first captured me.

I was on an earlier project, needing at least one photograph of working oxen. A man had arranged for his daughter to lead me to his logging site in the forest. As she and I hiked through a labyrinth of narrow hauling roads, the girl frequently stopped to listen. Cocking her head first one way and then the other, she kept pointing in her father's direction. All I heard was the soughing of the wind through the trees. After several miles there came a far off tinkling of bells and the teamster's sharp command: "Haw Lion! Back Bright! Back." We climbed over a ridge and saw the man and his team. They were yarding logs to a small staging area beside a rubber–tired wagon. It was very quiet: just the bells, the breathing of Bright and Lion—the huge oxen—and the occasional command from their teamster. Without question the work was hard: steel chain hooked around

An old bronzed bell on a working ox.

heavy logs, sweat and dirt, blackflies. Yet if one stepped back a few paces, this labor seemed but a gentle intrusion upon the forest. Even the shod hooves of the big team and the dragging of the logs made little noise on the mossy ground.

In the hours I stayed with the woodsman, he occasionally shattered this stillness with the racket of his chain saw. The cutting was quick, and as soon as he stopped, silence fell back over us. Bright and Lion knew their work. They dragged long logs through the maze of trees, ducking and turning their heads as one in order to avoid catching a horn. Taking cues from their driver's movements, following his whip motions with their eyes, they needed few commands. Despite their great size, their hooves did little damage to the tender forest floor. They worked mightily but with minimal impact, their presence signaled as much by the music of bells as by the removal of timber. I felt a rightness in the peace of their labor. That day I knew I wanted to tell the story of oxen.

In the months that followed, many ox–men welcomed me onto their farms and into their homes. With patience and good humor they attempted to educate Frances, my collaborator, and me in the ways of the ox. This is not mere animal husbandry; it is an entire way of life. As they gave us their words, into our tape recorders or in amiable conversation over kitchen tables, we realized their specialized knowledge might fill an encyclopedia. Could we possibly hint at this totality in a few words and

*They'll go through a lot more snow than a horse. You see, their stomachs takes up onto it. Oxen, their stomachs holds them up, they can go through more snow. They'll stay on the ground; they won't jump. They'll actually, what we call, waller snow.*

*Left:* Driving through the snow. January

A teamster and his Hereford oxen charge through winter snow. January

*They'll follow a road when you can't; they'll never leave it.*
*You can take a yoke of oxen back there in the woods, in the middle of the night.*
*You could take them oxen with no lights, dark just like it ever was,*
*and they'd stay in the center of that road.*

---

*Left:* Hitched to double–sleighs, oxen follow their teamster over winter ice. January

Dragging hardwood logs across a frozen lake. January

*You can't fool an animal. They know when it's a stranger around or when you're around. There's a lot of cattle that don't mind it, but then there's cattle that get nervous and worked up, same as anyt'ing else.*

Worn brass knobs on ox horns.

*Right:* An ox–man checks over his own pair amid several cor-raled teams at a country ox–pull. May

*Them oxen, they're very quiet. If you fell ahead of them, I know they'd stop right
in their tracks. They'd never go over you; I don't think so.*

*Left:* A quiet moment before the start of a country ox–pull. May    Youngsters wait by their father's team at a country ox–pull. July

*Dad would travel the countryside trying to find the oxen of his choice.*
*He'd travel for days until he could find a pair of cattle, as he called 'em, a pair of oxen*
*to his liking. And he would come home, and he'd be so proud of his oxen. Why, he'd get*
*them out on the highway, and he'd yell at them, "Haw Lion! Gee Bright!" And this*
*ox would try to do Dad's bidding, whichever way he wanted them to go.*

*Left:* An ox–man with his large pair of Durham–Simmentals.
July

A young Limousin–Durham pair, "well up in legs."
September

*You get some cattle that they train so easy. And you can get other ones
that can be just like mules; you can't learn 'em nothing. But you take a nice,
gentle pair of cattle, and they'll learn by experience, by themselves. Yes, it is
some things you gotta show 'em to do, but there's things they'll learn
on their own, as you work 'em.*

*Left:* A pair of Ayrshires stands ready to go winter logging.
January

Two–year–old Hereford–Durhams learn to "stand in,"
stand parallel to the wagonpole. March

*It's hard work to break a pair of cattle and break 'em right.*
*You gotta understand them bastards to know what to do to 'em. You gotta be*
*around 'em awhile. If they're big, you don't know where they're going to land neither.*
*No good to yoke 'em one day and in a few months yoke 'em again. Keep right at 'em,*
*and the first thing you're hauling something.*

Two–year–old Herefords yoked for the first time. May

*Right:* Hitched to a plow, a three–year–old team is carefully led alongside a previous furrow. May

# "Them Times, the Cattle was Worked"

T O ACCOMPANY A TEAMSTER INTO his barn in the dark of early morning and watch him yoke his oxen by the faint light of a lantern or a single, bare bulb is to witness a ritual that's been performed millions of times by the ox–men of North America. By this single act they have harnessed a power that can yard huge logs, pull stumps, break rocky ground, or haul a thousand board–feet of timber over winter trails.

"Harness" is, in fact, an exaggeration since the yoke—the device that extends the power of oxen to numerous tasks—is much simpler than a harness. Oxen work by pulling. In the case of head–yoked oxen, a single piece of yellow birch is precisely carved and fitted by the yoke–maker so that it may be securely bound to head and horns by leather or nylon straps. The load is then attached to small chain bows beneath the center of the yoke, and the yoke distributes the load's pressure to the horns, the back of the head, and especially the forehead, which is crossed by the yoke strap. A strong, flat forehead is desirable. The forehead is protected by a thick, leather head–pad.

To work effectively, oxen must be shod. With good shoes, oxen excel at traveling safely and surely across rough terrain, and will outdistance horses when pulling loads over difficult trails. Because an oxhoof is cloven, the ox requires two flat shoes per foot. During manufacture the blacksmith bends the ends of the shoes into calks. These provide the traction needed to harness the power and speed of a good team. In winter months, sharp ice–calks allow oxen to haul enormous loads of timber over icy trails or frozen lakes.

Working oxen need new shoes several times a year. So that each foot may be lifted safely, the ox is supported during shoeing by a "belly–pad," or sling, suspended within a stout, wooden ox–frame. Although it may disturb some to watch a blacksmith pare the bottom of a hoof with a keen chisel and then fasten shoes with sharp nails, shoeing is as painless as trimming one's fingernails.

Oxen are at their best in the woods. They excel at selective logging, a practice still championed by many traditionalists. Like the horse, the trained ox can maneuver adeptly through close spaces, leaving standing trees and forest soils in good condition. Because they are so surefooted, oxen do not require the ditched and graveled roads that tame the forest for modern–day machines. In previous decades, the woods were full of oxen. Teamsters were hired out to logging companies for the winter and sent home their pays. Others worked family woodlots to supply sawlogs and pulpwood to local mills and to bring firewood to nearby towns. Today there are still places where oxen haul timber on private lands or log delicate or inaccessible areas.

Although a single teamster can work his oxen in the woods, field work with oxen is labor intensive. Many field implements require two people: one to lead the team, the other to tend the machine. Sometimes a skilled teamster—with the considerable admiration of others—manages to train his oxen so that they can be driven from behind. Walking with a plow or seated on his mower, the teamster can then work alone.

There was a time when large farm families provided many hands to plant and harvest. Many hands were needed because the simple implements pulled by oxen performed only one task at a time. Even children led teams while the adults tripped a plow's moldboard or lowered the blade of a mower. Today, complex, powered machines push farming and logging operations at a noisy, sometimes reckless pace. Gone are the days of the breaking–up parties, where neighbors pooled their oxen to pull stumps and boulders and to plow new ground at the rate of an acre a day. Almost gone is the satisfaction in the quiet of the forest or the feel of a fresh furrow under one's boots. Although few want to return to these tough old days, there remain devoted ox–men who are not about to relinquish "them times."

*There was a time that's what you had to make a livin'. You yoked your oxen,
took 'em in the woods. You yarded out your load of logs; you loaded up on the sleds
and brought 'em home. And go again. I'll tell ya, she was pretty hard sleddin'
sometimes to make a living in the woods around here one time.*

A teamster hitches sleighs to his Hereford oxen. January

*Previous Page:* Tightening straps on a head–yoke.

*Right:* While the teamster stays well ahead, Hereford oxen race
loaded double–sleighs down a snowy slope. January

Steel dogs and steel chain hold a large log. January          *Right:* Hauling! January

*Well, most everybody had manure; it was farms them times.*
*Most every barn they'd have a pair of oxen, well, three or four cows, maybe more,*
*then some young cattle as they come along, and they all had manure to put on the land.*
*They had team spreaders before the tractors came out.*

Young Chianinas wait while their owner fills a manure spreader.
April

*Right:* A yoked pair of Chianinas. April

*I like the oxen for hauling Christmas trees because you come along,*
*say you got a bunch of Christmas trees here, well, stop here and the oxen'll stay*
*til you get the trees on. When you go ahead, there's no startin' it, no turnin'*
*the key to start the motor. All you do is tell 'em to come.*

*Left:* Loading Christmas trees on a wagon. November        Bringing out a load of trees. November

*I got no worry about getting hung up around the woods or anything,
getting bogged, because the ox will always bring a load out.*

*Left:* Heading down a logging trail with double–sleighs. January          Loading four–foot wood onto double sleighs. January

# "The Cattle Do Draw a Crowd"

THE DESIRE TO SEE WHOSE OXEN can haul the biggest load is a natural expression of a teamster's pride in his own abilities and his confidence in his team. In the days when oxen freighted heavy loads over country roads, teamsters were always ready to hitch their team onto the wagon or sleigh–pole of another whose load was mired. Not wanting to be outdone, the teamster in trouble often refused to unhitch and would insist that the helping pair be placed in tandem with his own. In logging camps the title of "king load" bestowed honorary recognition upon the teamster whose oxen hauled the largest single load in the course of a winter.

These traditions of informal competition in the arenas of work had their counterparts in ox–pulling contests at agricultural fairs and exhibitions. With its origins going back at least a century, ox–pulling has developed into a sport with established rules and procedures. Today there are more ox–pulls than ever, and since 1967 there have been regular international competitions in Nova Scotia and Maine. These international contests are the premiere events for competitive teamsters.

There are several different styles of ox–pulling. All employ a weighted drag. The drag is a wooden platform with runners, which holds a quantity of stackable weights. Teams take turns hooking onto the drag, and it is not unusual for an able team of heavy oxen to move drags with loads exceeding 10,000 pounds. The timed pull for distance is predominantly an American event. As seen in Nova Scotia at the International Pull in Bridgewater, this contest requires that teams weighing between 3,000 and 3,600 pounds haul weighted drags over the greatest possible distance within a five–minute period. Nova Scotians favor the short–distance pull; however, it occurs in New England as well.

The short–distance event is a pull for maximum weight. Although teams are divided into weight classes in both Nova Scotia and New England, only New Englanders compete on an equal footing against others in their class. Nova Scotians rank their results according to percentage values based on a team's maximum haul divided by its own weight. Though there are variations, in a typical short–distance pull, teams vie in round–robin order to pull an increasingly heavy drag over a three–foot distance. Successful ox–pulling requires psychology and finesse as well as brute strength. The rules prohibit profanity, cruelty, and other harsh behavior.

Exhibitions and fairs offer contests for ox–men in addition to pulling. Judges rank teams in competitions for show, best dressed, and best working pair. Nova Scotia teamsters lavish great care on prized teams, first trimming, washing, and then dressing their cattle with elaborate head–pads and bell–straps. With polished bronzed bells, brass knobs on their horns, brass and colored glass decorations studded over leather bell–straps and head–pads, and brightly painted yokes, a well matched pair of oxen lumbering into a show ring is a magnificent sight.

Although costs are considerable and the prizes modest, ox–pulling and other contests have grown in popularity. Knowing that oxen will draw a crowd, small communities combine ox–pulling with fund–raising suppers. Teamsters welcome the chance to demonstrate their abilities. Since the time and circumstances for traditional work on the land are no longer available to many, ox–pulling provides an opportunity to continue working with teams. It also provides a chance to socialize with other ox–men and their families and to offer a word of encouragement to a youngster entering the pulling ring for the first time. Week after week, summer after summer, teamsters load up their oxen and truck them to the pulls. There, amid bellowing cattle, clanging bells, and noisy spectators, something quietly momentous takes place: an ancient connection between man and beast is renewed as they work together to haul a load.

*My one ox was sharp, and the other was slow.*
*But I taught that fast ox to wait. He knew what he was waiting for;*
*he wouldn't let Bright get ahead of him. When he felt things comin'*
*tight on the other side, then he'd put on the power*

Hook–on–and–stay–on competition at à country pull. July          *Right:* Pulling! July

*They just get down, and they'll keep squeezing at it 'til it goes;*
*you can tell they're working at it.*

---

*Left:* A final pull for first place. May

A judge checks to see if the drag has been hauled three feet.
July

*You'll see a lot of 'em go in and haul a decent load and unhook and go out.*
*Well, that encourages their team. Every once in awhile you should do that, really.*
*And when the final time comes, when you think you gotta have that good pull,*
*then that time you can ask 'em.*

A Nova Scotia team in international competition. July

*Right:* An American bow–yoked team strives to follow its master in an international contest. Application of the whip is not allowed. July

*Well, the only place we can drive cattle now is around these pulls.*
*If you didn't go it wouldn't be worth keepin' cattle.*
*You wouldn't get no satisfaction.*

*That 4–H club; that learns the kids for to know about cattle.*
*If that wasn't done, why, maybe after awhile there'd be no cattle around.*

Ox–pull action. August          *Right:* 4–H competition. July

*Well now, you take Exhibition. You take the oxen out, what do you got?*
*You ain't got too much left, are you? You ain't got too much left.*

Judging teams for show. July

*No, it's not the money you get from it; it's not the trophies.*
*If you won 'em all, you wouldn't have anything. It's just the sportsmanship;*
*that's all it is with oxen. You just try to see who got the best team.*

Trophies, at a country ox–pull. May                    *Right:* First prize!

*When you grow up with the cattle, you don't want to give 'em up.*
*I could just sit there watching ' em for hours.*
*I like 'em that much.*